"The collection is a fine one, showing a variety of plots, settings and characters.... The husband and wife relationships are eminently recognizable—there's an excellent balance of faintly nostalgic sentiment and sharp, occasionally even acid, realism."
—*The Kirkus Reviews*

"The style of the stories is what one expects ...simple, unassuming, competent...(Pearl Buck) is a professional who writes with sure artistry." —*Chicago Tribune*

"Some of Pearl Buck's finest writing is contained in this collection. Such skillful development of character and plot suitable to her medium, combined with a compassionate treatment of individuals' problems, is rarely found these days.... Every story ends on an appropriately cheerful yet thoroughly sophisticated note." —*Library Journal*

The fourteen stories in HEARTS COME HOME AND OTHER STORIES originally appeared in the following short-story collections: *The First Wife and Other Stories, Far and Near* and *Today and Forever*, all published by The John Day Company, Inc.

Contents

Introduction

❦

PEARL S. BUCK'S place among contemporary American writers is unique. One cannot conveniently place her in one school or another of our short story writers and novelists. Though an honored member of the American Academy of Arts and Letters, she is not of the mainstream of her colleagues of the twenties, thirties and forties who brought the modern American short story to fruition. Acclaimed and beloved by peoples of the world, indeed the most translated American author next to Mark Twain, she belongs rather to the mainstream of world literature. And she is one of only five Americans to have received the Nobel Prize for Literature (the others being Sinclair Lewis, O'Neill, Faulkner and Hemingway).

If one considers the early life of Pearl Buck, one may find therein all the forces that shaped this remarkable woman. Born in Hillsboro, West Virginia, in 1892, she was taken to China at the age of four months, there to spend the first forty years of her life. For her parents it was but a return to the missionary life to which they were dedicated and to the land where they had already buried four of their short-lived children. To her long-suffering mother, with whom her relationship was wonderfully close, she has paid loving homage in *The Exile,* one of the two biographies singled out for special praise in the Nobel Prize citation. It was her mother who took complete charge of her early education. It was she, too, who taught her to find beauty in life and to record her impressions in words. From her stern, uncompromising father whose standards were so high and words of praise so few, she gained humility, a stubborn idealism and the capacity for long and willing work. She has told of his life in the companion biography, _Fighting Angel._ Then there was the beloved Chinese amah from whom the blond child begged stories for hours on end, the age-old Taoist and Buddhist tales of devils, dragons and priests, of fairies, gods, heaven and hell. Tiring of these, she once again heard from her parents tales of her pioneer ancestry, of the great western land they had left behind and of their own youth.

It has often been said of Miss Buck's style that it has the cadence of the St. James version of the Bible. Perhaps those who so compared it were thinking of the many hours the author must have spent in childhood listening to her father read it aloud to the gathered family. Actually, her style was more influenced by her study of the Chinese classics. Of the good Mr. Kung who instilled in her the principles of Confucius while teaching her to read and write Chinese, she has set down an affectionate portrait in her autobiography, _My Several Worlds._ Later, well schooled, she was to read and study those classics, whose wisdom and point of view became hers, rendering her the consummate interpreter of the East to the West.

And one must remember, too, the lasting impression made on the young girl by the traveling Chinese theaters from which, for centuries, illiterate peasants have learned of their great emperors and holy men, of virtuous ladies and tragedies of love. To witness the power of the drama and the dramatic narrative at work on the masses is an experience not given to many Westerners in their youth.

Miss Buck's fame as a novelist, as the author of _The Good Earth, Sons, Pavillion of Women, The Mother, The Townsman, Imperial Woman_ and a score of other favorites, has tended to draw attention away from her short stories, masterpieces in their own right. The stories in this collection are here reprinted for the first time in an inexpensive edition, making available a choice of the best stories from three volumes, *The First Wife, Today and Forever* and *Far and Near,* all published by The John Day Company between 1933 and 1947. Most of the stories originally appeared in the leading magazines both here and abroad.

The reader will find himself swept forward by the natural variety of their pace and structure, a variety growing out of the author's conviction that the form of each story must be adapted to its purpose. It is this deliberate evanescence of approach that has made it difficult for critics to identify the author with any particular school, and that may well explain the absence to date of a thorough and definitive study of her works. On the other hand, this very freedom from technical strictures and self-conscious experimentation has made possible the breadth of her content. For this she has herself said she is indebted to the Chinese novel. In the Nobel lecture delivered in 1938 before the Swedish Academy she said: "No, happily for the Chinese novel, it was not considered by the scholars as literature. Happily, too, for the novelist! Man and book, they were free from the criticisms of those scholars and their requirements of art, their techniques of expression and their talk of literary significances and all that discussion of what is and is not art, as if art were an absolute and not the changing thing it is, fluctuating even within decades!" And elsewhere in the same essay: "A good novelist, or so I have been taught in China, should be natural, unaffected, and so flexible and variable as to be wholly at the command of the material that flows through him."

Above all, the reader will find that these stories share the common denominator of universal themes. Here again the long years in China served the future author well in two ways that immediately come to mind. Forced by circumstance to look at an early age upon the extremes of the human condition and to mingle with all classes, she developed compassion at the same time that repeated exposure unconsciously trained her in the observation of detail. Many an American author spent comparable years of his youth in experience more restricted as to class and region, and either consciously set out later on a trek to find out about his fellow humans or turned his microscope or scalpel to that class of society best known to him. Then, secondly, coming a mature woman to the United States, where she now makes her home among the Pennsylvania hills, she brought to her observation of the American scene a fresh point of view, that of the older civilization. Her gaze, clear and warm as her own large blue eyes, took in family life and the relationship of men and women and saw their virtues, the presence and potential of which had long been forgotten, and weaknesses to which most pretended to be blind.

So Pearl Buck, obsessed with life, richly endowed with the capacity to feel and communicate human emotion, has used her storyteller's art as a mirror to the face of mankind in order that feeling, he may see, and seeing, may be moved to do better. Eschewing all association with the missionary heritage of her childhood, she has yet remained in the larger sense a missionary. In "Home to Heaven," with its portrayal of the fear and uncertainty underlying a callous indifference, are words of warning to an America grown insensitive to the murmur of the rising peoples of the East. In "The Quarrel" she writes with the indirection of Chekhov, leaving unspoken the secret of a human heart at once betrayed and freed by a single burning fickle gaze. The dreamlike quality of "Mrs. Mercer and Herself" leaves the reader speculating as to the symbolism of the desert in the hearts of today's frustrated wives. What is more understandable in any tongue than the plight of "The Old Mother" rejected by ungrateful children impatient with her outmoded ways? No disciple of the Freudian school, in "Mothers and Sons" the author has written a perceptive and moving story of siblings out of the intuition of her own mother's heart. "Enough for a Lifetime" foreshadows the author's own preoccupation with the theater and with the fascinating question of what is real and not real to the players themselves. "The Enemy," on the surface a suspenseful war story, probes the ever present dilemma of the man of science torn between the code of profession and the pressures of society. And then there is the humor, too, of "Home Girl" and "Mr. Right," postwar stories both tender and earthy with their setting in Japan.

Earlier it was said that in Miss Buck's life might be found all the forces that shaped the writer. We have touched upon a few of those influences. But from whence came the profound and warm humanity which passes all boundaries and all tongues? It matters not, for in this she belongs to the world as do Dickens, Chekhov or Tolstoy. In all humility the author herself has said: "I have been taught to want to write for these people. If they are reading their magazines by the million, then I want my stories there rather than in magazines read only by a few. For a story belongs to the people. They are sounder judges of it than anyone else, for their senses are unspoiled and their emotions are free."

The Enemy

DR. SADAO HOKI's house was built on a spot of the Japanese coast where as a little boy he had often played. The low square stone house was set upon rocks well above a narrow beach that was outlined with bent pines. As a boy Sadao had climbed the pines, supporting himself on his bare feet as he had seen men do in the South Seas when they climbed for coconuts. His father had taken him often to the islands of those seas, and never had he failed to say to the little grave boy at his side, "Those islands yonder, they are the steppingstones to the future for Japan."

"Where shall we step from them?" Sadao had asked seriously.

"Who knows?" his father had answered. "Who can limit our future? It depends on what we make it."

Sadao had taken this into his mind as he did everything his father said, his father who never joked or played with him but who spent infinite pains upon him who was his only son. Sadao knew that his education was his father's chief concern. For this reason he had been sent at twenty-two to America to learn all that could be learned of surgery and medicine. He had come back at thirty, and before his father died he had seen Sadao become famous not only as a surgeon but as a scientist. Because he was now perfecting a discovery which would render wounds entirely clean he had not been sent abroad with the troops. Also,

he knew, there was some slight danger that the old General
ight need an operation for a condition for which he was
being treated medically, and for this possibility Sadao
s being kept in Japan.

Clouds were rising from the ocean now. The unexpected
warmth of the last few days had at night drawn heavy
fog from the cold waves. He watched mists hide outlines
of a little island near the shore and then come creeping
up the beach below the house, wreathing around the pines.
In a few minutes it would be wrapped about the house,
too. Then he would go into the room where Hana, his
wife, would be waiting for him with the two children.

But at this moment the door opened and she looked
out, a dark blue woolen *haori* over her kimono. She came
to him affectionately and put her arm through his as he
stood, smiled and said nothing. He had met Hana in
America, but he had waited to fall in love with her until
he was sure she was Japanese. His father would never
have received her unless she had been pure in her race.
He wondered often whom he would have married if he had
not met Hana, and by what luck he had found her in the
most casual way, by chance, literally, at an American
professor's house. The professor and his wife had been
kind people, anxious to do something for their few foreign
students, and the students, though bored, had accepted
this kindness. Sadao had often told Hana how nearly he
had not gone to Professor Harley's house that night—the
rooms were so small, the food so bad, the professor's
wife so voluble. But he had gone, and there he had found
Hana, a new student, and had felt he would love her, if
it were at all possible.

Now he felt her hand on his arm and was aware of the
pleasure it gave him, even though they had been married

years enough to have the two children. For they had not married heedlessly in America. They had finished their work at school and had come home to Japan, and when his father had seen her, the marriage had been arranged in the old Japanese way, although Sadao and Hana had talked everything over beforehand. They were perfectly happy. She laid her cheek against his arm.

It was at this moment that both of them saw something black come out of the mists. It was a man. He was flung up out of the ocean—flung, it seemed, to his feet by a breaker. He staggered a few steps, his body outlined against the mist, his arms above his head. Then the curled mists hid him again.

"Who is that?" Hana cried. She dropped Sadao's arm and they both leaned over the railing of the veranda. Now they saw him again. The man was on his hands and knees, crawling. Then they saw him fall on his face and lie there.

"A fisherman, perhaps," Sadao said, "washed from his boat." He ran quickly down the steps and behind him Hana came, her wide sleeves flying. A mile or two away on either side there were fishing villages, but here was only the bare and lonely coast, dangerous with rocks. The surf beyond the beach was spiked with rocks. Somehow the man had managed to come through them—he must be badly torn.

They saw when they came toward him that indeed it was so. The sand on one side of him had already a stain of red soaking through.

"He is wounded!" Sadao exclaimed. He made haste to the man, who lay motionless, his face in the sand. An old cap stuck to his head, soaked with sea water. He was in wet rags of garments. Sadao stooped, Hana at his side, and turned the man's head. They saw the face.

"A white man!" Hana whispered.

Yes, it was a white man. The wet cap fell away and there was his wet yellow hair, long, as though for many weeks it had not been cut, and upon his young and tortured face was a ragged yellow beard. He was unconscious and knew nothing that they did to him.

Now Sadao remembered the wound, and with his expert fingers he began to search for it. Blood flowed freshly at his touch. On the right side of his lower back Sadao saw that a ragged gun wound had been reopened. The flesh was blackened with powder. Sometime, not many days ago, the man had been shot and had not been tended. It was bad chance that the rock had struck the wound.

"Oh, how he is bleeding!" Hana whispered again in a solemn voice. The mists screened them now completely, and at this time of day no one came by here. The fishermen had gone home and even the chance beachcombers would have considered the day at an end.

"What shall we do with this man?" Sadao muttered. But his trained hands seemed of their own will to be doing what they could to staunch the fearful bleeding. He packed the wound with the sea moss that strewed the beach. The man moaned with pain in his stupor, but he did not awaken.

"The best thing that we could do would be to put him back in the sea," Sadao said, answering himself.

Now that the bleeding was stopped for the moment he stood up and dusted the sand from his hands.

"Yes, undoubtedly that would be best," Hana said steadily. But she continued to stare down at the motionless man.

"If we sheltered a white man in our house, we would be arrested, and if we turned him over as a prisoner, he would certainly die," Sadao said.

"The kindest thing would be to put him back into the sea," Hana said. But neither of them moved. They were staring with a curious repulsion upon the inert figure.

"What is he?" Hana whispered.

"There is something about him that looks American," Sadao said. He took up the battered cap. Yes, there, almost gone, was the faint lettering. "A sailor," he said, "from an American battleship." He spelled it out, "U. S. Navy." The man was a prisoner of war!

"He has escaped," Hana cried softly, "and that is why he is wounded."

"In the back," Sadao agreed.

They hesitated, looking at each other. Then Hana said with resolution, "Come, are we able to put him back into the sea?"

"If I am able, are you?" Sadao asked.

"No," Hana said. "But if you can do it alone . . ."

Sadao hesitated again. "The strange thing is," he said, "that if the man were whole I could turn him over to the police without difficulty. I care nothing for him. He is my enemy. All Americans are my enemy. And he is only a common fellow. You see how foolish his face is. But since he is wounded . . ."

"You also cannot throw him back to the sea," Hana said. "Then there is only one thing to do. We must carry him into the house."

"But the servants?" Sadao inquired.

"We must simply tell them that we intend to give him to the police—as indeed we must, Sadao. We must think of the children and your position. It would endanger all of us if we did not give this man over as a prisoner of war."

"Certainly," Sadao agreed. "I would not think of doing anything else."

Thus agreed, together they lifted the man. He was very light, like a fowl that has been half-starved for a long time until it is only feathers and skeleton. So, his hand and arms hanging, they carried him up the steps and into the side door of the house. This door opened into a passage and down the passage they carried the man toward an empty bedroom. It had been the bedroom of Sadao's father, and since his death it had not been used. They laid the man on the deeply matted floor. Everything here had been Japanese to please the old man, who would never, in his own home, sit on a chair or sleep in a foreign bed. Hana went to the wall cupboards and slid back a door and took out a soft quilt. She hesitated. The quilt was covered with flowered silk, and the lining was pure white silk.

"He is so dirty," she murmured in distress.

"Yes, he had better be washed," Sadao agreed. "If you will fetch hot water, I will wash him."

"I cannot bear for you to touch him," she said. "We shall have to tell the servants he is here. I will tell Yumi. She can leave the children for a few minutes."

Sadao considered a moment. "Let it be so," he agreed. "You tell Yumi and I will tell the others."

But the utter pallor of the man's unconscious face moved him first to stoop and feel his pulse. It was faint but it was there. He put his hand against the man's cold breast. The heart, too, was yet alive.

"He will die unless he is operated on," Sadao said, considering. "The question is whether he will die if he is operated on, too."

Hana cried out in fear. "Don't try to save him! What if he should live?"

"What if he should die?" Sadao replied. He stood gazing down on the motionless man. This man must have extraordinary vitality or he would have been dead by now. But then he was very young—perhaps not yet twenty-five.

"You mean from the operation?" Hana asked.

"Yes," Sadao said.

Hana considered this doubtfully, and when she did not answer Sadao turned away. "At any rate something must be done with him," he said, "and first he must be washed." He went quickly out of the room and Hana came behind him. She did not wish to be left alone with the white man. He was the first she had seen since she left America and now he seemed to have nothing to do with those whom she had known there. Here he was her enemy, a menace, living or dead.

She turned to the nursery and called, "Yumi!"

But the children heard her voice and she had to go in for a moment and smile at them and play with the baby boy, now nearly three months old.

Over the baby's soft black hair she motioned with her mouth, "Yumi—come with me!"

"I will put him to bed," Yumi replied. "He is ready."

She went with Yumi into the bedroom next to the nursery and stood with the boy in her arms while Yumi spread the sleeping quilts on the floor and laid the baby between them.

Then Hana led the way quickly and softly to the kitchen. There two servants were frightened at what their master had just told them. The old gardener who was also a house servant pulled the few hairs on his upper lip.

"The master ought not to heal the wound of this white

man," he said bluntly to Hana. "The white man ought to die. First he was shot. Then the sea caught him and wounded him with her rocks. If the master heals what the gun did and what the sea did, they will take revenge on us."

"I will tell him what you say," Hana replied courteously. But she herself was also frightened, although she was not superstitious as the old man was. Could it ever be well to help an enemy? Nevertheless she told Yumi to fetch the hot water and bring it to the room where the white man was.

She went ahead and slid back the partitions. Sadao was not yet there. Yumi put down her wooden bucket. Then she went over to the white man. When she saw him her thick lips folded themselves into stubbornness. "I have never washed a white man," she said, "and I will not wash so dirty a one now."

Hana cried at her severely, "You will do what your master commands you!"

"My master ought not to command me to wash the enemy," Yumi said stubbornly.

There was so fierce a look of resistance upon Yumi's round dull face that Hana felt unreasonably afraid. After all, if the servants should report something that was not as it happened?

"Very well," she said with dignity. "You understand we only want to bring him to his senses so that we can turn him over as a prisoner?"

"I will have nothing to do with it," Yumi said. "I am a poor person and it is not my business."

"Then please," Hana said gently, "return to your work."

At once Yumi left the room. But this left Hana with the white man alone. She might have been too afraid to stay, had not her anger at Yumi's stubbornness now sustained her.

"Stupid Yumi," she muttered fiercely. "Is this anything but a man? And a wounded, helpless man!"

In the conviction of her own superiority she bent impulsively and untied the knotted rags that kept the white man covered. When she had his breast bare, she dipped the small clean towel that Yumi had brought into the steaming hot water and washed his face carefully. The man's skin, though rough with exposure, was of a fine texture and must have been very blond when he was a child.

While she was thinking these thoughts, though not really liking the man better now that he was no longer a child, she kept on washing him until his upper body was quite clean. But she dared not turn him over. Where was Sadao? Now her anger was ebbing and she was anxious again and she rose, wiping her hands on the wrung towel. Then lest the man be chilled she put the quilt over him.

"Sadao!" she called softly.

He had been about to come in when she called. His hand had been on the door so that now it opened. She saw that he had brought his surgeon's emergency bag and that he wore his surgeon's coat.

"You have decided to operate!" she cried.

"Yes," he said shortly. He turned his back to her and unfolded a sterilized towel upon the floor of the *takonoma* alcove, and put his instruments out upon it.

"Fetch towels," he said.

She went obediently, but how anxious now, to the linen shelves and took out the towels. There ought, also, to be old pieces of matting so that the blood would not ruin the deep floor covering. She went out to the back veranda where the gardener kept strips of matting with which to protect delicate shrubs on cold nights and took an armful of them.

But when she went back into the room, she saw this was useless. The blood had already soaked through the packing in the man's wound and had ruined the mat under him.

"Oh, the mat!" she cried.

"Yes, it is ruined." Sadao replied, as though he did not care. "Help me to turn him," he commanded her.

She obeyed him without a word, and he began to wash the man's back carefully.

"Yumi would not wash him," she said.

"Did you wash him, then?" Sadao asked, not stopping for a moment his swift concise movements.

"Yes," she said.

He did not seem to hear her. But she was used to his absorption when he was at work. She wondered for a moment if it mattered to him what was the body upon which he worked so long as it was the thing he did so excellently.

"You will have to give the anesthetic if he needs it," he said.

"I?" she repeated blankly. "But never have I."

"It is easy enough," he said impatiently.

He was taking out the packing now and the blood began to flow more quickly. He peered into the wound with his bright surgeon's light fastened on his forehead. "The bullet is still there," he said with cool interest. "Now I wonder how deep this rock wound is. If it is not too deep, it may be that I can get the bullet. But the bleeding is not superficial. He has lost much blood."

At this moment Hana choked. He looked up and saw her face the color of sulphur.

"Don't faint," he said sharply. He did not put down his exploring instrument. "If I stop now, the man will surely die." She clapped her hands to her mouth and leaped up and ran out of the room. Outside in the garden he heard her retching. But he went on with his work.

"It will be better for her to empty her stomach," he thought. He had forgotten that of course she had never seen an operation. But her distress and his inability to go to her at once made him impatient and irritable with this man who lay as though dead under his knife.

"This man," he thought, "there is no reason under heaven why he should live."

Unconsciously this thought made him ruthless and he proceeded swiftly. In his dream the man moaned, but Sadao paid no heed except to mutter at him.

"Groan," he muttered, "groan if you like. I am not doing this for my own pleasure. In fact, I do not know why I am doing it."

The door opened and there was Hana again. She had not stopped even to smooth back her hair.

"Where is the anesthetic?" she asked in a clear voice.

Sadao motioned with his chin. "It is as well that you came back," he said. "This fellow is beginning to stir."

She had the bottle and some cotton in her hand.

"But how shall I do it?" she asked.

"Simply saturate the cotton and hold it near his nostrils," Sadao replied without delaying for one moment the intricate detail of his work. "When he breathes badly, move it away a little."

She crouched close to the sleeping face of the young American. It was a piteously thin face, she thought, and the lips were twisted. The man was suffering whether he knew it or not. Watching him, she wondered if the stories they heard sometimes of the sufferings of prisoners were true. They came like flickers of rumor, told by word of mouth and always contradicted. In the newspapers the reports were always that wherever the Japanese armies went the people received them gladly, with cries of joy at their liberation. But sometimes she remembered such men as General Takima, who beat his wife cruelly at home, though no one mentioned it now that he had fought so victorious a battle in Manchuria. If a man like that could be so cruel to a woman in his power, would he not be cruel to one like this, for instance?

She hoped anxiously that this young man had not been tortured. It was at this moment that she observed deep red scars on his neck, just under the ear. "Those scars," she murmured, lifting her eyes to Sadao.

But he did not answer.

At this moment he felt the tip of his instrument strike against something hard, dangerously near the kidney. All thought left him. He felt only the purest pleasure. He probed with his fingers, delicately, familiar with every atom of this human body. His old American professor of anatomy had seen to that knowledge. "Ignorance of the human body is the surgeon's cardinal sin, sirs!" he had thundered at his classes year after year. "To operate without a complete knowledge of the body as if you had made it—anything less is murder."

"It is not quite at the kidney, my friend," Sadao murmured. It was his habit to murmur to the patient when he forgot himself in an operation. "My friend," he always called his patients, and so now he did, forgetting that this was his enemy.

Then, quickly, with the cleanest and most precise of incisions, the bullet was out. The man quivered but he was still unconscious. Nevertheless, he muttered a few English words.

"Guts," he muttered, choking. "They got . . . my guts. . . ."

"Sadao!" Hana cried sharply.

"Hush," Sadao said.

The man sank again into silence so profound that Sadao took up his wrist, hating the touch of it. Yes, there was still a pulse so faint, so feeble, but enough, if he wanted the man to live, to give hope.

"But certainly I do not want this man to live," he thought.

"No more anesthetic," he told Hana.

He turned as swiftly as though he had never paused, and from his medicines he chose a small vial and from it filled a hypodermic and thrust it into the patient's left arm. Then putting down the needle he took the man's wrist again. The pulse under his fingers fluttered once or twice and then grew stronger.

"This man will live in spite of all," he said to Hana and sighed.

*　　　*　　　*

The young man woke, so weak, his blue eyes so piteous when he perceived where he was, that Hana felt compelled to apology. She served him herself, for none of the servants would enter the room.

When she came in the first time she saw him summon his small strength to be prepared for some fearful thing.

"Don't be afraid," she begged him softly.

"How come . . . you speak English . . ." he gasped.

"I was a long time in America," she replied.

She saw that he wanted to reply to that but he could not and so she knelt and fed him gently from the porcelain spoon. He ate unwillingly, but still he ate.

"Now you will soon be strong," she said, not liking him and yet moved to comfort him.

He did not answer.

When Sadao came in the third day after the operation he found the young man sitting up in bed, his face bloodless with the effort.

"Lie down!" Sadao cried. "Do you want to die?"

He forced the man down gently and strongly, and examined the wound. "You may kill yourself if you do this sort of thing," he scolded.

"What are you going to do with me?" the boy muttered. He looked just now barely seventeen. "Are you going to hand me over?"

For a moment Sadao did not answer. He finished his examination and then pulled the silk quilt over the man.

"I do not know myself what I shall do with you," he said. "I ought of course to give you to the police. You are a prisoner of war. . . . No, do not tell me anything." He put up his hand as he saw the young man about to speak. "Do not even tell me your name unless I ask it."

They looked at each other for a moment, and then the young man closed his eyes and turned his face to the wall.

"Okay," he whispered, his mouth a bitter line.

Outside the door Hana was waiting for Sadao. He saw at once that she was in trouble.

"Sadao, Yumi tells me the servants feel that they cannot stay if we hide this man here any more," she said. "She says they are thinking that you and I were so long in America that we have forgotten to think of our own country first. They think we like Americans."

"It is not true," Sadao said harshly. "Americans are our enemies. But I have been trained not to let a man die if I can help it."

"The servants cannot understand that," she said anxiously.

"No," he agreed.

Neither seemed able to say more, and somehow the household dragged on. The servants grew daily more watchful. Their courtesy was as careful as ever, but their eyes were cold upon the pair to whom they were hired.

"It is clear what our master ought to do," the old gardener said one morning. He had worked with flowers all his life, and had been a specialist, too, in moss. For Sadao's father he had made one of the finest moss gardens in Japan, sweeping the bright green carpet constantly so that not a leaf or a pine needle marred the velvet of its surface. "My old master's son knows very well what he ought to do," he now said, pinching a bud from a bush as he spoke. "When the man was so near death, why did he not let him bleed?"

"That young master is so proud of his skill to save life that he saves any life," the cook said contemptuously. She split a fowl's neck skillfully and held the fluttering bird and let its blood flow into the roots of a wistaria vine. Blood is the best of fertilizers and the old gardener would not let her waste a drop of it.

"It is the children of whom we must think," Yumi said sadly. "What will be their fate if their father is condemned as a traitor?"

They did not try to hide what they said from the ears of Hana as she stood arranging the day's flowers in the veranda near by, and she knew that they spoke on purpose that she might hear. That they were right she knew in most of her being. But there was another part of her which she herself could not understand. It was not sentimental liking of the prisoner. She had come to think of him as a prisoner. She had not liked him even yesterday when he said in his impulsive way, "Anyway, let me tell you that my name is Tom." She had only bowed her little distant bow. She saw hurt in his eyes, but she did not wish to assuage it. Indeed he was a great trouble in this house.

As for Sadao, every day he examined the wound carefully. The last stitches had been pulled out today, and the young man would in a fortnight be nearly as well as ever. Sadao went back to his office and carefully typed a letter to the chief of police reporting the whole matter. "On the twenty-first day of February an escaped prisoner was washed upon the shore in front of my house." So far he typed, and then he opened a secret drawer of his desk and put the unfinished report into it.

On the seventh day after that, two things happened. In the morning the servants left together, their belongings tied in large square cotton kerchiefs. When Hana got up in the morning nothing was done, the house not cleaned and the food not prepared, and she knew what it meant. She was dismayed and even terrified, but her pride as a mistress would not allow her to show it. Instead, she inclined her head gracefully when they appeared before her in the kitchen, and she paid them off and thanked them for all that they had done for her. They were crying, but she did not cry. The cook and the gardener had served Sadao since he was a little boy in his father's house, and Yumi cried because of the children. She was so grieving that after she had gone she ran back to Hana.

"If the baby misses me too much tonight, send for me. I am going to my own house and you know where it is."

"Thank you," Hana said smiling. But she told herself she would not send for Yumi however the baby cried.

She made the breakfast and Sadao helped with the children. Neither of them spoke of the servants beyond the fact that they were gone. But after Hana had taken morning food to the prisoner she came back to Sadao.

"Why is it we cannot see clearly what we ought to do?" she asked him. "Even the servants see more clearly than we do. Why are we different from other Japanese?"

Sadao did not answer. But a little later he went into the room where the prisoner was and said brusquely, "Today you may get up on your feet. I want you to stay up only five minutes at a time. Tomorrow you may try it twice as long. It would be well that you get back your strength as quickly as possible."

He saw the flicker of terror on the young face that was still very pale.

"Okay," the boy murmured. Evidently he was determined to say more. "I feel I ought to thank you, doctor, for having saved my life."

"Don't thank me too early," Sadao said coldly. He saw the flicker of terror again in the boy's eyes—terror as unmistakable as an animal's. The scars on his neck were scarlet for a moment. Those scars! What were they? Sadao did not ask.

In the afternoon the second thing happened. Hana, working hard at unaccustomed labor, saw a messenger come to the door in official uniform. Her hands went weak and she could not draw her breath. The servants must have told already. She ran to Sadao, gasping, unable to utter a word. But by then the messenger had simply followed her through the garden and there he stood. She pointed at him futilely.

Sadao looked up from his book. He was in his office, the outer partition of which was thrown open to the garden for the southern sunshine.

"What is it?" he asked the messenger and then he rose, seeing the man's uniform.

"You are to come to the palace," the man said. "The old General is in pain again."

"Oh," Hana breathed, "is that all?"

"All?" the messenger exclaimed. "Is it not enough?"

"Indeed, it is," she replied. "I am very sorry."

When Sadao came to tell her good-by she was in the kitchen, but doing nothing. The children were asleep and she sat merely resting for a moment, more exhausted from her fright than from work.

"I thought they had come to arrest you," she said.

He gazed down into her anxious eyes. "I must get rid of this man for your sake," he said in distress. "Somehow I must get rid of him."

*   *   *

"Of course," the General said weakly, "I understand fully. But that is because I once took a degree in Princeton. So few Japanese have."

"I care nothing for the man, Excellency," Sadao said, "but having operated on him with such success . . ."

"Yes, yes," the General said. "It only makes me feel you more indispensable to me. You say you think I can stand one more such attack as I have had today?"

"Not more than one," Sadao said.

"Then certainly I can allow nothing to happen to you," the General said with anxiety. His long pale Japanese face became expressionless, which meant that he was in deep thought. "You cannot be arrested," the General said, closing his eyes. "Suppose you were condemned to death and the next day I had to have my operation?"

"There are other surgeons, Excellency," Sadao suggested.

"None that I trust," the General replied. "The best ones have been trained by Germans and would consider the operation successful even if I died. I do not care for their point of view." He sighed. "It seems a pity that we cannot better combine the German ruthlessness with the American sentimentality. Then you could turn your prisoner over to execution, and yet I could be sure you would not murder me while I was unconscious." The General laughed. He had an unusual sense of humor. "As a Japanese, could you not combine these two foreign elements?" he asked.

Sadao smiled. "I am not quite sure," he said, "but for your sake I would be willing to try, Excellency."

The General shook his head. "I had rather not be the test case," he said. He felt suddenly weak and overwhelmed with the cares of his life as an official in times such as these when repeated victory brought great responsibilities all over the south Pacific. "It is very unfortunate that this man should have been washed up on your doorstep," he said irritably.

"I feel it so myself," Sadao said gently.

"It would be best if he could be quietly killed," the General said. "Not by you, but by someone who does not know him. I have my own private assassins. Suppose I send two of them to your house tonight—or better, any night. You need know nothing about it. It is now warm— what would be more natural than that you should leave the outer partition of the white man's room open to the garden while he sleeps?"

"Certainly it would be very natural," Sadao agreed. "In fact, it is so left open every night."

"Good," the General said, yawning. "They are very capable assassins—they make no noise and they know the trick of inward bleeding. If you like, I can even have them remove the body."

Sadao considered. "That perhaps would be best, Excellency," he agreed, thinking of Hana.

He left the General's presence then, and went home, thinking over the plan. In this way, the whole thing would be taken out of his hands. He would tell Hana nothing, since she would be timid at the idea of assassins in the house, and yet certainly such persons were essential in an absolute state such as Japan was. How else could rulers deal with those who opposed them?

He refused to allow anything but reason to be the atmosphere of his mind as he went into the room where the American was in bed. But as he opened the door he found the young man out of bed to his surprise, and preparing to go out into the garden.

"What is this?" he exclaimed. "Who gave you permission to leave your room?"

"I'm not used to waiting for permission," Tom said gaily. "Gosh, I feel pretty good again! But will the muscles on this side always feel stiff?"

"Is it so?" Sadao inquired, surprised. He forgot all else. "Now I thought I had provided against that," he murmured. He lifted the edge of the man's shirt and gazed at the healing scar. "Massage may do it," he said, "if exercise does not."

"It won't bother me much," the young man said. His

young face was gaunt under the stubbly blond beard. "Say, doctor, I've got something I want to say to you. If I hadn't met a Jap like you, well, I wouldn't be alive today. I know that."

Sadao bowed, but he could not speak.

"Sure, I know that," Tom went on warmly. His big thin hands gripping a chair were white at the knuckles. "I guess if all the Japs were like you there wouldn't have been a war."

"Perhaps," Sadao said with difficulty. "And now I think you had better go back to bed."

He helped the boy back into bed and then bowed. "Good night," he said.

He slept badly that night. Time and time again he woke, thinking he heard the rustling of footsteps, the sound of a twig broken or a stone displaced in the garden, such sounds as men might make who carried a burden.

The next morning he made the excuse to go first into the guest room. If the American were gone, he then could simply tell Hana, and so the General had directed. But when he opened the door he saw at once that it was not done last night. There, on the pillow, was the shaggy blond head. He could hear the peaceful breathing of sleep, and he closed the door again quietly.

"He is asleep," he told Hana. "He is almost well to sleep like that."

"What shall we do with him?" Hana whispered her old refrain.

Sadao shook his head. "I must decide in a day or two," he promised.

But certainly, he thought, the second night must be the night. There rose a wind that night, and he listened to the sounds of bending boughs and whistling partitions.

Hana woke too. "Ought we not to go and close the sick man's partition?" she asked.

"No," Sadao said. "He is able now to do it for himself."

But the next morning the American was still there.

Then the third night, of course, must be the night. The wind changed to quiet rain and the garden was full of the sound of dripping caves and running springs. Sadao slept a little better, but he woke at the sound of a crash and leaped to his feet.

"What was that?" Hana cried. The baby woke at her voice and began to wail. "I must go and see." But he held her and would not let her move. "Sadao," she cried, "what is the matter with you?"

"Don't go," he muttered. "Don't go!"

His terror infected her and she stood breathless, waiting. There was only silence. Together they crept back into the bed, the baby between them.

Yet, when he opened the door of the guest room in the morning, there was the young man. He was very gay and had already washed and was on his feet. He had asked for a razor yesterday and had shaved himself, and today there was a faint color in his cheeks.

"I am well," he said joyously.

Sadao drew his kimono around his weary body. He could not, he decided suddenly, go through another night. It was not that he cared for this young man's life. No, simply it was not worth the strain.

"You are well," Sadao agreed. He lowered his voice. "You are so well that I think if I put my boat on the shore tonight, with food and extra clothing in it, you might be able to row to that little island not far from the coast. It is so near the coast that it has not been worth fortifying. Nobody lives on it because in storm it is sub-

merged. But this is not the season of storm. You could
live there until you saw a fishing boat pass by. They pass
quite near the island because the water is many fathoms
deep there."

The young man stared at him, slowly comprehending.
"Do I have to?" he asked.

"I think so," Sadao said gently. "You understand . . .
it is not hidden that you are here. . . ."

The young man nodded in perfect comprehension.
"Okay," he said simply.

Sadao did not see him again until evening. As soon as
it was dark he had dragged the stout boat down to the
shore and in it he put food and bottled water that he had
bought secretly during the day, as well as two quilts he
had bought at a pawnshop. The boat he tied to a post in
the water, for the tide was high. There was no moon and
he worked without a flashlight.

When he came to the house he entered as though he
were just back from his work, and Hana knew nothing.
"Yumi was here today," she said as she served his supper.
Though she was so modern, still she did not eat with him.
"Yumi cried over the baby," she went on with a sigh.
"She misses him so."

"The servants will come back as soon as the foreigner is
gone," Sadao said.

He went into the guest room that night before he went
to bed, and himself checked carefully the American's
temperature, the state of the wound, and his heart and
pulse. The pulse was irregular but that was perhaps because of excitement. The young man's pale lips were
pressed together and his eyes burned. Only the scars on his
neck were red.

"I realize that you are saving my life again," he told Sadao.

"Not at all," Sadao said. "It is only inconvenient to have you here any longer."

He had hesitated a good deal about giving the man a flashlight. But he had decided to give it to him after all. It was a small one, his own, which he used at night when he was called.

"If your food runs out before you catch a boat," he said, "signal me two flashes at the same instant the sun drops over the horizon. Do not signal in darkness for it will be seen. If you are all right but still there, signal me once. You will find fish easy to catch but you must eat them raw. A fire would be seen."

"Okay," the young man breathed.

He was dressed now in the Japanese clothes which Sadao had given him, and at the last moment Sadao wrapped a black cloth about his blond head.

"Now," Sadao said.

The young American without a word shook Sadao's hand warmly, and then walked quite well across the floor and down the step into the darkness of the garden. Once . . . twice . . . Sadao saw his light flash to find his way. But that would not be suspected. He waited until from the shore there was one more flash. Then he closed the partition. That night he slept.

*   *   *

"You say the man escaped?" the General asked faintly. He had been operated upon a week ago, an emergency operation to which Sadao had been called in the night. For twelve hours Sadao had not been sure the General would live. The gall bladder was much involved. Then the old man began to breathe deeply again and to ask for food. Sadao had not been able to ask about the assassins. So far as he knew, they had never come. The servants returned, and Yumi had cleaned the guest room thoroughly and had burned sulphur in it to get the white man's smell out of it. Nobody said anything. Only the gardener was cross because he had got behind with his chrysanthemum cuttings.

After a week Sadao had felt the General was well enough to be spoken to about the prisoner.

"Yes, Excellency, he escaped," Sadao said. He coughed, signifying that he had not said all that he might have said, but was unwilling to disturb the General further. But the old man opened his eyes suddenly.

"That prisoner," he said with some energy, "did I not promise you I would kill him for you?"

"You did, Excellency," Sadao said.

"Well, well!" the old man said in a tone of amazement. "So I did! But you see, I was suffering a good deal. The truth is, I thought of nothing but myself. In short, I forgot my promise to you."

"I wondered, Your Excellency," Sadao murmured.

"It was certainly very careless of me," the General said. "But you understand it was not lack of patriotism or dereliction of duty." He looked anxiously at his doctor. "If the matter should come out, you would understand that, wouldn't you?"

"Certainly, Your Excellency," Sadao said. He suddenly comprehended that the General was in the palm of his hand and that as a consequence he himself was perfectly safe. "I can swear to your loyalty, Excellency," he said to the old General, "and to your zeal against the enemy."

"You are a good man," the General murmured, and closed his eyes. "You will be rewarded."

*   *   *

But Sadao, searching the spot of black in the twilighted sea that night, had his reward. There was no prick of light in the dusk. No one was on the island. His prisoner was gone—safe, doubtless, for he had warned him to wait only for a Korean fishing boat.

He stood for a moment on the veranda, gazing out to the sea from whence the young man had come that other night. And into his mind, although without reason, there came other white faces he had known—the professor at whose house he had met Hana, a dull man, and his wife, who had been a silly, talkative woman, in spite of her wish to be kind. He remembered his old teacher of anatomy, who had been so insistent on mercy with his knife, and then he remembered the face of his fat and slatternly landlady. He had had great difficulty in finding a place to live because he was a Japanese. The Americans were full of prejudice and it had been bitter to live in it, knowing himself their superior. How he had despised the ignorant and dirty old woman who had at last consented to house him in her miserable home! He had once tried to be grateful to her because she had, in his last year, nursed him through influenza, but it was difficult, for she was no less repulsive to him in her kindness. But then white people were repulsive, of course. It was a relief to be openly at war with them at last. Now he remembered the youthful, haggard face of his prisoner—white and repulsive.

"Strange," he thought. "I wonder why I could not kill him."

Hearts Come Home

❧

YOUNG DAVID LIN stood moodily in the corner of the large parlor and watched the eight or ten couples of his friends gravely dancing. The music of an industrious brass band blared forth from behind a clump of palms planted in pots. He knew, of course, it was a very rich and expensive room, since it belonged to Mr. Fang, who was one of the leading bankers in the city of Shanghai. Mr. Fang would not tolerate anything that was not rich and expensive. The walls therefore were hung in modern oil paintings and also in very delicate and exquisite old scrolls, for, Mr. Fang always said, his fat and shining face expanding into great thick wrinkles of laughter, "I have the best of everything, new and old. There is room for it all in my house."

Mr. Fang sat now watching the young people dance, and beside him sat two pretty girls. One of these was his daughter, Phyllis, and the other was his latest concubine, a young actress. They were about the same age, but they were very different. Phyllis, David had decided earlier in the evening, was the prettiest girl in the room. He did not understand how anyone so fat and ugly as Mr. Fang could have this slender bamboo of a girl for a daughter. For she did look like a bamboo. She was pale and a little tall, almost as tall as himself, and she wore a soft green long robe, and her face was not painted, so that it was the color of new ivory. And her hair was not like these other women's hair. It was not clipped or frizzed or curled or any of those things. It was long and straight and very black and drawn back from her face into a firm knot on her neck. She sat placidly watching her guests, an expression of tranquil pleasure about her pretty lips. As for the concubine, she looked like an actress. She made great eyes and moved her body about and her hair flared out from her too pink and rounded face. David, staring briefly at her, hated her instantly. She would chatter—she would chatter in some barbarous mixture of English and Chinese.

He had for some ten minutes been planning to go and ask Phyllis to dance with him, but he had been held back by this actress. Suppose, he said to himself, that this actress put out her hand—she was forever putting out her hand to the young men who approached her—and before he knew it he would have to dance with her; he would not, he said to himself, dance with any more frizzy-haired women, no, nor women with painted, powdered faces. Their hair tickled his neck and their faces ruined his foreign coat. He glanced down at his shoulder and brushed it off with the palm of his hand. There was a patch of powder upon it. That was because Doris Li's face had lain there earlier in the evening. He hated Doris Li—a silly creature who pretended she had forgotten how to speak her own tongue because she had been in Paris so long.

With Phyllis he had never danced, because this was the first time he had seen her. She worked somewhere in a school, not in this city, and now she was home for the spring holiday. Mr. Fang had said, introducing her, "This is my one industrious child. The others are content to do nothing."

"You must be proud of her," David had murmured, not looking at her face. He was very tired of girls' faces.

But Mr. Fang only laughed loudly. "She doesn't make enough money for me to be proud of her," he said cheerfully. "She does it to amuse herself."

Then he did look at her—a girl who worked to amuse herself! He had never seen such a thing. For the first time in months he was interested even for a moment in a girl. With something more than his usual fixed smile he said, "May I have a dance?" But she had already promised every dance. For a moment he was sorry. Then he said to himself it did not matter. After all, she was only old Fang's daughter and another girl. He danced desultorily through the afternoon with several girls. He could scarcely remember them now. They all left powder on his coat, though, he remembered gloomily.

Then old Fang had decided they would not stop at the end of the program. He loved dancing, bounding about the room like a huge balloon in his floating silk robes, his round face glittering with smiles, and his laughter roaring out when he stepped on someone's foot as he passed. Now he shouted at the musicians, peering at them through the palms, "Play three more numbers and you shall have a double tip!" So saying, he seized his concubine and they were off. Against his protruding bulges she leaned herself gaily, her eyes roving away from him and about the room.

It was David's chance. Hastily, for he saw converging upon Phyllis three dapper, beautifully dressed young men, he hastened himself and appeared before her. "May I—"

But the young men also hastened themselves— "May I—" "May I—" "May I—" Their voices were like the rounds he used to have to sing in the American school where he was educated. He stood back stiffly—let her choose. She chose very easily, rising and moving toward him. "You were first?" she said in a pleasant little voice. "Yes," he said, and they moved out into the room.

In the noise of the music it was impossible to talk. That was like old Fang, too, to go and hire a double brass band for a tea. The room shook in the noise. He held her to him in the approved modern fashion, breast to breast, thigh to thigh. Her cheek was against his shoulder. He danced well and he knew it, but then, he found, so did she. She gave and swayed so easily to his body that he grew suspicious and looked down at her. Was she being perhaps a little too easily yielding? He was tired of girls who yielded too easily. But her small pale face was quite cold, and her eyes, when she turned them up to his prettily were passionless. She smiled and said something, but he could not hear her voice. He raised his eyebrows and she laughed, and they did not try again. At the end of the dance the young men were waiting for her solidly, so he let her go with no more than his usual carefully effusive thanks. "You dance swell, Miss Fang. Gee, it's good to get a good partner!"

"Thank you, Mr. Lin. You dance swell, too," she answered easily.

He did not dance again, although there were girls without partners. Doris Li was one of these, and she came languishing and laughing past him. But he bent ostentatiously to tie his shoestring. He wasn't going to dance again. He pondered on Phyllis a moment, although he had now for a long time not thought about any girls at all. He thought in fact about nothing except his work, which he liked very much. It was that of a manager in his father's printing house. He thought all the time about how to improve the printing of their books. He used to think about girls a great deal, but that was before he tired of them. They were so much alike. Every girl in Shanghai, he had long ago decided, was like every other. He listened cynically when his friends grew excited over a new beauty. There was not such a thing.

The tea ended and people began to go away, gay couples hand in hand going off together to some other amusement. The band was silent, and instead the air was filled with a clatter of thanks and farewells, Chinese and English mingled in word and sentence. It was very smart to speak so, just as it was smart to take foreign first names. He could speak the jargon, too, when he must. He had, in fact, many ways of speaking. He could speak American college boy or Oxford English or the precise old Chinese his father still demanded of him, or this jargon of English and Chinese his friends now practiced. It all depended on where he was.

But he secretly liked the Chinese best, although he made fun of it to his own friends. They all said over and over "There are so many modern things we cannot say in Chinese. How, for instance, do you say—" He always agreed, and they had fun trying to twist the old staid words to say even such things as "Hot mamma," "You're my baby," "I'm nuts about you." But afterwards he felt uncomfortable, as though he had taught a child to say innocently an obscene thing. For the old words would not say these things. Twisted thus, they made no sense, saying nothing at all, remaining serenely themselves and refusing to be perverted.

He joined the ebbing crowd at the door. Phyllis stood there, smiling, answering gaily, putting out her hand freely to her guests. He looked at her and said to himself gloomily that he was probably wrong in thinking she was different from any of the others. Just now she seemed like any of the others—like any girl. Probably she powdered too. He looked down at his shoulder involuntarily. But no, it was quite clean. He made up his mind instantly.

"May I stay a little while and talk?" he asked.

She hesitated. "I am going to the Casino with friends," she said.

"May I come with you?" he asked at once.

"I suppose you may," she answered.

A servant was there with her coat, and he took it and put it about her shoulders. Suddenly he saw the small fine hairs upon her nape, black against the ivory pale smooth skin. He felt a strange shock of pleasure in him.

That was the beginning, but the end was almost instantly there. For before the night was over he was wildly in love with her, though the accumulated hatred he had for all girls was worse than ever. He loathed every girl he saw at the Casino that night. They were the worst of their kind, he thought, his heart scornful behind his smiling face. He danced with them when he could not get Phyllis, practicing all the little attentions of smart behavior while he hated them. When he took a hand, he hated it for its prettiness and its scarlet nails. It made him curious to know what Phyllis's hands were. He must look the first moment he could. In the little alcove where he sat out a dance with another girl he kissed her coldly, when she leaned toward him for his kiss. It was nothing to kiss a girl, nothing to him. He rubbed his lips secretly while he was pretending to wipe his face with his handkerchief. He hated rouge—Phyllis's lips—he began wondering about her lips.

There it was. Once he began this sort of wonder he could not stop it, and day after day of spring sunshine hurried him. Besides, she would be going away again. He had to hurry. He begged a holiday from his father and beset her daily, using all his technique. After all, he told himself, she was a modern girl, and probably she liked all this stuff. He sent her flowers and candy, and found copies of freshly printed books and had them under his arm when he appeared before her, so that he never went without gifts.

But of course all these gifts—they must have meaning. He watched her to see if they meant anything. "Like candy, kid?" he inquired of her carelessly, presenting her with a five-pound box of foreign chocolates. Did her face fall a little? But her voice came with careful enthusiasm. "Oh, swell, Dave," she replied. They spoke English almost entirely, and since they had both gone to an American university they spoke what they had learned there. "Sure you like it?" he pressed her. "Crazy about it," she replied. He stared at her. She talked as they all did, but somehow it never seemed her language. She opened the box and exclaimed cheerfully, "Oh, aren't they lovely—oh, how nice." Then she put it down on the table.

Yes, he used his technique, all the modern technique they used on each other. He took her everywhere, to dance, to the theater, and she went willingly. In the taxicab he reached for her hand and held it, and once he seized her by the shoulders and would have kissed her, but unexpectedly she bent her head quickly and his lips touched her cheek and not her lips. He had planned the kiss with some enthusiasm, too—more enthusiasm than he had felt in such things for a long time. But, foiled, he had no enthusiasm at all. Her cheek was quite cold. She did not take her hand away from his, but it lay there passively, and he wished it would not be rude to put it down.

Yet he loved her more all the time. Because he could not

seem to get at her he loved her. She did not repulse him, she never repulsed him. She took her part in all his plans, she refused him nothing. If he took her arm, she leaned against him a little—she had no old-fashioned ways. But so she was. She did all these things as though it were a pattern she had been taught to do. It was a technique with her. It was a technique of love for them both. He wanted her to know he loved her, and he had no way to tell her except this modern way. "I'm crazy about you, kid," he said. "Sure, I'm crazy about you, too," she answered politely, and his heart chilled in him.

And all the time the days were passing, the days of the short month he had, and he could not break away this barrier of modern technique. Once at the door after a late dance he leaned to her, "Kiss me good night, Phyllis?"

"Yes," she answered readily, and touched his cheek easily with her calm lips.

It was all nothing. They were growing not nearer but further apart. Words and touch only were pushing them apart. He did not know what to do, so he kept on doing what they were doing.

Then suddenly the day before she went away they discovered each other. They were dancing together at the Casino again, close, welded together, when suddenly she stopped and pulled away from him and looked at him.

"Do you truly like this?" she asked him. He was startled. Her voice was changed, softer, deeper. She was speaking in Chinese, in their own tongue! Why had they never spoken in Chinese? There had been some nonsense of different dialects. She was not native to Shanghai—her family had come from the north—English was smarter, and so they pretended it was easier. But it was not. He understood her perfectly in Chinese. He looked back at her intensely. The tawdry dancing hall faded from around them. "I do not like it," he replied. "I cannot tell you how greatly I do not like it."

"Then let us go away," she said simply.

She was quite different from anything he had known of her before. In the car she sat with such reserve and dignity that he did not want to take her hand. At this moment he was nearer to her when he did not take her hand. At her door he hesitated. But she said, "Will you come in? I think there is speech we wish to have together."

"I have many things to say," he answered.

It seemed indeed that they had never talked at all. All the foolish foreign words they had interchanged had said nothing. Now crowding to his tongue were other words, their own words. Everything remained yet to be said. She sat down on the satin-covered couch, and he sat on a chair near her. She looked at him, and then she looked around the room. "I dislike all of this," she said, sweeping her hand through the air. "You do not know me at all. You do not even know my true name. I am not what I have seemed to you. Now that I am about to go away I want you to know that I am very old-fashioned. I have been all this month doing things with you which I hate. It is better for you to know. I do not like to dance. I dislike foreign sweets. I do not like to kiss people. It makes me feel ill to kiss anyone or to feel anyone's lips upon my face or hand—even yours I do not like."

"Wait," he interrupted. "I see now I have felt what you were all along. I see why we were never near to each other. Why did you come with me to dances, and why did you let me kiss you? If you had said you did not like it I would not have done so."

She dropped her head and looked at her hands tightly

clasped in her lap. She answered, shyly, "I thought you liked these foreign ways and I wanted to be what you liked. I thought if I refused you might not—come again." Her voice was very small indeed when she finished.

"What is your true name?" he demanded of her.

"It is Ming Sing—Shining Heart," she replied.

"Mine is Yung An—Brave Peace," he said.

They were silent a moment.

Then he went on. He leaned forward in his chair. "You mean—you do mean truly that you like our own ways best?"

"Much, much best," she faltered.

"You would not like a house like this?" he questioned her sternly.

"No," she faltered.

"Nor dancing nor motoring nor any of these things the women do all day?"

"No."

"We need never waste our time so any more," he said, after a moment.

"Never any more," she answered.

He waited another moment. "I also do not like to kiss," he announced.

"Then let us not kiss each other any more," she said.

"We will speak our own language and I will take off these foreign garments and put on my robes again and we will live in old comfortable ways and I will smoke a water pipe."

"I will never wear leather shoes again," she said. "And I will never eat butter again, which I hate, nor any foreign foods, and our table will always be set with bowls and chopsticks, and I shall have a house with courts and no stairs, and I want many children."

He saw it all as she spoke, their house, their home, everything their own, and themselves as they really wanted to be. He began to pour out his words, "Will you then marry me? Shall we——" Then he stopped. He rose to his feet and stood resolutely before her. "No," he said. "Miss Fang, my father will write your father a letter. It will come soon—at once—" he was already halfway to the door. Now he was at the door, and he looked back at her. She rose and bowed, and stood looking at him, too, waked, and warm as a rose. He saw her for the first time. This was how she truly was, this lovely, natural creature of his own kind. They would raise lotus flowers in the pool in the court, and they would have a little bamboo grove and read poetry there in the summer—old four-lined verses. He had always wanted to have time for it.

"Are you going, Mr. Lin?" she asked in the old formula of farewell.

The words came so sweetly from her tongue that his feet had carried him back a step before he knew it. Then he caught himself. "No more foreign ways," he said firmly. He went out into the hall, and then he put his head in to look at her once more. She was sitting quietly upon the couch, her little hands folded, her little feet placed neatly together, exactly as his own old mother might have sat as a girl. She was looking ahead of her, seeing, he knew, the house, the court, the many children, the safe old ways of living. She was there waiting, so pretty, so pretty— "At least not yet," he amended, hurrying.

The New Road

❧❦❧

LU CHEN kept a hot-water shop on the corner of the street of the North Gate, where the alley of the Hwang family intersects it. As everyone knows, that was one of the chief places in the whole length of that street. Not only did the silk shops fling out their banners of orange silk, but down the alley of the Hwangs lived other great families. A score of times a day the clerks idling about the dim shops sent the tea coolie for pots of scalding water to brew the tea that they sipped the whole day through. A score of times a day the ladies of the alley, gambling delicately as a pastime in one another's houses, sent their slaves to get water from Lu Chen. It was a thriving business and had been a thriving business even in his grandfather's time, when an emperor had lived but a few miles away and that very street had ended in a prince's pleasure grounds.

From his father Lu Chen had received the shop, together with a rice sack full of silver dollars. The rice sack had been emptied to pay for his wedding, but gradually it had been filled again to pay for the schooling and then the wedding of his son. Now, after this last emptying, it was a fifth full again, and Lu Chen's grandchild ran about the shop, terrifying the old man with his venturesome spirit and his curiosity regarding the great copper caldrons built into the earthen ovens.

"When I was a child," Lu Chen proclaimed at least daily to his small grandson, "I never ran near the caldrons. I obeyed my grandfather and did not eternally run about like a small chicken."

Of this the grandson understood nothing. He was as yet too young to speak clearly, but he was able to understand that he was the center of his grandfather's heart, and he continued to stagger about near the ovens under the old man's agitated eye. He had become accustomed, of course, to being lifted suddenly by the collar of his small coat and to dangling in the air while his grandfather set him in the inner room.

"I cannot understand this child of yours," remarked Lu Chen to his tall young son. "When will you teach him obedience?"

Lu Chen's son, who had been inclined to idleness and discontent ever since finishing his fourth year at the government middle school, shrugged his shoulders in reply and said half petulantly, "We do not so worship obedience these days."

Lu Chen glanced at him sharply. He would never acknowledge that his son was at all idle. Even at night, when he lay within the curtains of his bamboo bed beside his wife, he would not acknowledge it.

Sometimes she said: "The boy has not enough to do. The shop is small, and there is really only one man's work. If you would only rest now—are you not fifty years old? —and allow our son to manage the business, it would be better. He is twenty years old, and he feels no responsibility for his rice or for the rice of his wife and the child. You do everything. Why did you send him to school if he is to be idle?"

Lu Chen threw back the thick blue cotton-stuffed quilt.

This talk of giving up his work in the shop always stifled him. The real reason why he had allowed his son to continue in school year after year was that he might have the shop to himself.

"That bigger caldron," he muttered, "is never so bright as I could wish. I have said to him a dozen times, 'Take the ash from the oven and wet it a little and smear it upon the copper and, when it is dried——' but he never will do it."

"Because you are never satisfied when he does," said his wife. She was a large, stout-bodied woman; Lu Chen's small, dried figure scarcely lifted the quilt at all in comparison with the mound of her flesh beneath it.

"He will not do it as I command him," he said in a loud voice.

"You are never satisfied," she replied calmly.

This calmness of hers irritated him more than any anger. He sat upright and stared down at her placid face. Through the coarse linen curtains the light of the bean-oil lamp shone with a vague flicker; he could see her drowsy eyes and her full, expressionless lips.

"I do as my father taught me," he said shrilly.

"Ah, well," she murmured. "Let us sleep. What does it matter?"

He panted a moment and lay down.

"You care nothing for the shop," he said at last. It was the gravest accusation he could think of.

But she did not answer. She was asleep and her loud, tranquil breathing filled the recesses of the curtains.

The next morning he rose very early and himself scoured the inside of the two caldrons until they reflected his lean brown face. He would have liked to let them remain empty until his son awoke and so show him how they could be made to look. But he dared not, since the slaves and servants came early for hot water for their mistresses' baths. He filled the caldrons, therefore, with water from the earthen jars and lighted the fires beneath them. Soon the steam was bubbling up from under the water-soaked wooden covers. He had filled and refilled the caldrons three times before his son sauntered in, rubbing his eyes, his blue cotton gown half buttoned around him and his hair on end. Lu Chen gave him a sharp look.

"When I was young," he said, "I rose early and scoured the caldrons and lighted the fires beneath them, and my father slept."

"These are the days of the Revolution," said the young man, lightly. Lu Chen snorted and spat upon the ground. "These are the days of disobedient sons and of idle young men," he said. "What will your son be, seeing that you do not yet earn your rice?"

But the young man only smiled and, buttoning his coat slowly, went to the caldron nearest him and dipped into a basin water wherewith to wash.

Lu Chen watched him, his face quivering. "It is only for you that I value the shop," he said at last. "It is that the business may go to you and the child after you. This hot-water shop has stood here sixty years. It is well known. All my father's life and my life and your life have come from it—and now the child's."

"There is talk of the new road now," said the young man, wringing a steaming cloth from the water and wiping his face.

That was the first time Lu Chen heard of the new road. It meant nothing to him then. His son was always away, always full of talk of new things, ever since the Revolution had come into the city. What the Revolution was Lu

Chen did not clearly perceive. There had certainly been days when his business was very poor and when the great shops had been closed for fear of looting and when the families he regularly supplied had moved away to Shanghai. His business then had been reduced to the petty filling of tin teakettles for the poorer people, who haggled over a copper penny. People said it was the Revolution, and he had become anxious and cursed it in his heart. Then suddenly soldiers were everywhere, and they bought water most recklessly. That was when he began filling up the rice sack again. That was the Revolution, too. He was mightily puzzled, but he no longer cursed it. Then the great shops opened and the old families came back and soldiers drifted away again and things were much as they had been except that prices were high, so that he could raise the price of water too, and was relieved.

"These revolutions," he said to his son one morning, "what are they about? You have been to school—do you know? It has been a great stir. I am glad it is over."

At that the son raised his eyebrows. "Over?" he repeated. "It is only begun. Wait. This city will be the capital of the country, and then everything will be greatly changed."

The old man shook his head. "Change? There is never great change. Emperors and kings and presidents or whatnot, people must drink tea and must bathe—these go on forever."

Well, but this new road? On the very day his son had mentioned it, that impudent young slave girl from the third alley down had turned up the corner of her lip at him and said: "I hear talk from our master of a great new road sixty feet wide. What then of your caldrons, Lu Chen?"

Lu Chen's arm was bare to the elbow and wrinkled and reddened by the continued steam from the water. He scarcely felt the heat. But now, as the slave girl spoke, he dipped his bamboo dipper more deeply into the water and grunted. His hand trembled and slopped a little water over the edge of the caldron into the hot coals of the fire. A hiss rose from them. He did not speak but made a pretense of stirring up the fire. He was not going to speak to that silly creature. Yet, after she had gone, he remembered that she was a slave in the house of Ling and that, since the eldest son of Ling was an official, there might indeed be talk of the road. He gazed about on the gray brick walls of his little shop in a sort of terror. They were darkened with smoke and dampness and had cracks that he could remember even from childhood. Sixty feet wide? Why, it would mean the whole shop ripped away!

"I will ask such a price that they cannot buy it," he thought. "Such a price——" He cast about in himself for a sum enormous enough to stagger a government. "I will ask ten thousand dollars!"

He was happy then. Who would pay ten thousand dollars for this twelve square feet of space and the two caldrons? Where was so much money in the world? Why when his father had been a young man, the Prince Ming-yuan had built a palace for that. He laughed a little and was more lenient with his son and forgot the new road and daily preserved the life of the child from the caldrons. Everything was as before.

One morning midway to noon he sat down to rest and drink a little tea. He always brewed his own tea after the fifth emptying of the caldrons, just before he began to fill them again for the noon call. In this interval, when people had bought for the morning tea and the hour had not yet approached for the midday meal, he could enjoy a little leisure. He took the grandchild on his knee and let him drink also and smiled to see him grasp the bowl in two hands and drink, staring gravely over the rim.

All at once there was a sharp rap like a sword-cut at the door. Lu Chen set the child down carefully and moved the teapot out of his reach. Then he went to the door and, fumbling a little, drew back the wooden bar. A man stood there in a gray cotton uniform. He was a young officer of some sort, with an arrogant eye, but he scarcely looked at Lu Chen.

"Sir," said Lu Chen a little timidly, since the young officer carried a gun and a belt stuffed with cartridges. But he was interrupted.

"The new road passes your shop. What is your name, old man?" The officer rapidly consulted a sheet of paper drawn from his pocket. "Ah, yes, Lu! Thirty feet off your house. Fifteen days from today your shop must be gone. Else we will tear it down for you." He folded the paper carelessly and put it back into his pocket. Then he turned to go away. At his heels were three common soldiers, and they turned also and fell into step. Lu Chen could not speak. He swallowed but his throat was dry. No sound came forth. One of the soldiers glanced back at him, a curious, pitying glance. That pity suddenly released the knot in Lu Chen's throat.

"Ten thousand dollars!" he called hoarsely after the young officer.

The officer halted instantly and wheeled about. "What is that?" he said sharply.

"The price of the shop is ten thousand dollars," faltered Lu Chen. The young officer grasped his gun, and Lu Chen shrank in alarm behind the door and closed it. But the

young man would not have it. He walked back and thrust
his gun so suddenly against the door that Lu Chen staggered and bumped into the child, who began to cry. Every
time in the child's whole life that he had cried, Lu Chen
had rushed to him. But now he did not even hear. He
was gazing fixedly at the young officer, murmuring over
and over, unconsciously, "Ten thousand dollars, ten thousand dollars."

The officer stared at him and then broke into a chilly
laughter. "It is your contribution, then, to the new capital,"
he said, and, shouting a sharp command, he went away.

Contribution? What contribution? The child lay on the
earthen floor, wailing. He was used to lying wherever he
had fallen, since someone always picked him up, but now
no one came. Lu Chen stood looking out through the door
after the young man's figure. His heart lagged in his body
so that he could scarcely draw his breath. Give up his
shop, his life? What was all this talk of a new capital? It
was none of his business. He turned and, seeing the child,
dazedly picked him up and put him on his feet. Then,
with the child in his arms, he sat down. Why, the shop was
the child's! No one could take it away. Anger rose up in
him and relieved him then, since it drove out his fear. He
never would give up the shop—never! He would sit there
in it until they tore the last tile from over his head. He
set the child on the floor again and bustled mightily and
filled the caldron and started roaring fires, so that within
the hour the water bubbled and steamed and lifted the
wooden covers. He was very sharp with his customers and,
when the impudent slave girl came with her cheeks pink
and her black eyes saucy, he skimped her a little on water
and would not fill the kettle for all her scolding.

"It will be a good thing for us all when the new road

comes and takes away your shop, old robber," she flung
at him when she saw that he would give her no more.

"Nothing can be taken from me," he shouted after her
and, when her mocking laugh came back to him, he
shouted, "That for the new road!" And he spat.

After a while the door opened and his son came in.

"What of the new road?" he asked indolently, feeling
of the teapot to see whether it was still hot.

"Now then," said Lu Chen. "You still return for your
food, do you? Where have you been today?"

"But it is true of the new road," said the boy, sipping
the half-cold tea from the spout of the pot. "Quite true.
It comes straight past us. The shop—'thirty feet off'—will
leave but half of the two bedrooms at the back."

Lu Chen stared unbelievingly. He was all at once so
angry that his eyes grew dim. He raised his hand and
knocked the teapot from his son's hand, and it fell upon
the ground and broke into three pieces.

"You stand there," Lu Chen muttered thickly, "you
stand there and drink tea—" and, seeing the young man's
astonished face, he began to weep and walked as fast as he
could into the room where he slept and crawled into the
bed and drew the curtains.

In the morning, when he rose, he was still angry with
his son. When the young man ate his rice, innocently, Lu
Chen twitched his eyebrows and muttered: "Yes, you eat
and your son eats, but you do not think where the money
is to come from." But for all of this he did not believe that
they would really take away his shop, and he went on
about his work as before.

The eleventh day after he was warned by the officer,
his wife came to him with unwonted consternation on her
face. "It is true that the road is coming," she said. "If

you look up the street, you will see a sight. What shall we do?" She began to weep softly, her large face scarcely disturbed.

Lu Chen, seeing her, felt himself quivering. He went to the door and gazed up the street. Always the street had been so narrow, so winding, so darkened with the overhanging shop signs of varnished wood and colored silk, that one could see for only a few feet. But now there was the strange light of the sun shining upon the damp cobbles. A score of feet away all the signs were gone, and men were tearing down houses. Heaps of age-stained bricks and tiles lay on the street, and caravans of donkeys with baskets across their backs stood waiting to carry them away. The same officer that he had seen was walking about, and behind him followed four angry women, their hair streaming down their backs. They were cursing and wailing, and Lu could hear them say, "We have no life left, no life left—our homes are gone!"

Lu went into the shop then and shut the door and barred it. He sat down on the short wooden bench behind the caldron, his knees shaking, his mind in a maze. Inexorably the road was coming. The child ran out of the inner room and leaned against his knee, but Lu beheld him apathetically. The child, seeing his remote gaze, looked roguishly up and touched the great caldron with a tentative finger. But Lu, for the first time in his life, did not cry out at him. A dim thought went through his mind. "Burned? It is nothing. You will starve at last."

There was a thunderous knock at the door at that moment, and Lu's heart leaped. With his whole body taut, he went to remove the bar. It was the officer in a very clean new uniform, and behind him stood the three soldiers. No one could dream from their appearance that they had been bitterly cursed but a few moments ago, so sure and confident did they seem. Lu, looking at them, suddenly felt that he was a very old man and that it was best for him to die.

"Four days," said the officer, "and your shop must be gone. Tear it down yourself, and you will have the materials. Otherwise we will confiscate it."

"But the money?" faltered Lu Chen.

"Money?" repeated the officer sharply, tapping his shining leather boot with a small stick he carried.

"The price is ten thousand dollars," said Lu Chen a little more firmly, gathering himself together.

The officer gave a sharp, short laugh.

"There is no money," he replied, each word as clear and cold as steel. "You are presenting this to the Republic." Lu Chen looked wildly about. Surely there was some redress. Surely someone would help him.

He began to scream out in a broken, shrill voice to the passers on the street. "Do you see this, sirs? I am to be robbed—robbed by the Republic! Who is this Republic? Will it give me food and my wife and my child?—"

He felt himself twitched slightly by the coat. The soldier who had looked back at him the other day whispered hurriedly, "Do not anger the officer—it will be worse." Aloud he said: "Do not complain, old man! In any case your shop would have to go. In the new day that is coming we shall not want hot-water shops. Hot water will come pouring forth from the self-going pipes."

Lu Chen would have answered him, but was at that moment pulled backward by his son, who stood there in front of him, facing the officer. The young man spoke anxiously, courteously: "Sir, forgive an old man who cannot understand that the Revolution has come and brought new light. I will answer for him. We will pull down the house, sir. It is an honor for us to sacrifice all we have to the country."

The red anger that had been rising over the officer's face faded: he gave a short nod and walked quickly away.

The young man barred the door against the curious, half-pitying crowd that had gathered to see the scene. Then he stood against the door and faced Lu Chen. Lu Chen had never seen him thus, firm and decided. "Shall we all be killed then?" he demanded. "Are we to die for the sake of a shop?"

"In any case we shall starve," said Lu Chen, seating himself on the other side of the table, opposite his wife. She had continued to weep the whole time, without noise or disturbance, merely wiping the large tears from her cheeks with the corner of her blue jacket.

"I have found work," said his son. "I am to be an overseer of workmen on the new road."

Lu Chen looked up at him, then, without any hope in his heart. "Even you, my son?" he whispered.

The young man pushed back his hair restlessly from his forehead. "Father, there is no use in fighting against it. It will come. Think of it, a great new road sweeping through our city! Automobiles, passing to and fro! Once at school I saw a picture of a street in a foreign city—big shops and automobiles rushing back and forth. Only *we* have wheelbarrows and rickshas and donkeys crowding against one another in the streets. Why, these streets were made a thousand years ago. Are we never to have new ones?"

"What is the use of automobiles?" muttered Lu Chen. He had seen them often in these past weeks, crowding, pushing, insistent, making people rush to doorways and side alleys. He hated them. "Our ancestors," he began.

But the young man snapped his fingers. "That for them!" he cried. "I shall get fifty dollars a month from the new road."

Fifty dollars a month? Lu Chen was stunned. He had never seen such an amount of money. He was diverted a little, and his wife stopped crying.

"Where will so much come from?" he asked, half fearfully.

"The new government has promised it," replied his son in a complacent tone.

"I shall buy myself a new black sateen coat," the young man's mother said, a light beginning to break over her face. And then, after an interval during which she thought about the coat, she gave a rumbling, hoarse laugh.

But to Lu Chen, when he had pondered the matter, it seemed that there was no hope for his shop, now that it was no longer their only means of support. He sat all day without lighting the fire, and the great caldrons for the first time in threescore years were cold.

When people came to buy water, he said: "There is no more need. You are to have pipes. Until then heat your own water."

The saucy slave girl stuck out her tongue at him, a small, red tongue, as red as a cherry, but he shook his head at her without anger or interest.

The next day his son asked, "Shall we not call the masons to tear down the house, lest we lose everything?"

That roused him a little. "No," he cried. "Since they will rob me, let them rob me utterly." And for four days he sat in his house, refusing to eat, refusing even to open his door, although he heard approaching nearer and nearer the destruction—the crash of falling bricks, the groaning of timbers placed centuries ago and now lowered to the ground, the weeping of many people like himself, whose homes were thus demolished.

On the morning of the fifteenth day there was a great knock upon his door. He rose at once to open it. There stood a dozen men, armed with picks and axes. He faced them. "You come to destroy my shop? I am helpless. Here it is." And he sat down again upon his bench while they crowded in. There was not one touch of sympathy in their faces. In this fashion they had already destroyed hundreds of shops and homes; and to them, he saw very clearly, he was only an old man and one more troublesome than others.

His wife and his son and his son's wife and child had gone away that morning to a friend's house, and they had taken with them everything except the bench whereon Lu Chen sat and the two caldrons. His son had said: "Come with me, Father. I have prepared a place—I have rented a little house. They advanced me some money on the first month." But Lu Chen had shaken his head stubbornly and sat still as they went out.

There were the great copper caldrons, firmly embedded in the clay of the ovens. Two workmen hacked at them with pickaxes. "My grandfather put those in," he said suddenly. "There are no such workmen nowadays."

But he said nothing more while they took the tiles from the roof and the light begun to seep down between the rafters. At last they took the rafters, and he sat there within four walls with the noonday sunshine beating on him. He was sick and faint, but he sat on through the long afternoon, and, when evening came, he still sat there, his shop a heap of bricks and tiles and broken rafters about him. The two caldrons stood up naked out of the ruins.

People stared at him curiously but said nothing, and he sat on.

At last, when it was almost dark, his son came and took him by the hand. "The child will not eat because you have not come, Father," he said kindly, and then Lu Chen rose, like a very old man, and, holding his son's hand, went with him.

They made their dwelling, then, in a little thatched house just inside the North Gate, where there are fields and empty lands. Lu Chen, who all his life had lived in the bustle of the streets, could not endure the silence. He could not bear to look out across the blankness of the fields. He sat all day in the little bedroom that belonged to him and his wife, scarcely thinking. Since there was no need for him to work any more, he became very soon an old, old man. His son brought home at the end of the month fifty round silver dollars and showed them exultantly.

"It is more than the shop ever yielded," he cried. He was no longer indolent and careless, and he wore a clean gray uniform buttoned neatly about him.

But Lu Chen only muttered, "Those two big caldrons used to hold at least twenty gallons of river water."

One day his wife, as placid again in this house as she had ever been, showed him her new sateen coat, smoothing it over her great bosom. But he only stared at her. "My mother," he said heavily, "once had a gray coat that was bound in silk." And he fell to musing again.

No one could make him go out of the door. He sat day after day, his hair getting quite white and his lined face loosening from its former busy tenseness. His eyes, which had always been narrow and watchful and snapping, grew dull and hidden behind the veil of dimness that belongs to old people. Only the child sometimes beguiled him for a brief moment.

It was the child at last who beguiled him beyond the door. He had sat all through the shortening days of early winter, gazing out of the small window of his room. His day was marked off into the three periods of his meals; and at night he slept fitfully, sometimes still in his chair with his head on the table.

There came then, after a week of rain, one of the mild, deceptive days that are an interlude of autumn before the intense cold sets in. He had been conscious all morning of the soft, damp heat. The sun, shining obliquely through gray clouds, lighted up the landscape. He was restless, and he pushed open the window. The fresh smell of earth and moisture rose up. "I could have caught a caldronful of the rain water," he said, sniffing the dampness. Rain water in the old days could be sold at a high price.

Just then the child came tugging at his hand. "Out, out!" he cried, laughing. "Come and play!"

Lu Chen felt a stirring in him. Well, he would go out just a little, perhaps. And, rising slowly, he took the child's hand and went out. It was very warm, and the sun felt heartening to him. He straightened himself with an effort and began to walk toward some houses near by. He would just go and learn what news there might be. Not for a long time had he heard any. His son was busy all day, and, as for the women, who would talk with a woman?

The child was chattering and a small cheeping of autumn insects filled the air. It was almost like spring. He looked about curiously. Where was he, exactly? There was the North Gate yonder. Ah, that would be the end of the street where his shop had been. He would just go and

look at it. Could he bear it? He walked a little more
quickly.

Then he turned a corner, and the street lay before him.
The street? What was this? A great wide sweep of emptiness, straight through the heart of the city! On all sides
the same narrow, winding, dark streets and alleys that he
had always known, and straight through them, like the
clean swath of a sword blade, this—this new road!

He stared along it, suddenly smitten with fright. Why,
it was enormous—what would they ever do with a road
like this? The men working on it were like midgets—like
ants. All the people in the world could go up and down it
and not jostle one another. There were people standing
about, like himself, subdued and silent. Some poignancy
in their expression drew his interest. "You lived here?"
he hinted to a thin-faced man who stood near him. The
man nodded slowly. "The house was all I had," he said.
"A good house, built in the time of the Mings. It had ten
rooms. I live in a hut now. You see, the house was all I
had—I rented the rooms."

Lu Chen nodded. "I had a shop—a hot-water shop,"
he said with difficulty. He would have liked to say more;
it was on his tongue to say, "There were two huge copper
caldrons." But the man was not listening. He stood staring down the vast new roadway.

Someone drew near, and Lu Chen saw it was his son.
The young man broke into a smile and came running. "My
father!" he cried. And then, "Father, what do you think
of it?"

The old man's lips trembled. He felt that he might either
laugh or weep. "It—looks as if a mighty storm had swept
through the city," he answered.

But the young man only laughed and said eagerly:

"See, Father, this is my bit of the work. Look, at the side there will be pavements, and, in the middle, room for the electric cars and on both sides great space for vehicles of all sorts—room for everything! People from the whole world walking and riding on this road—the road through the new capital!" Someone called him, and he walked away, bustling a little.

Lu Chen stood still, gazing up the road. Infinitely wide, it stretched on both sides of him, infinitely long it extended into the distance. How far did it go, he asked himself solemnly. He had never seen anything in his life like it for space and straightness. Far at the other end, as far as his eyes could pierce, it went on and on, astounding, magnificent, new! Well, here was a thing. Not even emperors had made a road like this! He looked down at the little child beside him. This child, he supposed, would take the road for granted. The young always took things for granted—the way his son had taken the destruction of the shop, for instance. For the first time he did not use the word "robbery" in his mind when he thought of his shop. Instead, this question occurred to him: Had it taken this new road to make his son a man? He perceived that, as he had cared for his shop, so his son cared for the road. He continued to stand with the child, looking up it soberly, absorbed, pondering its import. This Revolution—this new road! Where did it lead?

Enough for a Lifetime

❦❦❦

MISS WILLEY hesitated a moment before she opened the door into the courtyard. Each autumn she dreaded more sharply these wintry mornings of cold, yellow, sandy winds.

"May and June don't make up to me for it," she thought miserably, staring through the square of glass set into the door.

The court was full of dim yellow light. Standing a little on tiptoe, since she was very short, she found she could not even see the ragged pine tree in the middle of it. It was a very bad sandstorm, bad even for a Peking November. She put her hand on the wooden bar of the door. "I *must* go," she told herself.

Then her small childish face wrinkled anxiously. Which had she better do—run quickly through the dust and risk catching her foot on an unevenly laid tile, or go slowly, clinging to the side of the veranda? If she kept her head down . . . She sighed a little. She didn't feel like running today. She must go. The school bell clanged sharply, and in the courtyard she saw the huddled figures of the girls creep through the sandy cloud.

She set her teeth and said faintly, "O God . . . please . . ." She whimpered again. It was the beginning of a prayer she never finished nowadays. She used to pray a great deal, telling God everything. But now she went no further than that preliminary cry. Not that she expected anything . . . not now; it was only a habit, perhaps. But really it was a little more. She had to cry out to somebody, and there was no one else to whom she could tell how she hated everything. She could not even tell God, for that matter. How could she, when this school and the mission were all His work? No, she made the little cry involuntarily. . . . Although God might perhaps . . .

She fumbled for the door of the classroom, choking. The fine sand was in her very lungs. She held her breath and pushed open the door and closed it. It was better now —better in the schoolroom. She found her handkerchief and wiped her eyes and looked about her. Eight girls sat waiting for her. They were all dressed alike in the cheap blue cotton coats the mission school provided. They turned their similar faces to her, without expectancy, and their eyes were unlighted. She was suddenly afraid of them again. She had taught this class in Old Testament History for sixteen years and still she was afraid of it. No one was ever interested.

She sat down timidly behind the table which was a little too high for her, and opening the Bible she said, trying to make her voice firm, "Today, we have the giving of the Ten Commandments."

Through the morning she sat, one class after another passing before her. The room grew very cold. The wind tore at the lattices and forced the sand between the wide crevices in the wood. Upon the table the sand lay thick. Her hands were cold and gritted. The pages of her book would not lie smooth for the sand. Through the inset of glass above the papered lattice she could see the circle of the sun, pale and flat against the yellow sky.

At noon she must go into the court again and to the bare dining room where she would have her tiffin with old

Miss Benton. The food would be full of sand, and Miss
Benton would sit silent through the meal or, if she talked,
she would talk about how much the straw cost for the
kitchens and where they could cut down on the food, and
how the cook was taking too much squeeze, and how the
new revolutionary government was making wicked laws
against the teaching of religion, and how they must never
give up the purpose for which they came, which was to—
Miss Willey sent out her little cry again, "O God . . .
please . . ." forgetting the stout Chinese girl standing
patiently before her, plodding through the Thou Shalt
Nots.

It was on the afternoon of this day that Miss Willey first
thought seriously about Mr. Jones. It began by her looking
at Miss Benton while she talked and suddenly seeing how
ugly she was. She was very ugly. Her scant gray hair was
yellowed, and her skin was dark and leathery. She had
lived forty years in these winds and sands.

"I shall look like that," Miss Willey thought sadly. "In
twenty more years I shall look like that."

She remembered that even now she had to struggle very
often at night to make herself put cold cream on her face.
It seemed scarcely worth while when no one ever came to
see her. And then she was always so tired at night and
there was so much to do. Sometimes she thought she had
not strength to say her prayers and put the cold cream on,
too. But she dared not leave off prayers, at night at least,
and somehow she still could not quite let herself go and
look like Miss Benton. . . . Even Mr. Jones, she thought,
could scarcely be worse to see across the table three times
a day.

"I might as well. . . ." she thought.

That was how she began to think about Mr. Jones.

She thought about him often during the afternoon school. She thought of him as he now doubtless was, sitting in his study in the big square mission house at the north end of the compound, where he had lived a long time with Mrs. Jones until she died last month. She had not been dead a month before Mr. Jones wrote Miss Willey the letter. She had been sitting in her room reading when the letter came. She was reading secretly—that is, she was reading a book she kept in her cupboard where Miss Benton could not see it. Even so, when Miss Willey read it, she drew the bolt softly in the door, because Miss Benton had a way of giving a thump and bounding in without waiting. As it was, she had once driven Miss Willey into a lie.

"What have you got the door locked for?" she demanded indignantly.

"I am dressing," Miss Willey called faintly through the crack. It was a great lie. She was not dressing at all—she was reading the book.

The book contained the sonnets of Elizabeth Barrett Browning. It had been sent to the school among a lot of old books from America, and Miss Benton, sorting them, had picked it out with her thumb and forefinger and snorted, "We don't want that kind of thing here." Miss Willey gathered it up, then, with the trash. But afterwards she took it to her room and looked at it and saw what it was. There were pictures of Elizabeth Barrett and Robert Browning in the front pages and Miss Willey looked at them earnestly, because once, in high school at home in Ohio, the English teacher had said she looked like Elizabeth Browning. But Miss Willey had not seen a picture of her until now. She stared thoughtfully at the curl-shadowed face . . . not pretty, that face. . . . After she began to read the poems she was glad she was like Elizabeth, although she looked more often at Robert. On one night when she was sure Miss Benton had gone to bed, she even took down her hair and curled it around her fingers and peeped shamefacedly at herself in the mirror. With her hair like that she did look like Elizabeth. She stared at herself a moment and then she brushed the curls all out quickly and braided them down her back and went to bed. But, of course, it gave her a special interest in the lovers.

She was reading the book when Mr. Jones's letter came, and that was what made the letter so dreadful. By this time, she had read the book over and over again and to her shame and terror she could not stop reading it. She ran quickly to her room after tiffin to read until the two o'clock bell rang, and often she had to read a while before she could go to sleep at night. It was sweet . . . sweet . . . to love like that! She could so clearly see those two lovers—Robert tall and handsome and dark, and Elizabeth small and clinging, her heavy chestnut curls half hiding her face. She saw them always standing together, Elizabeth clinging. It would be sweet to cling to someone like that . . . a man, tall and strong, with whom she could be safe.

But she knew no men at all. Of course, there were men in Peking—many men. One saw them sometimes on the streets if one went there, and there were always some men, a very few, in the English church where she went on Sunday afternoons. She went regularly to the English church, alone, because Miss Benton went to Chinese services three times on Sundays, and anyway she did not think the English church was important, since what they had come out for was to save the natives. But Miss Willey went because it was her one chance in the week to sit

among white people, and it made her feel at home again.
It was like Ohio to see only white faces. No one ever
spoke to her, it is true, but this she did not expect, because no one knew her, not even a woman, and of course
not a man. There was nothing about her, of course, to
attract a . . . a . . . gentleman. Besides, the school was so
far away—in a country village—a half hour from the city.
As for Chinese men . . . well, it was not the same. And
they were always married, anyway. There was only the old
Bishop who came to see them once a year and who always
shouted heartily, "Wonderful privilege, Miss Willey, for
a young woman like you to work with a wonderful old
saint like Miss Benton! Wonderful school she has built out
of a handful . . . After she is gone it will be your job. . . .
wonderful opportunity, you know!"

Miss Willey agreed, smiling her pretty smile, her color
a little more faded each year. By now, the only pleasure in
the Bishop's speech was that he called her "young woman."
She was thirty-eight, and of course, she told herself soberly, she must remember that the Bishop was very, very
old. Thirty-eight was not really young for a lady. So she
lived quite alone in the midst of all the blue-coated school-
girls, and though she was kind to them and she knew they
liked her well enough, still she was alone, and she warmed
herself secretly in the passion of the two dead lovers. It
made a thing to look forward to after supper—something
to go back to in her room. The days were so alike.

Of course, she had never thought of Mr. Jones as a
man at all. There was, for many years, Mrs. Jones, and it
was not easy to remember him when she was alive. She
and Miss Benton were great friends, and when the four
of them came together to talk about the work Mrs. Jones
and Miss Benton talked and Mr. Jones and Miss Willey

listened. He was a small pale man, bald and unbearded, and there were freckles on his cheeks and across the backs of his hands, which were unexpectedly large and white and hairy. Mrs. Jones planned his sermons for him, and he preached them in a small high voice which did not vary its tones in an hour's talking. It was strange to hear Mrs. Jones's positive doctrines coming forth in his mild voice. He was not very strong and Mrs. Jones bustled about him continually. They never took a meal at Miss Benton's without her saying, "Now, Archie, you know you can't eat that hot bread. . . . His stomach is so delicate, Miss Willey. You wouldn't believe the trouble it's been to me all these years!"

Mr. Jones obediently laid down the hot biscuit and looked about him despondently.

"A little toast, very hard and dry, please, Miss Benton," said Mrs. Jones firmly.

But in spite of his stomach, it was Mrs. Jones who died first, very suddenly, of typhoid fever. In three days it was all over, and Mr. Jones was left alone.

Still, Miss Willey did not think of him as a man. It would take much longer than three days for Mrs. Jones really to be dead. It would perhaps be years before one saw no longer beside Mr. Jones that large thick body, the square face, the reddish-gray hair brushed up from the forehead, the reddish hairs about the lips and chin. In her house, one still waited for her heavy footsteps upon the bare floors. But more than that, Miss Willey by now thought of a man only as tall and dark and handsome, as a strong breast upon which a little dark-haired woman might lean, where she might cling and hide her face.

So Mr. Jones's letter had come as a great surprise to her. She could scarcely grow used to it, although three whole days had passed since it came. . . . He had been very clever about sending it, too, choosing an evening when he knew Miss Benton was having a night class. It would never have done if she had been in the house. She would have opened it at once. "I thought of course it was mission business," she would have said grimly.

But she was away, and Miss Willey had just locked the door and opened the book to her favorite sonnet. She had just read, "How do I love thee? Let me count the ways," when there came a knock at the door. She thrust the book quickly under the edge of her full skirt.

"Yes?" she called.

"A letter," the servant's voice answered.

She opened the door a little and took the letter and glanced at it, wondering. She never had any letters. When she saw what is was, she felt faint. No one had ever proposed marriage to her before. The servant waited. At last he asked, "Is there no answer?"

She looked up from the letter, startled. Why, of course . . . there must be an answer.

"Oh . . . tell . . . say there is an answer later!"

She shut the door and now she made sure of the bolt. She sat down again and looked at the letter. It was very short. It said:

My dear Miss Willey,

I hope you will not think ill of me that so soon after my dear wife's demise I should write you this letter. I miss her sorely. Nevertheless, in writing this letter I do not think of any other than you. We have long known each other and we are engaged in the same noble work. I have always deeply respected your gentle and ladylike qualities. To this respect I now add affection. Will you, my dear Miss Willey, return my emotion and consider me as a suppliant for your hand?

Faithfully yours,
ARCHIBALD JONES

She read it through three times. Then her eyes fell upon the book. She had left it open upon the table just where she was reading it. Now the lovely burning words flew to her heart. "How do I love thee? Let me count the ways." She read it through again slowly. The letter dropped from her hand to the floor. She laid her head down upon the page and began to weep softly.

*   *   *

During the three days she avoided all chance meetings with Mr. Jones. The sandstorm was really a blessing to her in this, because he had asthma, and when the winds blew from the desert he had to shut himself up in a little inner room and hold a wet towel to his face and breathe through it. Miss Willey knew this as everyone did, because Mrs. Jones would describe his suffering so clearly that Miss Willey's vivid imagination could see him gasping and choking alone in that little room, sighing every now and then in a way he had. Poor Mr. Jones! He would be very lonely shut up like that. She was a little sorry for him. For, of course, neither she nor Miss Benton could think of going into the house where he was—not now, with Mrs. Jones dead and gone. She perceived that after all Mr. Jones was a man. Without Mrs. Jones he became a man.

On the afternoon of this third day, therefore, since it was Saturday and there were no afternoon classes, she went to her room and locked the door and took out the letter again. A flutter came into her throat as she read. After all, it was a real proposal of marriage. She held it in her hand and stared out of the window thoughtfully, afterwards. She saw the low tiled roofs of the village houses and she looked across them to the bare hills in the west. The sky was chill and of the same hue as the dry, sandy earth. There was no color anywhere.

"After all," she told herself sadly, "it's the only proposal I'll probably ever have. No one will ever want to marry me except Mr. Jones."

*　　　*　　　*

She sighed and turned away from the gray window, and since it was Saturday she made the fire in the little iron grate and lit the kerosene lamp on the table. The room was changed, more cheerful and more cosy in the yellow light. She drew the curtains and pulled her rocking chair to the fire and fetched the book and began to read it here and there. It fell open of itself in many places, and now sitting so warmed, she let it open where it would and read and dreamed. In the quiet and warmth Mr. Jones's letter, lying on the table, gave reality to the poems. Did she not know now in her own experience what a man's love was? She, too, might, if she liked, write a letter which would bring a man to her. She began to plan what she might perhaps say to Mr. Jones if she should decide. She dreamed a little, the book sliding upon her lap, her eyes fixed on the flames. She did not think of Mr. Jones exactly while she was imagining the answer to his letter. She was making an answer worthy of the poem.

But still it was a good thing she did not write it down, because the very next day the extraordinary thing happened to her. She went to bed almost happily Saturday night, the letter shaping in her mind. She would not, she thought, write it just yet—perhaps on Sunday night. She was always a little low on Sunday night because no one spoke to her in church and because she knew when she woke up the next morning it would be Monday again. . . .

All Sunday morning, during the school exercises and during Sunday school, she thought about the sort of letter she would write. Once, it is true, she thought about Mr. Jones, and was confused by the knowledge that it was to Mr. Jones she was planning to write such a letter. Would he perhaps be shocked by it or think it unmaidenly? For an hour or so after this occurred to her, she devoted herself to her Sunday-school class.

But as the day wore on she could even bear to remember that the letter was to be sent to Mr. Jones. For the dust had given Miss Benton a cold, and nothing Miss Willey could do was enough. Miss Benton went to bed with a gray flannel petticoat about her head, and she complained that it was strange that Miss Willey still did not know how to get the water right in a hot water bottle, or where, after all these years, she kept her aspirin, in the left-hand corner of the small shelf in the closet in the bathroom. Miss Willey, running to and fro, silently panted under her breath, "O God . . . please . . ." Surely, Mr. Jones could not be worse than this? She was very late to church and would almost have not gone, except that it gave her an excuse to get away from Miss Benton.

Then, on that very day, the thing happened for which

she long ago had given up any hope. Someone spoke to her after church. She was just sidling out of the end of her pew, and there he was at the end waiting for her—a man —young, tall, dark, handsome. She had sat drearily through the service, her feet aching a little. The church was very cold, and Dr. Henry preached. Her spirit sank when she saw him rise, stooped and gray, to his usual sermon. "Brethren, in these evil days, when so many have forgotten the true teachings of the Scriptures and have turned aside to pleasure . . ."

Pleasure! Miss Willey turned her head straight away from him and stared out of a high window. She could see nothing but pale sky until a gust of wind tossed up a bare branch. What a day it had been, trying to do her own work and Miss Benton's, too! She went over it all, not hearing the old man. At the end she rose when the hymn began and felt faint with fatigue while they sang, "Fight the good fight!" Her small lower lip trembled, and she stared earnestly at the window, now quite dark.

After the benediction she turned to go out as she always did, her eyes down, not expecting to hear anyone call her name. And then she heard him call her name, and she looked up and saw him and saw his kind, happy dark eyes. He smiled a little.

"I hope I didn't startle you? Forgive me . . . I shouldn't have spoken so suddenly. I wanted to catch you before you went home. You see, the Dramatic Club here in town wants to give *The Barretts of Wimpole Street* and we can't find anybody for Elizabeth, and Julie Barnes said she had seen you in church one day and you looked exactly like Elizabeth, so I said I'd ask you. I came especially. I'm to be Robert."

Miss Willey stared at him, opened her mouth, and shut

it again. Her lips began to tremble again piteously. The young man said quickly, "I say . . . I . . . you aren't feeling ill, Miss Willey?"

She shook her head. "No," she whispered. "No." Then she cleared her throat. She was being absurd. What would he think of her? But it was all absurd. As if she, of all people . . .

"I couldn't do it," she said, looking up at him tragically. "I couldn't possibly do it. I've never . . . I have done nothing at all dramatic. I teach in a mission school . . . and . . ."

"Now, Miss Willey, don't say no so quickly," the young man interrupted warmly. "If you knew how we've looked. . . . I say, don't answer me now. Anyway, this is no place to put such a question, but nobody's ever seen you anywhere else except in church. Look here, I'm coming to see you tomorrow, and I won't take no for an answer. No, no, no—don't say another word. Tomorrow, about teatime, Miss Willey!" Then, smiling and lifting his hat, he was gone.

There it was. She looked about and saw that almost everyone was gone, and so she went out of the church into the dusk and climbed into a ricksha. It was impossible to believe what had happened. She held herself rigid in the swaying vehicle and saw nothing in the crowded street. A play! She had never even seen a play. . . . She got out at the school gate and did not hear the whining of the ricksha puller for money money. Thirty cents was the right fare, but she was always so distressed when they were not satisfied that she usually gave them more. But tonight she did not notice the fellow. She walked lightly into the house. Miss Benton called out wearily, "Is that you, Amy?"

For a moment Miss Willey thought of answering gaily, "I'm not exactly sure myself, Miss Benton! I think I'm somebody else, tonight!" But Miss Benton would think she was mad. So instead she went into Miss Benton's room and asked gently, "Shall I fill your hot water bottle for you?" And when Miss Benton fumbled for it with her feet and pushed it out onto the floor Miss Willey picked it up and said fervently, "I'll do my very best to get it just right this time."

*　　*　　*

But by teatime next day she was more sure than ever that she could not do it. She had been foolish enough during the evening to think that perhaps she could. Not so much that she could, perhaps, as that it would be so nice if she could. She spent the whole evening in her room dreaming over the book, imagining the words said aloud, herself saying the words aloud—to Robert. She heard herself saying them over and over, passionately.

When she stood up to get ready for bed at last, something fell out of the book. It was Mr. Jones's letter. How had it come into those pages? She must have tucked it there without knowing that she did. Suddenly, she could not bear to think it had been against those poems and she opened a drawer in the table and thrust it among her papers.

But of course she couldn't do the play. Monday morning brought her to reality again—the school bell, the shuffle of feet across the tiles, the cold schoolroom, the Old Testament open before her, Miss Benton's cold a little better, enough better to make her irritable and shouting commands everywhere. There was only one good thing, and it was that Miss Benton could not get up. That meant, Miss Willey thought agitatedly, that she would see the young man alone and tell him she couldn't. . . . She appreciated the invitation so much but she couldn't do it.

But it was not so easily done. The young man sat holding his cup of tea and he bit once into the rather stale little cake—for of course she had forgotten to see about fresh cakes with everything else on her mind—and he listened to Miss Willey. Then he put down his tea and laughed.

"You are exactly like Elizabeth!" he declared. "Do you know, Miss Willey, you might be rehearsing the first act with me! I wish you could see yourself. And I am going to play my part. I am Robert Browning—not Ted Hall of the American consular service—and I won't take no!"

She had never been so overridden in her life, not even by Miss Benton. He was laughing at her and refusing to let her speak, and when she stood up he had her by her two elbows and held her tight, shaking his head and laughing at her in his great, round, deep voice. She fell silent and stood before him, drooping, all but leaning upon him. She was not used to . . . she was very, very tired. She felt his eyes upon her face. But she could not raise her head. He said quietly, "Now take down your hair, and let me see it done like Elizabeth's. It's curly, I can see."

She obeyed him, fumbling, shocked at herself. What if someone came in, a servant or a student? They would think her mad. But his fingers were at her hair, skillful, quick. He said, his voice soft with astonishment, "I never could have dreamed of such a likeness—the play's made!"

He turned and took up his hat swiftly, and said with decision, "Miss Willey, you are going with me this very minute! I don't dare let you out of my sight until I have you thoroughly committed before witnesses! Our first rehearsal is at six, and I'll bring you home safely afterward.

Go and get your hat and coat, and I'll wait here for you."

Miss Willey, hearing him so command, obeyed him. By now she was past any will of her own at all. She crept by Miss Benton's door and flew upstairs, holding her curls with her hands. Then she smoothed them back and put on her brown coat and her brown toque and ran down softly again. In the ricksha, following behind his broad back, very upright before her and solid and clear in the dusk, she sat tense and amazed, her hands clenched together. She had not the least idea what she was going to do.

When she found herself in a large cheerful drawing room full of people and light and the roaring warmth of a great fire, she was completely lost. She saw a host of faces turned to her and cries went up all about her, "Oh, Ted, swell!" "Ted, you persuaded her!" "Now that's fine, Miss Willey!" She looked at them all, and she felt herself fainting a little. Before she knew it she had gasped out the beginning of her prayer, "O God . . . please . . ."

There was a silence and the mistiness in front of her eyes grew darker. She clutched the knobby back of a carved Chinese chair. Then someone came up to her and a light young voice, a girl's voice, said very clearly and kindly, "Don't you see she is frightened? She is as pale as she can be. Here, Miss Willey, sit down and drink this hot tea. And all of you go on talking and leave her alone a little while, until she is used to us."

So Miss Willey found herself sitting in the big Chinese chair drinking good hot tea, and the others stopped looking at her and went on with their own talk. Soon she felt better, well enough to look at the girl beside her. She saw at once that this was the prettiest girl she had ever seen, a girl with a round rosy little face set about with very fair, curly hair. The girl met her eyes and smiled so

quickly and delightfully that Miss Willey felt she must
say something. "I am so silly. . . . I don't know what came
over me. . . ."

"I understand perfectly," the girl interrupted eagerly.
"You came in so suddenly out of the cold and silence, and
we all began shouting at you. It was perfectly natural."
Then, still smiling, she said, "Isn't it going to be fun? I'm
to be Henrietta. You are simply perfect for Elizabeth.
And isn't Ted handsome as Robert? Look at him over
there talking to Mrs. Howett—she's our director."

Miss Willey looked earnestly. "Yes, he is quite what I
imagined," she replied.

They were all very kind to her then. When they saw
that she was better they came crowding about her and said
kind things. "It is so good of you, Miss Willey, you must
be so busy. . . ." "We feel the play is quite made now,
Miss Willey. . . ." And then Mrs. Howett gave out the
parts, and she had hers, pages of it. How could she ever
learn it all! Then before she could do more than glance at
it, they were asking her questions. Did she think Elizabeth
should wear gray or brown? Where ought the couch to be?
She turned over the pages and scanned the lines, surprised
now at her own ease, answering, she thought, very well.
She felt their approbation warm about her. She looked
about at their faces. Why, how kind they all were—so
kind and good and approving. It was lovely to be approved. She thought to herself, "I shan't mind a bit if
Miss Benton is cross when I get back."

Then it was over, and people began to scatter quickly.
"Darling, I've a dinner in twenty minutes. . . ." "Do drop
in for cocktails, Julie darling, you and Ted. . . ." "Dance
at the Grand tonight—Mary, m'dear, you and Jack coming? Ah, come on!"

She did not know exactly how to get away and then she found herself with only three of them, Mrs. Howett, whose house it was, and Mr. Hall, and the pretty girl named Julie. "I must go," she murmured.

"I'll go with you," the young man said, and then he looked at the pretty girl. "Be a little late, Julie."

But this Miss Willey could not bear. "Oh, no, Mr. Hall, it isn't at all necessary—not at all—I am quite safe. . . ."

"He'd better go with you, Miss Willey," the young girl said earnestly.

"Oh, no, it isn't . . . I assure you. . . ." Miss Willey cried in distress, "I am used to going about alone—I don't want him to be late on my account—"

"Well, Miss Willey, if you are quite sure," the young man broke in.

And really he was very kind. He went with her to the street and helped her climb into the ricksha, and he tucked the rug so snugly about her feet that she was quite cozy. Then he smiled kindly and he said, cheerfully, "Good night —Elizabeth," so cheerfully that she grew bold. "Good night, Robert," she replied over her shoulder, smiling very shyly.

She turned her head once to look back, after the ricksha had started. He was running gaily up the steps. The door opened and the pretty girl came out. For a moment, against the warm light pouring out into the darkness, their two figures met together. Then the door closed.

*   *   *

Of course, Miss Benton could not be nice about it. She shouted at once when she heard the front door shut, "Where have you been, Amy Willey?"

Miss Willey thought it best to tell everything at once, now that she still had the strength of their kindness to help her. She went into Miss Benton's room. "I am going to be in a play, Miss Benton," she answered, before she even took off her toque. "It is *The Barretts of Wimpole Street,* and I am to be Elizabeth. They asked me because I look like her."

She waited, her heart beginning to beat very hard. But it was not so dreadful, after all. The very strangeness of the thing crumpled Miss Benton's attack.

"Whoever heard of such a thing!" she said loudly.

Miss Willey did not answer, since Miss Benton said this of many things of which she did not approve. She sat down and looked at Miss Benton quietly, and began to take off her gloves. Then Miss Benton sneezed and could not find her handkerchief. When Miss Willey saw it on the floor and pressed it into her hand she could only gasp, "What will the Bishop say?"

But standing there above Miss Benton and looking into her wrinkled face and at her dry gray hair scattered sparsely upon the pillow, Miss Willey suddenly felt young and strong. She answered, "The play will take only three weeks and the Bishop is not coming until after Christmas. He needn't even know. And I promise you it won't make any difference in my work. The play and the rehearsals are all at night—you won't see any difference."

"It'll be scandal in the school," Miss Benton muttered.

"I won't tell any of them—and anyway, Miss Benton," said Miss Willey, clasping her hands together a little wildly, "I've told them I am going to do it, and I am!" Miss Benton blew her nose loudly and without waiting Miss Willey went to her room.

That night after her supper she sat down to study her

part. She began this very first night to make a ritual of it. First, she read the book softly aloud to herself, until she felt the words come to life in her voice and until she felt Elizabeth's passion transfused into herself. Then she took up the typed sheets and like a miracle the words of the play printed themselves upon her brain. What the hour was when at last she went to bed she did not know. She would not look, for what did it matter? She had been so happy all evening. The little plain room was a theater for love to play in.

*   *   *

In those three weeks she scarcely spoke to anyone beyond the necessities of her work. She managed somehow to get through the long days. She taught her classes, collected her papers, made out her marks, and waited for the nights. Three times a day she sat across the table from Miss Benton. They never spoke of the play any more, and after supper each night Miss Benton ignored Miss Willey entirely. Once at breakfast she said, "I'm worried about poor Mr. Jones. The servants say his asthma is so bad he can't get out of his room. He misses Mrs. Jones—she knew what to do for him better than any doctor."

But Miss Willey scarcely heard her. She had quite forgotten the letter in the drawer upstairs.

At night, after Miss Benton had scraped back her chair and gone to her room, Miss Willey began to live. She put on her coat and toque and rode through any wind or rain. She felt new life rise in her, warm and eager, however cold the night ride was. They were rehearsing now in the Masonic hall. It was always cold, and the others grumbled and blew on their fingers and pretended their teeth were chattering so that they could not say their lines. But Miss Willey was never cold. She came always on time and was ready in her place, serious and quiet, and she brought the sonnets with her, and read them between acts, so that the spirit of the play might not be broken for her.

She knew all her lines very soon. After the first week, they were her own speech. She waited without impatience while the others stammered and halted. When Robert, holding her in his arms, faltered, she prompted him softly beneath her breath. He whispered under her curls, while she clung to his breast, "You're swell, Miss Willey!"

But that she did not like. She liked nothing which broke the spell. She was not Miss Willey now, she was Elizabeth, and Robert was her lover. She avoided every sight of Ted Hall. When he made merry off stage and laughed and danced a tap dance to warm himself, she looked away, pretending to be busy over her lines. He was Robert— Robert—she wanted him to be nothing but Robert. When Mrs. Howett called to them to take their places, she welcomed him back again in passionate silence. Now they were themselves again, Elizabeth and Robert. The play was all for them; the others only built up the story of their love.

She began to be Elizabeth all day long. In the morning when she rose she was Elizabeth. Somehow, she dreamed through the day twisting the duties of it into Elizabeth's duties. She walked and talked as Elizabeth would. She let dark eyes look up quickly and full of fire, and then drop again. She altered her dresses a little, and loosened the sides of her hair. When Miss Benton sniffed, she pretended not to hear it.

At the rehearsals she grew used to praise and no longer needed its warming for strength. When they said, "You are wonderful," she accepted it, smiling as Elizabeth smiled, shyly yet with mischief. When Mrs. Howett said, "Really, Miss Willey, I have nothing more to suggest. I don't see how a professional could do it better," she was silent. Of course, no one could do it better. She *was* Elizabeth.

Thus every night she fed her soul. She who had starved all her life now poured into herself nightly this great hot love. She clung to Robert, she was timid and fearful, she grew strong and sure, she gloried in him and in love. Nightly she knew what it was to lay her head against a man's breast, to hear a man's voice plead most beautifully for her love. And she made him so plead. For her own passion made the man passionate. His voice took on the deep tones of sincerity. He held her to him with gentle power. Nightly the triumphant hour of flight came to its great moment of crisis, and nightly she cried, "I go—to my husband!"

Afterward, she hurried as quickly as she could into her wraps and went away. They grew used to her instant disappearance. She did not want anything to spoil that moment —not his voice saying other things to other people. She must keep that moment quite perfect every night and hurry away with it like a lovely jewel in her palm.

*   *   *

Still, with all this, there was one place in the play which worried her. She had in one scene, before Robert came, to weep—to weep desolately, alone in her dark room at night, an invalid, hopeless, the moonlight shining in at her window meaningless, because she was alone. At first, she did it rather well. She could turn her face to that moon and weep for loneliness. It was natural to weep like that. But then it grew harder and harder. She was so happy. She knew that in the very next act Robert was coming. How could she keep on weeping desolately?

Mrs. Howett grew uneasy. "Miss Willey, it's all so perfect—except somehow you've let the life slip out of that weeping scene. Could you practice it by yourself a little at home?"

But she could not even weep at home. Nothing seemed to make her weep any more. She had been used to weeping rather easily, but now she went blithely through her days and mounted to the great crescendo of the nights. She could not weep.

Then something came to help her. It came just in time for the opening, the night of the dress rehearsal. She had not, in fact, done the weeping well at all that night. She felt less like it than ever. The ruffly brown dress was so becoming and her hair had gone just right. Julie, whirling by her in a crinoline, saw her and gave her a great hug. "You are adorable, Elizabeth!" she cried. "Look at her, Ted! How can you keep from falling in love with her really and truly?"

There was Robert at the door. Miss Willey smiled up at him, the blood crowding into her heart. But before she could protest, they were both gone. Then while she sat, still smiling, through the open door she heard his answer, not made to her, but to Julie. She could hear his voice, Robert's voice, saying most passionately, "Julie, Julie, I can't bear you to talk even in fun of my loving anyone except you. I love you. . . . I love you. . . ."

There was silence. Miss Willey got up softly after a little while and closed the door. Then she sat down before the mirror. Elizabeth looked back at her, alone.

A moment later Mrs. Howett came in. "Miss Willey," she began anxiously, "I hate to criticize . . ."

But before she could finish Miss Willey turned to her quietly. "I know what you mean, Mrs. Howett. It's the weeping. But I think I have the idea now—I think I can do it."

* * *

So she wept the next night very well, the night of the grand performance. Out there beyond the footlights were hundreds of staring faces, white and dim. She had thought she might be afraid of them. But she was not. She did not know them and they were nothing to her. In the familiar room upon the stage, which was now more her room than any other in the world, she lay upon her couch and bade the maid turn out the lights and leave her. Then alone, she gazed quietly into the moonlit sky beyond the window. She let herself think fully of what she had not dared until now to think. Now she knew. She was only Amy Willey, after all, and Robert was Ted Hall, and he loved a girl named Julie, who was pretty and young.

After tonight it would all be over—everything. She would go back to her place again. It was only a play. The tears rose brimming to her eyes and she began to sob softly. She had let herself live as though this were to go on forever. She dropped her head upon her arms. It was Amy Willey who wept now, and she wept utterly and with her whole heart. There was silence in the hall, and her sobs beat into it. Then there was the crash of hands clapping and the curtain went down.

She rose very quickly, then. Mrs. Howett ran to her exclaiming, "My dear, it was perfect!"

But Miss Willey did not seem to hear her. She hurried into her dressing room, terrified. She had lost Elizabeth! She was not Elizabeth any more—she was only Amy Willey again, and she couldn't go on with the play. . . . She stumbled into the dressing room and shut the door and locked it and sat down and wrung her hands. Why, she couldn't even remember her lines! How silly she had been to think she could—she remembered nothing except his voice last night—Robert's voice—saying over and over again, "I love you, I love you. . . ." At that moment she had begun not to be Elizabeth.

Someone knocked at the door. A voice called, "Five minutes, Miss Willey!"

She did not answer. She could only sit there with her hands wrung together. Then she saw her book. She had even forgotten to take it home last night and had not missed it. It lay on her dressing table, open as she had left it yesterday. She picked it up and turned the pages desolately. It had no meaning now. . . .

But suddenly it had meaning. After a moment the lovely, rich, full words began to take on their old habit of meaning, the meaning they had before ever the play began. She knew them by heart. She said them softly aloud, turning the pages here and there. The love was in them still, deathless. No one could kill a love like that. It did not matter what Ted Hall said to anybody. She did not even know who Ted Hall was. She only knew Robert, to whom she had written these songs of love. How silly she was—this last night was her greatest night—her night of marriage.

"Curtain's going up, Elizabeth!" a voice shouted.

"I am ready," she answered steadily.

So she forgot how Amy Willey had wept, and she went out to finish the dream of love.

She knew, of course, that the play was a success. She did not need them crowding about her to cry at her, "How could you be so wonderful!" "You are a great actress, Miss Willey!" "You were glorious!" She smiled at them all, saying nothing.

Then Julie, in her wide, ruffled white skirt swept up and wrapped her tenderly about with warm young arms. "You made it a great experience for us all. Dear Miss Willey, I want you to know first before anyone. Ted and I are going to marry each other. Somehow, seeing him with you like that—I know now that I love him."

And there he was, still dressed as he had been. But looking at him she knew him no more for Robert. No, Robert was safe forever in her own heart. This was Ted Hall, and when he said in his hearty boy's way, "You made us all do our best, Miss Willey," she smiled and took his hand and pressed it against Julie's, which she held.

"I am so glad," she said gently. Then she slipped her hand out between those two, and left them joined together.

It was quite easy to leave them quickly, partly because everybody was used to it, and partly because now everybody had for the moment forgotten even the play in the excitement of Julie's announcement. She fetched her coat and went quietly away in her ricksha, just as she had done on any other night.

*   *   *

So it was all finished and she was back again in her old life. The play was over. There was a note or two, one from Julie, and another from Ted, saying that they must meet. But the days went by and they did not meet. It was easy to see them as very happy and gay, and of course the school was not near and they would think her busy. All she had left of those three happy weeks was the typed manuscript of her part. The days began to pass in their old steady, graven fashion, two days and three days, and then day upon day.

But, still, everything was not quite the same. One night when she lit her fire and prepared for the evening she opened the drawer to her table. She must look over her papers which she had so long neglected—her few bills and things. It was then she saw Mr. Jones's letter, lying where she had thrust it. She had forgotten all about him. She took out the letter and read it again. It seemed quite new and strange to her. She sat with it in her hand, staring thoughtfully into the fire for a while after she had finished it. Of course, it was really a proposal. And now at her age she couldn't expect . . . It would be hard to grow old and never be married at all, never know what it really meant to . . . She should have answered the letter long ago, of course, but it was not too late yet. She could still write to him the letter that she planned.

But now she remembered him very clearly. Why, she could never write that letter to Mr. Jones, never, never! It was a letter she could write only to Robert, to Robert who had come out of the book and who in the play had taught her what love really was, what a glorious, glowing, tempestuous, shining thing love was. She smiled a little, remembering Robert. What did it matter whether she ever married or not? It wasn't marrying that mattered. It was love. She could keep whole and beautiful within her always her knowledge of love. She knew she could, she knew she was able, to write a letter of love—only it could not be to Mr. Jones. No . . . no . . . no . . . it was better to keep the gift ungiven except in her dreams rather than . . . She leaned over and carefully laid the letter in the middle of the flames, and when it was ash she turned to her papers again, smiling a little too steadily.

At dinner that night she saw Miss Benton looking at her secretly. She looked back in inquiry. Miss Benton must have something on her mind. "Yes, Miss Benton?" she said gently.

For a moment Miss Benton looked as though she would not speak after all. Then she changed and said gruffly, "Play's all over, is it? I saw about it in the paper."

"All over," said Miss Willey.

"Well," said Miss Benton, "all I can say is, it was a queer business for a missionary. But as long as it's over now . . . And I suppose you're satisfied?"

"Quite satisfied," said Miss Willey.

Heat Wave

IT WAS GOING to be another hot day. He stood by the
window, stared down the street, and gave a gust of a sigh.
There was a thick gray haze over the city. It was hot
already, and it was only five o'clock. . . . He wished he
had not got up so early. But he was so hot—he had been
hot and restless all night. He had waked up and felt his
skin tickling. The sweat was running down his neck, over
his ribs, in small slow streams. He heard Mattie's loud
breathing by his side and was wide awake. Still, if he had
turned over and shut his eyes and waited a minute, he
might have dropped off again.

But it had been hot so long he was all on edge—nine
days and nine nights! Mattie slept through anything. Hot or
not, she slept. If he could have felt her threshing around beside him and heard her groan out, "Ain't it awful, Hansie!"
he could have borne it better. But she slept no matter what,
lying as stiff and still as a small dead woman, except for
her heavy, regular breathing, blowing in and out, in and
out, all night long between her full, puffing lips. She was
hot enough, too. This morning, when he couldn't stand it,
he had leaned over and stared at her. She lay on her
back, sleeping, her mouth open, her little stubby hands
with their bright red nails crossed tightly on her rounding
stomach. Her cotton nightgown was wet over her small
breasts and clung damply to her legs. She was hot, but she
could sleep.

He had grunted petulantly then, and got up quickly, young and impatient. "Ain't no more sleep for me, and I might as well work," he said aloud, looking at Mattie. "The way some folks can sleep," he muttered. But she did not hear him. She puffed in and out, in and out. "Like sleepin' with a railway ingin," he said.

Then he looked gloomily toward the open door of the bathroom. "If I wash now . . . I don't know. . . ." he thought. He might go and clean up the shop and then wash before breakfast. If he washed now, it would be waste. Standing there in his blue pajama trousers, his short, thick upper body bare and ruddy under his sweat, he was suddenly tired of the day before it was begun. Usually, he jumped out of bed like a shot of a gun and was in and out of the bathroom before Mattie had opened more than one eye. He would dance in wet and dripping to shout at her, "Hey, you lazy block-a-wood, I'm ready for breakfast!"

That waked her, and she would smile sleepily and begin to stir, stretching her arms above her head and yawning loudly and cheerfully. Then she'd bustle—oh, they got on well enough—until it got so hot. They quarreled a good deal one way and another, now.

And it was hotter than ever today. He was tired of it—tired of everything, tired of washing and shaving and dressing, of eating and working and sleeping. He wouldn't wash—he'd let himself sweat. "I'd be wet through by breakfast, anyway," he thought.

He pulled a cotton undervest over his head and put on his old blue trousers, taking no pains to be quiet. But Mattie did not waken. Well, let her sleep. He didn't care if he ate or not on a morning like this. He wouldn't be able to eat even pork chops and buckwheat cakes and maple syrup, not if they were set before him. He walked heavily into the hall and down two stairs. Then he halted and listened. She was still sleeping, breathing in and out as loudly as ever. Well, he couldn't stand any more of that —not after a night of it. He'd be able to hear her 'way down in the shop. He stomped back and shut the door firmly. He had a glimpse of her between the door and frame. She was lying there exactly as she had lain all night, small and square and stiff. He was tied to her, as surely as a ship is tied to a dock.

But then everything in his life had him by the nose. This shop he'd bought—he opened the door. The close smell of spiced meats, of warm foods shut into a small room, wrapped about him. Everything would be spoiling on him if this heat went on. He couldn't put everything on ice. That fruit cake delivered yesterday—he bent over the counter. Yes, it was molding already, a faint powdery frost upon its black, rich surface. He took the cake up and blew over it, and then ran his finger over its crust. Why, even sausages couldn't hold up these days. This was life, to go and put everything he had into a delicatessen and make it look nice and paint it all up, and then along came this heat the very first summer!

He wasn't sure he'd ever wanted a delicatessen, anyway. When Mamma died and left him his five thousand, he didn't know as . . . but Mattie was all for the delicatessen. Her grandpa had had a delicatessen, and she couldn't get over what a nice kind of a business it was, refined and nice and sure, because people had to eat, didn't they? Well, he had wanted a good bar where you could sell beer and soft drinks too, but she had said, "I couldn't serve in a bar, Hansie . . . it would look so . . . But a delicatessen—well now, I wouldn't mind. Nice people come to a delicatessen, and I could help out real well."

Yes, and how much had she helped out? She hadn't hardly come into the shop since the heat began. He couldn't even get to a stadium concert once a month. There the stadium was, only five blocks away, and he read in the paper every day about the concerts and what they were going to have. He always spelled carefully through the long names. He didn't really know one piece of music from another, not by the names, but he liked to sit out under the stars in the dark, and maybe watch the moon come up as big as a yellow pumpkin over the high houses, and listen and think about something else than sliced ham and potato salad. He thought about a lot of things, things he read in the paper, politics and fights and sometimes a little piece of poetry that was nice, and now things like the Germans and the Reds. Not that he had any use for Reds! The only concert he had got to this summer, the mayor gave a speech and there was a lot of noise in the crowd and people said it was the Reds yelping again. They kept it up even when the music began and spoiled the night for him, and he had a hard enough time getting a while off, too. He'd had a regular fight with Mat about it. She hadn't wanted to keep shop for three whole hours. "I've had my day's work, too," she pouted. "If you'd seen the wash today . . . and besides I ain't so good this summer with the baby coming and all this heat. . . ."

Well, he was nearly tired of the baby before it was even born. She made it an excuse for everything she didn't want to do. God knows his own mamma had had babies every summer and nobody thought anything of it, and neither did she. But then Mattie was a sort of fancy girl—black hair all fuzz, and eyes big and black, but the eyelashes not real. It was the first time he had even known girls could have eyelashes not real. After they were married he told her to cut 'em out.

Well, they had a sort of row about it, but he needn't have bothered. She soon wouldn't have taken the trouble, anyway. They had only been married six months and look at her now. She was like all the other married women. . . . Didn't care how she looked now that she had got him. She'd say, "It's the baby, Hansie. . . ." Well, he'd— He pulled himself up abruptly and scrubbed hard at a counter. He couldn't curse his own child, he guessed, not before it was even born.

So he had gone to the door and opened it and looked down the street. But no coolness came in. The air from the street was heavy and full of the heat of the day before, and the day before that, and many days. There were no winds in the night to blow the streets clean.

He drew up an empty box and sat down outside the door. Right and left of him stood garbage cans. In front of him was his own that he had filled last night. Soon the truck would come. . . . But, first, he saw a small, shambling, bent figure come creeping by, the trousers too long and covering the torn shoes. This figure pushed a ruined baby carriage. In one hand it held a stick, and it began to turn over the garbage in the cans slowly and silently.

Above him, a woman's frowsy blond head thrust itself form a window. She screeched down into the street, "I'll thank you not to mess everything over the sidewalk! There's nothing in my can you can eat. I don't throw good food away. . . ."

The figure moved speechlessly away and drew near. Five minutes before, Hans had felt something bristling in him. This wasn't quite thieving, he had been thinking, but the next thing to it. But then the woman screamed—he knew that gabbling woman Mattie was always running with—

"Hey, you!" he shouted at the small gray thing. "There's a loaf of stale bread in my can. . . . *I* don't care . . ."

He watched gloomily while the creature fished desperately to find the loaf. This, he supposed, was what the Reds were always talking about. Well, would they call him, Hans Reder, a capitalist maybe, letting this fellow get his food out of his garbage. . . . Still, God knows, he was no capitalist. . . . He was a worker. . . . Couldn't even get to a people's concert.

If Mattie had not come down at this moment, he would not have known what he was. But she came in. He could hear her heels dragging in those silly bedroom slippers she had bought at a sale—mules, she called 'em—and the heels clattering till he couldn't stand it. Then she was there beside him in the open door, wrapped in her faded green kimono. She leaned against him. She hadn't washed. He could smell her, sour with sweat. Then she saw the thing at the garbage can, and before he could speak she screamed out as bad as that hag, "Get out of my garbage, you! Why don't you go and get something decent to do, 'stead of living on other people's leavin's?"

In that moment he was a Red. He growled at her, "Have a heart, can't you, Mat? A fella can't go out and get a job anywhere these days. . . . And you don't want the garbage, do you?"

"Yeah?" she sneered, turning to look down on him, one hand on her hip. "Well, say, it don't matter about my wantin' the garbage or not. It makes me sick to see a human bein' snooping around like a alley cat."

"Yeah?" he bawled. "Well, you make me sick, see? Selfish! Women are all selfish . . . crabbin'. . . . Don't want a thing themselves and then won't let anybody else have it. . . ."

Mattie drew herself up and put both hands on her thin hips. Her kimono hung open and her nightgown was drawn tight over her knobby stomach.

"Yeah . . . sez you!"

The gray ghost at the garbage can, hearing their loud voices, peered at them from under the brim of a torn felt hat, and put the lid on the garbage can softly and crept away, pushing the wrecked baby carriage.

"Now . . . look what you done, Mat!" said Hans gloomily. "There was a loaf a stale bread in there he might as well a had . . ."

"Let him go," said Mat loudly.

He looked at her. She was hideous, he thought suddenly. Her hair was a snarl, her lips pale, and her black eyes cold. God, how a fellow got let down after marriage! He used to say her mouth was like a red rose—it made him sick when he remembered what he used to say. She didn't care now how she looked. He shouted at her, "Pull your clothes over yourself, can't you?" She shouted back at him, "Who made me look like this, I'd like to know?"

He got up. He wasn't going to have her start talking about the baby out here. Let her show herself. . . . He didn't care. . . . He'd get to work. But he lingered to stare remorsefully after the gray ghost, now five houses away. He said gloomily, "It's enough to . . . They're right, them Reds. Things ought to be fixed so nobody needs to starve like that. Let the rich give it up. . . . There ought to be some way so . . ."

"Yeah," Mat interrupted loudly, "and if we had Reds, they'd come and take everything in your shop."

"Yeah, and if they was starvin', I'd let 'em," he threw at her.

"Nice lookout for your family," she sneered. "Nice thing for a woman to hear when she's about to . . ."

"Aw, go on and get some clothes on you, will you? The truckmen are coming and you look like hell. . . ."

"Yeah? And whose fault . . ."

A wave of heat swept over him. He had forgotten for a moment about being hot. Now the rumble of the truck drew near. Cars began to rush by. With the noise, the heat rose, stifling, thick, roaring, about him. He slapped his sturdy leg. He wouldn't speak to her—he'd get to work. But as he passed he looked at her, and he could not bear her. All the heat and sickness in him rose and burst out of him. He shouted at her over and over, "Shut up . . . shut up . . . shut up!" He could not leave off, his teeth set, his eyes glaring into hers, the sweat starting out over his whole body. "Shut up! Shut up . . . shut up . . ."

Her soft full face changed in surprise. She stared at him as though he had gone insane. Then, breaking into a wild howl of tears, she rushed away.

*　　*　　*

He did not follow her. He was tired of following her. He knew what he would have to do if he did. He'd have to tell her he was sorry and coddle her and lie down beside her on the bed and coax . . . Well, he wouldn't . . . not today . . . not in all this heat. He wouldn't hold her against him on this hot day on that messy bed.

"Every way, the Reds is right," he muttered to himself willfully. He took out his dusting cloth and began wiping the counters off again. This business of a man's tying himself to a woman when he was young—the Reds had it right—easy divorce, and no questions asked. And the woman had to work, too, in Russia. Gee, he'd like to see Mat work for once, a real day's work! She said she used to work in a ten-cent store, but he didn't believe it. She wasn't working when they met . . . just living with her married sister and taking care of the kids when she felt like it. He moved a pie, wrapped in cellophane, and wiped under it. If it wasn't sold today, it would be no good tomorrow. Beer, now, and bottles, you could keep forever . . . What had possessed him!

The morning wore on. The sun streamed in at the door, an oblong patch of solid white heat upon the floor. He'd have to buy an awning or he couldn't keep anything in the window.

The door opened. He saw Mat's sullen face. "Breakfast," she said coldly. She hadn't brushed her hair . . . probably hadn't washed her face, even. "Don't want any," he said. "It's too hot to eat." The door slammed—nice way to start the day!

It didn't get any better, either. Two women came in during the morning, one to buy six eggs, the other a quarter of a pound of butter. That was all. He was shut up in the idle shop. "No use goin' back upstairs," he thought, and let the hours wear on.

Toward noon the sun went under, but it was no cooler. The sky pressed down—thick, dark, hot as a woolen blanket. The shop was a pocket, full of smells. The sausages reeked, the cheese stank. He went to the door and leaned against the frame and stared down the street. He'd sell the shop. He'd . . . He might do anything. It was a rotten city. He might go off somewhere—no chance for a young man here, not in these days. He watched the cars rolling by and chose one to hate especially. It was a large black and silver car. The traffic light changed, and it paused near where the garbage can had stood in the early morning. Some difference! He stared at a chauffeur, at a handsome, cool, white-haired woman. Well, she didn't worry about anything—going out to her country place with her bags, he guessed, and he couldn't even get to a concert five blocks away. Yeah, the Reds were right, all right.

The door opened behind him and Mat came in and passed him. She was all dressed up in her green dress and hat and white fixings. The dress was getting too tight for her, but he wouldn't say anything, or she'd yell for something new.

"I'm going to Roselle's," she said shortly. "Your dinner's on the table."

"All right," he said as briefly. Her mouth was painted very red now, and her black hair was carefully waved where it showed under one side of her green hat.

"Hope it doesn't rain before I get back," she said anxiously, not looking at him. "This dress won't stand it. Well, g'by!"

She stepped jauntily down the street and he stared after her against his will. From the back, you wouldn't know anything was wrong. He used to think she had style when she was all dressed up—he used to like it. But today it made him tired. He felt a drop of rain on his face. It was going to rain. But there was no wind, no coolness in it, even in the clouds. The very rain came down warm, a meager, tepid shower.

Anyway, he would eat. And if it was going to rain all afternoon and Mat was away, he'd sleep. Nobody would come to the shop in the rain, and Mat would be late. . . . She and her sister would probably go to a movie. He was

tired clear through. The wet heat made him dizzy. He'd
eat only a little something and then get into a tub of cool
water and throw himself on the bed. When he woke, he'd
think some more about selling the shop. He couldn't stand
this. . . . He couldn't stand another day.

*   *   *

But when he woke he had slept so heavily he scarcely
knew where he was. Where was he? What time was it?
Not night, for the pale twilight streamed gently in at the
window. But something had happened to him. His body
felt light and relieved, his very bones rested, his skin
dry. He drew a great breath. Why! . . . he was cool! The
bed was cool, the room was cool. There must have been
a storm somewhere and now it was over—well, he could
hardly believe he was cool!

He stretched himself and smiled. He was as hungry as
hell. He didn't believe he had eaten anything, after all
. . . went and took a cold bath and threw himself on the
bed to sleep a few minutes before he ate and then hadn't
waked again. Now, here he was cool. . . . He'd forgotten
how it felt to be cool.

The door opened softly a little way and Mat stuck her
head through, smiling, mischievous. "Great big lazy!" she
cried. "I've been back ages. . . . The shop's been full and
I've been getting supper, too. Honey, you haven't eaten
anything this whole day! I've got a grand supper for you
—everything you love—beefsteak, honey boy, and fried
potatoes and sweet corn! And I made a dessert . . . and
it's turned so cool you can eat and eat!"

He leaped up and roared at her, "Gee, I'm hungry
enough to eat you up, Mat. . . . You look swell to me!"

She gave a little squeal of pretended fear and was gone. Never mind. . . . He'd catch her and give her a good hug yet—he hadn't kissed her in an age—several days maybe —since it had been so hot. Anyway, he was starved. He began to put on his clothes. Well, just for once, since it was so cool, he'd wear a tie, Mat's favorite red one, and a clean blue shirt. She liked blue to go with his eyes, and red to go with his hair, she said. Gee, he wasn't a bad-looking fellow—he rushed down, ravenous, shouting, "Don't let me get into the shop till after supper, will you, hon? I'd eat everything I saw!"

That night, after a rush of business, he sat out in the dark cool street with Mat. The sky was black and full of stars. He sat on the milk box, but he brought out the canvas folding chair for Mat. She'd been swell to him. She hadn't gone to the movies at all. She'd come back in the rain, God knows why, and found him asleep and seen that he hadn't eaten his dinner, and she'd stayed in the shop the rest of the afternoon and sold a lot. The pie was gone, too. Now, she lay back in the canvas chair and hummed a little. Under the dim street lights she looked pretty, her hair all curly about her face and her lips red and full—like a big rose, her mouth was. He bent over and gave her a kiss. Well, he was glad about the kid, too. And she'd look as good as ever, after it was over.

"You're swell," he whispered suddenly. "I'm just as crazy about you as I ever was."

"So'm I about you," she laughed, and slapped him playfully on the cheek.

So they sat there in the coolness, watching the people go by. He strained his ears in a brief moment of quiet between traffic. Did he hear faint music? No, not quite . . . not quite . . . Still, he knew it was there. The music was going on. It would be there every night, every summer. In his lifetime he'd get to hear a good deal.

When they rose at last to go to bed and were straightening the shop out for the night, Mat asked him suddenly, looking at him very straight out of her black eyes, "Say, Hansie, I've been wantin' to ask you something all day. You didn't really mean all that stuff you talked about Reds, did you? You scared me."

Reds? He stared at her. Oh, that—"Forget it," he said shortly. "I was so hot this morning I guess I was crazy." He lifted the garbage can and set it out on the street.

But when she was gone upstairs, he waited a moment. He looked thoughtfully at the loaf of cake on the counter. It had molded the night before. It wouldn't keep much longer. Still, it was so cool tonight. . . . And he might sell it tomorrow yet. Then, suddenly, he picked it up and wrapped a piece of paper about it.

"Oh, well . . ." he said aloud, and stalked across the sidewalk and dropped it in his garbage can.

The Quarrel

THE MAN stared angrily about the crowd in the little street of the hamlet where his home was. There his neighbors stood about him and about his wife, a circle of some thirty or forty people, men and women, their faces grave and listening. Little children, naked in the summer heat, squeezed themselves restlessly through the legs of their elders in order that they might reach the empty spot in the center where the man and his wife stood, and so miss nothing of the quarrel. The man would not look at his weeping wife and he hung his head sullenly and so saw these children, and seeing, saw one of his own among them, a child of eight or nine years. Yes, and there were his two younger ones, come also to see what was happening, and the three stared up at their parents in astonishment.

Suddenly the man could not bear it. There had been enough else, his wife's tears and scolding all these days, her hidden angers and suspicions which she would not speak. The man gave a great bellow and darted at his third son and cuffed him and roared at him,

"Get you home, you little dog!"

The child burst into loud wails and rubbed his shaven head and stood wailing, sure of sympathy from the crowd. The woman cried out then in the midst of her subdued weeping, turning her tear-wet face to this one and to that one among the crowd, "You see how he is, neighbors— this is how he is nowadays!"

The crowd stared unblinkingly at the man and in perfect silence. They had listened to everything: to the woman's accusation, to the man's short answers, to the silences. But disapproval of him was now thick in the air, and the man felt it. He looked down at his bare horny feet, and began to scuff his toe back and forth slowly in the dust. The dust made him think of his dry fields, waiting for his watering. He muttered, "There is all my work waiting for me and here am I wasting the good afternoon!"

This thought simmered in him awhile and suddenly his round dark face turned crimson and the veins stood out black on his temples. He lifted his head quickly and threw one furious look at his wife and he shouted at her. "What is it you want, you bitch? Tell me and let me get back to the fields! How can I get money to feed you and all your—your—"

"You see how he is," the woman wailed. "You see how he speaks to me now! Two months ago he was the best and kindest man. Sisters, you have often heard me say how I was blessed by the gods in the man to whom I am given. Always has he put into my hand every penny he earned, and he would come like a child and ask me for a bit to shave his head with before a feast day or to game a little with, or to buy some tobacco. And I was glad to give him pleasure. Now these two months I have not had a penny from him, no, not although he sold the rice, the last rice we had, and sold it well, and he has not even told me what he gained for it!"

She fell to louder weeping, her small brown wrinkled face streaming with tears, and then she took up her blue apron and flung it over her head and wept aloud.

Still the crowd was silent, and the children stared avidly. The man's two younger children crept up to their mother, and hiding their faces in her baggy blue cotton trousers began to weep convulsively. In this silence and weeping the man looked up cornerwise and as though unwillingly at a certain door in the street.

Yes, there was someone standing there, a young girl in a long green robe, such as young women in towns wore these days, and her hair was cut short about her neck. She had a sharp mischievous pretty face and she was smiling a little as she listened to the quarrel, leaning against the door frame with an indolent grace. Now when she caught the man's stolen look she took a rounded comb out of her shining black hair and passed it quickly through her bangs, cut long to her clearly marked eyebrows.

But the man was looking down again. His face had grown paler and he said in a smothered voice, "I do not know why you want money all the time. There is rice in the house and there is flour and there is bean oil and we have cabbages in the garden."

The woman pulled the patched apron abruptly from her face and leaned towards him, her eyes dried with sudden anger. She put her little hard wrinkled hands on her narrow hips and leaned her thin hard little body from the waist and shouted at him shrilly:

"Yes, and is bare food clothing too? Are not the shoes gone from the children's feet? Look at me, neighbors— look at these patches on my coat. When have I ever had any new clothes? Three years ago he got the gains from that money club he belongs to—ten silver pieces he gained in his turn, and he bought two bolts of coarse white cloth of the strongest, cheapest sort, and I dyed it dark blue with these hands of mine and I cut him two suits and me one suit and the eldest boy a suit and we wear them still and I have patched and patched. Now I can patch no more——must I not have cloth even for patches? I have not shoes for my feet, and with my feet bound how can I go barefoot as the children do? Only this morning I asked him again for a little money to buy stuff for shoes, and what does he do? He cursed me and gave me naught, and he was even so angry he would not come home this noon, but went and bought some bread at the inn and all the good food going to waste that I had made for him! And he said he had no money, but he could go and buy bread to feed his anger against me——" Her anger broke into tears suddenly again. "It is not as if I asked him for money to buy a long robe such as some women wear these days. Oh, well I know he would have money to buy a long robe for some woman but not for his wife!"

At this a terrible look came over the man's face. He leaped forward, his arm raised to strike the woman, but out of the crowd several stepped and caught his arm, and the women pulled his wife back. One of the men who held him said to him gently, "Remember she is your wife and the mother of your children."

"I have borne him sons——I have borne him sons," wailed the wife in a low voice of agony.

At this moment a gentle voice was heard. It came from an old woman with a quiet wrinkled face, who had stood all this time on the edge of the crowd, a little apart from the others, and leaning upon her staff. Now she called out with concern:

"You two, you are no longer young. Li the First, you are forty and five years old. I know, for I was with your mother when you were born. Your wife is forty and four. I know for I was at the wedding and helped her from the bridal chair at your father's door. You have been married twenty-eight years, and you have had twelve children and there are seven of them left. Your eldest son would have been twenty and seven years old, had he lived, and you would have now been a grandfather and your wife grandmother. Your youngest child here is but three years old. Think of all these things and of all the years you have lived together upon your land and let there be peace between you now."

This the old woman spoke in a quavering clear old voice, and because she was the oldest woman in the hamlet and mother to the richest man, everybody respected her and listened to her while she spoke. When she had finished the man's wife was softened and she turned to the old woman and said with earnestness, "Grandmother, you know I have always said my man was good—the best and kindest man. So was he ever until two months ago. Now see how he looks!" She turned her eyes on the man and all the eyes of the crowd turned to him also. The man's head drooped again and a slow dark crimson came creeping up out of his neck. "See how he looks, Grandmother! Ever the gentlest good man he was, and now always angry and sour! Yes, he can go out and smile and laugh and be merry before some, but when he comes home he is dark and silent and there is not a merry word in him and he never speaks except to blame me because my hair is not smooth or my coat not clean or some such thing wrong. And I have but this one coat to my body, and how can I be always clean? I have the house and the children and the work in the fields, and how can I sit as some women do and put powder on my skin to make it pale and oil on my hair to make it smooth?"

Suddenly the man could not bear it again. He shook himself restlessly, his strongly knit body straightening itself.

"I ask you, what is it you want of me?" he muttered thickly. "All this noise and talk over nothing—what do you want of me?"

"What do I want of you?" repeated the woman passionately. "I want this one thing. I want you to be to me as you have ever been until two months ago. That is all I ask. Your heart is changed—your heart is turned away from me! I ask but this one thing—be to me as you were!"

It was now as though the crowd were not there. There were but the two, the man and the woman, solitary in a world beating with passion, the passion of the woman. She stretched out her little horny hands to him, hands swollen at the knuckles, the nails hard and black and split. "Oh, be to me as you were—be to me as you were!" she moaned.

A sigh went up from the crowd. The man wet his lips two or three times, quickly, and out from the edge of his stubbly black hair two small streams of perspiration began to trickle towards his jaws. He glanced again, secretly and unwillingly, at the door where the slender pale green figure leaned in the afternoon sunshine. The girl's robe was such a green as are young leaves newly full on fruit trees in spring, pale, but very pure and green. He would not look so high as her face. But he knew perfectly how her face was, her pale skin, the full red lips always smiling, her eyes black and fearless, never downcast or turned away from him. It was that look of hers that caught him whenever he passed by—he passed by often just for that look, although he never spoke one word to her. How could he speak since she was the granddaughter of the richest man in the hamlet and he but a farmer who did not even own his land but must have all he had from off the bit he rented? He had been saving these two months even for a long blue cotton gown such as most men have as a matter of course, and for a pair of white town-made stockings and a pair of town-made shoes.

When he thought of this bitter saving he set his heart against that wailing wife of his. Well, he had been faithful all these years. He was forty and five years old and he had never taken a bit of pleasure for himself, no, not once had he gone into a common pleasure house where even a poor man may go and for a little piece of silver take some joy and change. Day in and day out he had labored for his wife and for his children until now he was forty and five years old, and he had but one old robe to his body and never anything else but these old patched clothes for his labor.

Yet there was this one thing that troubled him. Did she look at all men like that, with her eyes so wide open and lingering, or was it only at him? This was what had kept him uneasy all these days and nights. How could he know if she only looked at him like this? Every time he passed the door he stole his glance at her and every time she gave him back the look, so free, so bold. He had heard men talking together sometimes as men will and he had heard them say that nowadays women were changed, fearless of any man they were, taking anyone they chose, free and enticing in all they did.

He wet his lips again and felt the perspiration down his neck. How could he know if she looked at all men so, or was the look saved and for him? Somehow he must know the truth.

"Oh, be to me as you were!" his wife whispered broken-ly, and she lifted the corner of her apron to her eyes and wiped them, her anger gone from her utterly, and only agony left.

He lifted his head suddenly and looked full at the doorway. Must he not know the truth?

The whole crowd looked with him. When they saw his head lift and his eyes turn thither, they lifted their heads and looked. There the girl stood in the doorway, preening herself. She had the little white comb of bone in her hand, and her fair arm was upraised, and she smoothed back the glistening black hair from her little pale ears, where gold rings hung. The women stared at her with hostility. "That long robe like a man's—" some woman muttered suddenly. But every man looked at her in silence and in secret wonder.

Now the old lady at the edge of the crowd when she saw them all looking, she looked, too, and with astonishment. This girl to her was but her great-granddaughter and a naughty child whose town parents had spoiled her. Had she not said a score of times to her son how the child had been spoiled until she was fit for no man to wed, and that she pitied the man to whom she was betrothed? But now she stared with increasing sharpness at this girl. For the first time she saw the pretty pettish face, lit with secret wantonness and mischief, turned to someone in the crowd. The dry red came up into the old lady's wrinkled cheeks. She thumped her way to the door, her stick knocking on the cobblestones, and stared in the direction of the girl's gaze. That gaze fell straight as any beam upon a young man who hung about the door. At first he had been in the crowd, listening to the quarrel, but now he had turned his back upon it and was staring at the girl, his sheepish eyes half shamed, too, his jaw hanging, a little water at the corner of his mouth.

The old lady thumped her stick hard upon the stones.

She knew that lad, son to the innkeeper who owned no land and was but a sort of public servant.

"Get you into the house, you shameless, wicked child!" she cried suddenly, her voice very shrill and cracked, but full of such anger and authority that the girl, pouting a little, turned half away. "Into the house, I say!" the old lady cried again, lifting her staff so menacingly that the girl slipped within the shadow of the door.

But her little hand was still on the lintel, a little slender pale hand, with a gold ring on the tiny last finger. The old lady went up and struck this hand sharply and it was withdrawn into the shadow also.

"Never have I seen such a maid as this," the old lady shouted, still shrill. "Standing at the door, a betrothed maid, and staring at any man who passes! So they tell me all maids do nowadays, and what the world is coming to I swear I do not know!"

In the crowd the passion died away softly. The wife smiled a little, somehow comforted, the women were less sullen, and the men looked obliquely here and there and cast their eyes at sky or field or spat in the street's dust. A child cried and the crowd moved apart and made ready to scatter, its interest gone. Only the innkeeper's son stood still bemused, staring at the empty door.

But he was not the only one to have seen that beam-like look. The man had seen it and his wife also. Out of the man's face had ebbed every drop of blood, leaving him yellow as a sere leaf. He stood looking down into the dust. Now he knew.

But the old lady was not finished. She understood everything suddenly and she was not finished. She turned and shook her stick slightly at the man and pointed it at him.

"Li the First," she said firmly, "you are a fool. Go back

to your fields. But first give your wife that money you have in your girdle."

Slowly the man fumbled in his belt and brought forth four pieces of silver. He did not turn his head but he held the silver in his outstretched hand. Then his wife put forth her hand until he felt beneath his finger tips the hard dry palm of his wife's hand. He dropped the money there and with it all his dreams.

Then he straightened himself quickly and looked about the parting crowd, his face a little bleak, but serene again, and he spoke in his routh and usual voice.

"I do not know why my woman has made all this quarrel," he said. "All she needed to do was to tell me for what she wanted the money. As she says herself, I have ever given to her all I had."

He stooped and picked up again the hoe he had thrown upon the ground when he was called there, and shouldering it he went, without once turning back his head, to his own life once more.

The Truce

❦

ACROSS THEIR HEARTH Elizabeth Bond looked at Martin, her husband. They had decided, the last time they quarreled, that they would not quarrel for thirty-six hours. They could not go on quarreling. They were degraded by their endless quarreling. In the midst of it she had looked at him over the breakfast table, quivering, and she cried, "Oh, Martin, stop!" And he groaned out, "If we only could! What is the matter with us?" He looked up at her, his face twitching.

Then the idea had come to her. "Let's make a truce," she said slowly, staring at him. "Let's agree not to quarrel about anything more until tomorrow night. We're alone tomorrow night. Then let's sit down and talk it all over and see what we can do. We cannot go on like this. Either we must understand each other . . . or we must . . . separate."

It was the first time that she had used the word aloud, and though she had said it to herself many times, said aloud it frightened her. But he did not seem to notice it.

"No," he agreed thoughtfully, "we cannot go on like this." He had folded his napkin up neatly and come to kiss her gravely on the forehead, and then he had left the room.

She did not move while he put on his hat and coat and went out of the front door. She sat immobile, her head leaning on her hands. He tried so hard, she tried so hard, and still it was like this. It was not as though they were cheap, common people—not like that Mr. Beel and his silly little wife next door, who were continually fighting. Martin was not like that—not interested in stenographers and secretaries—and she wasn't interested in anybody else. There was no triangle at all. They did not want to love anybody else. They wanted to love each other. They wanted to be happy, to do what was right, to fulfill their vows to each other.

Yet she was, she realized with horror, glad to see him go out of the house, her husband! For now the house was her own again. It never seemed her home while he was in it. He was always like a guest in a hotel, who sees nothing beyond what is necessary for his comfort, and it was she who had made the home, planned it, decided on every shade and color. He said he liked it, of course, approving —that is, most of the time approving—when he noticed it, or if she asked him. But when there was something he did not like. . . . He had never liked that lovely, old, dull blue Japanese print because he had said he did not know what it was about. He liked a picture he could understand. It looked, he said, silly—a pale, flat face staring out of swirling blue cloth. Maybe the Japanese liked their own pictures, but he was an American. . . . There she was, remembering the stolid things he said! Why could she not remember his kindnesses? He had brought her a box of chocolates last night. But she did not like chocolates—she liked nougat. He never remembered, because he liked chocolates. She rose quickly and drew her breath in deeply. Anyway, she had the picture, and it was hanging there where she had put it.

*　　　*　　　*

Still, it had been terrifying to them both to realize, even in those short thirty-six hours, how often they had looked at each other and stopped the bitter words upon their tongues. Without knowing it, they had made a very habit of quarreling. He had not come into the house last night before he had wanted to know why it was that his particular coat hanger in the closet downstairs was the one she always seemed to use for her fur coat, and she had begun to answer coldly she didn't know he had had a particular coat hanger, and he had started to say that she didn't realize . . . when they both looked at each other and remembered. A score of times, they had remembered. By the end of this second day she felt as though she had scarcely spoken to him. She felt checked and hampered at every turn of speech with him, and tonight he had sat all through dinner, silent, effortless.

Now, the thirty-six hours were over. They looked at each other, she on one side of their fire and he on the other. She had taken care to look rather nice. She put on a dull red dress that they both liked . . . one of the few dresses they were agreed upon. He liked to see her in plain things, straight and simple and without a touch of the bizarre that she loved. So he liked the red dress because it was straight and fitted her straightly, and she liked it because it was red.

He had, she saw, taken an unusual care with himself, too. He had changed into his dark suit and had put on a fresh tie. He was still good to her sight, she thought, rather sadly, blue-eyed and blond-haired. Perhaps that had been the whole trouble. . . . He had been so very handsome that she had seen nothing beyond that. She had always been rather weak about handsome people—why, she had even loved to look at a pretty woman—perhaps because she had never been really pretty herself. She was too dark, too tall, her features a little too large. Sometimes, people said she was handsome when she was looking her best, but she had secretly, wistfully, always wanted to be small and fair and pretty—the sort of woman men would call "little girl." Martin never called her "little girl." Why should he, when she stood as tall as he in her stocking feet? If he had, they'd probably both have burst out laughing.

Still, there was the secret wish, and he had never divined it. She had tried to be always the sort of woman he admired, dependable and capable and ready, even, to help him in his work in the laboratory. Her music had made her fingers sensitive, fortunately, and she learned quickly enough the technique of his work. They quarreled less in the laboratory than they did at home. Indeed, there she admired him more than anywhere else, and there he commended her briefly. "Good worker . . ." he said sometimes, or he said, "You're a smart girl, Bet." Well, that was praise enough in a laboratory . . . but somehow, not enough at home, at night, by a fireside.

"Well, Martin?" she said quietly.

"Well, Elizabeth," he answered after a second.

There was a pause. She felt the old familiar anger rising swiftly to her lips. Of course, he would wait for her to begin. Of course, it was like him to make her take the initiative, to force her to a commitment. He was always so cautious, so guarded—the scientist in him, perhaps. Then she pressed her lips firmly together. She would not be forced, either by him, or by her anger. She made her voice come out lightly, easily, and she smiled as she spoke. "And what is the end of it in your opinion, Martin . . . say, as a scientist?"

He felt for his pipe. "You mean . . . the end for us?"

Ah, she thought a little maliciously, he was putting it off again!

"Yes, for us."

He lit his pipe carefully and put the match in the fire, and puffed. She could wait, she would wait, she told herself.

"What do you think?" he asked.

"For once," she answered instantly, "I am going to wait until I hear what you think. I seem to remember one of your complaints against me is that I am always too ready with my own opinions."

"I seem," he said, after a long staring into the fire, "to rub you the wrong way. Everything I do seems to be not wrong in itself, but somehow wrong because it is done in a way you don't like. I seem just to *be* wrong, rather than to *do* wrong." He hesitated and then added, "Perhaps, if we'd had children, we wouldn't have had time to notice each other so much."

At the word "children" her heart became rigid. She could not have children—she hadn't known it when they were married—not until afterward. She couldn't hear the word "children" mentioned without that rigidity, that stillness, that putting away. She fixed her eyes on the blazing fire. It was a lovely fireplace, and she had designed the hearth. The whole house was lovely . . . the house she had so longed to have a home as well as a house. Perhaps, if they had had children . . . She pushed them away again. He had put it exactly—he seemed always to be wrong.

"And I?" she asked rather sadly. "I suppose you find me the same way."

"I don't know," he answered.

He had let his pipe go out and now he was scratching

a match again . . . silly, but the way he scratched a match even had been a thing to quarrel over. She could not bear his slow, firm scratch—she hated the sound of a scratching match—it shivered down her spine. He had forgotten this again, and now he was scratching in long slow strokes. . . . She held herself tightly, waiting for the burst of flame to end it. At least she would not speak of it at this moment— it was too small of her.

"I suppose," he said, puffing vigorously, "that I do not find all that you do pleasant. It is natural, when one is so often criticized, to become critical in turn. I think if you had been able to accept me more and to let me have— well, my little habits—that I would not have seen things in you."

"What, for instance?" she said dangerously. So there had been things in her, too?

"Well," he said, with surprising readiness, "the way you keep stirring your coffee and stirring your coffee while you talk. There is no sense in it. The sugar melts instantly, and yet you go on stirring and stirring."

She swallowed hard. "I didn't know that I did it," she said.

"No," he agreed, "of course, I know that."

"Why didn't you speak if it?"

"I thought maybe I would, sometime," he replied calmly.

"You've spoken of enough else," she cried hotly. "You don't like the way I dress, you don't like the way I play. . . ."

"Those are more important things," he interrupted. "You don't know how to dress to bring out your good points, and you are too tall a woman to sway at the piano the way you do."

"Even if I don't know it?"

"I've told you that you do it."

"You certainly have, my dear Martin, again and again and again. . . ." There was the old, frequent swelling of anger in her throat and the ringing in her ears. Oh, she would like to hurt him. . . . She wanted to hurt him terribly, terribly. . . .

But before she could do it, he began to speak again rather mournfully. "Even before we were married I used to notice it. . . ."

"Did you, indeed?" she murmured, biting her lip.

But he refused to notice the interruption. ". . . and I thought I would mention it as soon as we were married, knowing how sensitive you were. . . ."

"Did you think I would be less sensitive afterward?"

"No, but I thought we'd be nearer together then, so that I could do it more easily, but we never have seemed to get much nearer. In fact, Elizabeth, I sometimes think we were nearer before we were married than we have ever been since."

She felt her anger subside a little in surprise. Now, that was rather clever of him. She pondered it. They had been near those first days. She was still in the old manse, a girl fresh from college, wondering what she was going to do with herself. There seemed a score of things that she could do, but, of course, her music was the one thing she knew she must do. She had gone on with it steadily all through college . . . college because her mother so wanted it, her little starved mother, who died before she could see her girl graduate and get the diploma she herself had always longed to have had . . . but after college, music . . . music. She and Dad had been planning how to get the music, he giving what he could from his little salary at the church and she earning something by lessons in the village while she commuted to the conservatory.

And then, suddenly, Martin had come that summer to visit some cousins in the village. They had met on a country picnic, and instantly they had become friends. He talked about his work, and she . . . she thought about his square shoulders and his strong hands and his serious, too-good-looking face. There were no young men in the village like him—and she had gone to a college for women and had not seen many men, and somehow she was ready for friendship with men. And he had never had time for girls, he said, and he was glad, he said, that his first real friendship with a girl could be with one so sensible as she. "I hate silly girls," he said darkly. Of course, she knew there must have been girls enough about him because he was so good-looking. There were many women who thought of nothing else in a man except his looks. She had been astonished by a throb of jealousy in her breast. Why should she be jealous?

But, still, she was jealous that summer, a strange jealousy that made her lean to him in a new way and let the sparkle come into her eyes. She laughed more easily, and she teased him a little and was different without wanting to be exactly, until one day he had seized her in his arms, one day when they had been walking over the wind-swept hills, and had kissed her hard.

"There," he said gruffly. "That's what you have been asking for."

"I haven't. . . . I haven't!" she cried furiously. It was their first quarrel. While they were friends they had never quarreled, but once he had kissed her they quarreled again and again, and she lived in a strange state of despair and delight—strange delight of the body, strange despair of the heart, because after he had kissed her she was lonely.

But they were engaged and married. She wanted to be married quickly, because there was no reason why she shouldn't be and because she thought that after they were married she would not be so lonely with him. She wanted to be married. . . . She was in a fever to be married. There was old Dad saying wistfully, "What about your music, darling?" And she had put him off airily: "Oh, music doesn't seem to matter these days, beside Martin. And I can take it up again any time I like, and I shall keep practicing. . . ."

She didn't even know until after they were married that Martin did not really like music. When he worked in the evening it disturbed him a good deal if she played.

Now she said aloud, moodily, "You've never really liked music at all."

He took his pipe out of his mouth. "What the devil has that to do with it?"

"Everything, everything!" she cried, looking at him in great accusation. "It's just like you to understand nothing of what my music means to me. Why, it means to me what your work means to you. . . . It means my life, that's what it means! I've let it go—I've let this thing and that interfere with it—getting the house settled and then trying to learn to run it the way you wanted it and thinking I had to help you in your work . . . the hours I've put in at the laboratory . . ."

"For God's sake," he broke in, his voice thick, "never come near the laboratory again—I can do without you! I'd rather work alone the rest of my life than have you come as a favor. Why did you come, if you didn't want to?"

Why did she not speak the truth? She had wanted to come at first so as to be near him, to try somehow to be less lonely when she was with him. It had frightened her to discover that even after they were married she was still lonely with him. But other words crowded them out.

"I never will come again if it means no more to you than that. You said . . ."

Across their angry voices the doorbell rang suddenly, and she paused. It rang again and again, sharply, insistently. He drew himself together, preparing to rise. But she was already on her feet swiftly, ahead of him. She was running to the door before he was out of his chair, and she flung it open. There stood a telegraph messenger. She signed quickly the slip he held out to her and took the yellow envelope. Martin came sauntering up behind her.

"For me?" he inquired. "I've been expecting word from Baker, the chemistry man. . . ."

"No," she said, astonished. "It's for me. I don't believe I've had a telegram since Mother died."

She tore it open quickly and turned to him, crying aloud, "Oh, Martin, it's Dad. . . . He's very ill!"

*   *   *

So they could not come to the end of their quarreling, after all. She had to lay aside everything else and tend this old, trembling man, whom she had gone to fetch home with her. She could not believe it was Dad. Surely, it was not Dad. She poured out the story to Martin in their room when the old man was safely lying in the comfortable bed in the guest room. She had written him many times during the two years since she had seen him. "You must come and visit us, Dad. . . . We have such a pretty guest room."

And of course he always said gratefully that he would come. But he kept putting it off—he was so busy in his church—it was hard to get a supply, and he had to pay for it himself. But he was surely coming to see his girl— and to see Martin, too, of course, and the new home. He missed her very much about the manse, but of course it was nice to think of her. . . .

And here he was, come in such a way as she would not have dreamed!

"Oh, Martin," she cried, forgetting all else, "if you could have seen! I went rushing to the manse, thinking of course he was there. But he had—they had made him resign two months ago, Martin! And he hadn't told us— he was so broken up he couldn't tell us—he doesn't seem to realize it, not even now. There was a young man in the manse, a boy just out of school, and he seemed ashamed enough. He took me to Mrs. Wick's boardinghouse and there Dad was, in one of those awful cheap rooms where the traveling salesmen stop—you know—and he has been living there two months . . . and all the time saying nothing to me at all, and when he saw me he was so ill he thought I was Mother!"

She fumbled for her handkerchief and looked at Martin's face in the mirror. It was after dinner, and he was changing his tie carefully, knotting it compactly beneath his chin.

"It's a shame, old girl," he said gravely. Then he said cheerfully, "Well, don't worry about him now. . . . He's here safe and sound and we'll look after him."

"My father, Martin . . . my old Dad!"

She looked at him piteously, longing to go over to him and put her head down upon his shoulder.

"Yes, yes," he said kindly, "it's awful. Well, we'll look

after him. I've got to go now, my dear. . . . Got an appointment in twenty minutes." He turned and bent and kissed her, and went downstairs. She heard his footsteps echoing sturdily upon the floors, heard the door slam, and then his footsteps echoing upon the walk. She was suddenly alone in the house, alone with an old sick man—with death, perhaps—with things she did not understand. She was afraid. For a moment she was afraid even to go into the guest room where that guest lay. It did not seem like Dad, that old vague terrified man who kept calling her "Allie." But of course she must go . . . of course she must go and take care of him. The doctor would be here in a few minutes. And Martin did not mean to be unkind. He was only practical. She rose and entered the room.

*　　　*　　　*

"You see, Allie," her father's high, trembling voice said, "you see how it was. I didn't want to tell the child. . . . She's so young. And there was no one to talk to—"

"I see, dear," she answered gently. Day after day now she had said those words, and day after day he poured out his tragedy to her, always the same tragedy. Once, at first, she had called him "Dad," and he was troubled for a moment, staring at her. Then she remembered that her mother had never called him anything but Robert, and so she said quickly, "I must have heard Elizabeth . . ."

"Yes," he said relieved. "But I like it that you never called me 'Dad' as some women do when they have children. It always seemed to me as if they forgot their husbands. . . . You always have kept me . . . your lover. . . ."

She smiled, trembling a little under the necessity to speak. She could not . . . could not . . . say Robert, not as she remembered her mother used to say it with that deep caress in the words—"My Robert—" so she said unsteadily, "Yes, my . . . my dear."

But his mind was flying off again, as it did these days, continually. "You see, Allie, they thought I was older than I was. You remember my birthday is on September the sixth. They said a man seventy-five years old is too old for the church. But you see the point is, Allie, I am not seventy-five—I won't be seventy-five yet for a long time—not until next September . . . on the sixth of September . . . I said." He began to tremble and tried to sit up in bed, his faded old blue eyes gathering energy. He faced his foes. "I said, 'Mr Jones, you are mistaken, sir. . . .' "

"Yes, yes, dear," she said sobbing. "Lie down . . . dear heart . . . lie down and rest. . . ."

"But I want you to understand everything, Allie. . . ."

"I do understand, dear."

Over and over, until he slept, she murmured the comforting words, "I understand, my dear. . . . I understand. . . ."

* * *

But in the morning, when she had left him sleeping in the care of the nurse, she went running to her own room to throw herself upon her bed and weep, and, weeping, Martin found her and listened to her as she poured it out to him.

"Oh, Martin, he is so pitiful—he worked there forty years, on that tiny wage—plowing through the snow to visit the sick and never taking any vacation in summer and doing without things—and in the end they threw him off—his own people, Martin!"

"It's a darn shame," he said, sitting down beside her and taking her hand.

In his way he was very kind to her these days, she thought, clutching his solid strong hand gratefully. He never reproached her for anything. Even when she sat down sorrowfully to play sometimes, he did not say anything. But she tried to remember, too. If he were in the room she held her body quiet, and she remembered about the coffee. She would never forget again—not if she could help it. Yet these things were now strangely unimportant. Their own life seemed quite in abeyance. Those two quarrelsome, vigorous young creatures—where were they? She found herself even behaving like her mother, being quieter, less argumentative, more patient than she naturally was. When he slammed the front door as he always did, she did not cry out at him quickly, not even though she winced at the noise. She was able to be silent.

For nothing mattered now except this—she had in these few short weeks, perhaps not more than days, to see her father safely through to the end. She began to feel what her mother would have been at such an hour, how she would have spoken, and how comforted an old dying man. Day by day, she seemed to be her mother, even to herself.

"Don't distress him," the doctor said. "It won't be long at best—let him have the comfort of thinking your mother is by him."

So she let him think so.

"When I am well, Allie," he said with feeble brightness, "I am going to start again. I am going to apply for a country church somewhere, with a little country manse that has a garden. With a garden we won't be dependent on whether or not they pay my salary quite promptly. I find it so distressing, dearest, to ask for money. I think if it were not for you and the child I never could do it. If I were alone, I would just do without it. And with a garden . . ."

His voice trailed off and he fell into one of his little sleeps.

To Martin that night, she cried angrily, "I don't believe they have paid him properly all the two years I've been away. Oh, I ought to have gone back—I didn't dream what was going on—and he never said anything."

"Just as well, perhaps, you didn't," Martin said practically. They were at the dinner table, and he poised his knife carefully above the beefsteak. "After all, my dear, he was a very old man, and I daresay the last ten years he hasn't been able really to fill the pulpit."

"I don't care," she said sharply. "Forty years deserves something at the end . . . if religion means anything. . . ."

"I suppose religion means dollars and cents, like anything else," he replied calmly.

But she could not swallow her portion of the meat. She sat there aching, aching.

Martin glanced at her, and then said kindly, "You mustn't let yourself get so worked up. It's only what happens to any of us. . . . We've got to face things as they are, you know. You let yourself feel things too much. You always have."

"It's my own father, Martin," she said.

"Yes, of course it is," he agreed. "Of course I know how you feel and all that, but the point is, there probably is another side to it. Probably the old man did hang on too long and didn't take any hints, and so they had to be plain with him. You know he always was rather absentminded and dreamy. I used to think, that summer I was there, that things weren't too happy in the church, but he didn't notice anything."

"What do you mean?" she asked. "Why didn't you tell me?"

"It wasn't any of my business," he said. "I'm not interested in churches. But I heard Uncle Jim say something about his sermons being long and too vague for these days. The young people had stopped coming, you know."

She was silenced, remembering. It was, perhaps, very true. She could not honestly deny it.

"All the same," she repeated, "they might have remembered what he had been . . . and what Mother was . . ."

"Of course," he said amiably. "They ought to have remembered. But you know how people are. There's no use in expecting anything much from people. One has to be practical about life."

Practical! She rushed passionately back to her father's bedside. He had had a restless day.

"I'll take care of him tonight, Miss Carew," she said to the nurse. "I'm sure you'll be glad of a straight night's sleep." The nurse wavered. "I can't leave him tonight," Elizabeth added quickly.

"I'll be here, in case," the nurse answered wearily.

She sat by him in a very madness of devotion through the long hours. But he slept quite peacefully and as he had not slept for several nights. He wanted her to take both of his hands, and she sat holding them in her grasp, frail as sea shells worn and dried by wind and the sands, and she watched him sleep. Only once he woke, and then he stared at her a little while and said, troubled, "Is it night, Allie, and you not asleep?"

She answered, "No, indeed, dear . . . it's the afternoon. . . . I have the shades drawn against the sun."

"You mustn't . . ." he began and then wavered off into sleep again.

*   *   *

Somehow, it did not seem their house at all, this house. It did not seem the house she had made for herself and for Martin. Some other life stronger than theirs had taken it. Their life, and what had been their love, stood in abeyance upon this other life, this greater love.

For now, as the end drew near, this was all the old man had. Everything left him except this passionate clinging to Allie. Elizabeth went away from him only when he slept and when he woke he cried for her, and she had to become Allie for him again. He was not her father any more, nor was Allie her mother. They were two people, two other people, two lovers, eternally married to each other. The reticence, the sense of vague shame she had had at first when her father poured out his heart to her, left her now. He was telling things he would never have told Elizabeth, and so she put away Elizabeth and became Allie, and he told her everything. In her necessity for release somewhere at first, she had told Martin the piteousness of the secret things she heard. "Oh, Martin, he's fighting for faith—I always thought his faith in God was so sure—the one thing in life for him . . . for which he gave up everything . . . but he isn't sure—oh, what ought I to do?"

"Face the facts," said Martin briefly. "Nothing else to do. Keep your perspective, Elizabeth. Keep saying to yourself, 'He's only one man dying as we all must die.'"

"He's my father. . . ." she said brokenly.

She could not say that Martin was wrong, nor even that he was unkind. He was helping her all he could. But he could not understand why she felt she must help the old dying man not to face facts—help him to believe what was not true, even, so that he might die happy. Yes, Martin was very kind. In the sickroom he was strong, and he lifted the old man capably and easily from one side of the bed to the other. But the old man always looked at Martin bewildered and asked always the same question, "Allie, who is this young man?"

At first she had said cheerfully, "Don't you remember Martin, dear?" But he did not remember. So she said, "He married Elizabeth, you know . . ."

Then he said, "But Elizabeth is not married—Elizabeth would have told us if she were married." And after a moment he said, "Elizabeth is only a little girl. . . ."

He was so distressed then that Martin said comfortably, "Oh, I'm just one of your neighbors, Doctor."

The old face relaxed and smiled vaguely. "I'm always glad to see young men." The voice began quaveringly, "I am always glad to see young men in my study between four and six in the afternoon. Allie, tell the young man . . ." The words trailed away.

"Funny, he doesn't even remember we are married," said Martin, as they stood and watched the gentle, sleeping face.

Perhaps, she thought later, he did remember. For when he waked he said suddenly, "Elizabeth wasn't married. She was never really married."

"What do you mean, dear?" she asked, her breath bated. But he did not answer and she did not know.

*   *   *

So she must let herself become Allie completely as the swift days passed—the few days left to him. He clung to her then unceasingly and he whispered out the innermost fear of his life. "Allie . . . what if . . . I've been wrong? What if I've staked my life on something . . . not true? Suppose there isn't . . . God?"

Years ago, she had asked herself that question, and years ago had answered it. If she had not, those two years with Martin would have destroyed faith utterly—Martin in his laboratory, announcing confidently over his slides, "You see how matter divides itself, Bet—divides and dies —no meaning in it, except that endless division and death." Martin was right, of course. . . .

"I know there is God," she said calmly to the anxious dying face.

"You're sure . . . Allie?" he asked, listening, his whole face listening.

"Sure," she answered.

"If you're sure, Allie . . ." he said contentedly, and fell into sleep.

Over and over again in the last day, in the last night, he asked the question and she answered it. He would forget, for he could remember nothing except the vague fear of the end.

"You're sure, Allie?"

"Sure . . . sure . . ."

But at the very end she added the two words she had heard so often from her mother's lips which until now she had not been able to say. She had not been able to say them because of some final shyness, since she was after all Robert's and Allie's daughter. But it was as though Allie at this last moment broke through her shyness completely and completely took possession of her. "Sure . . . sure," she said to the glazing, beseeching eyes, and then she added, sobbing, "my Robert . . ."

He smiled suddenly, brilliantly.

* * *

When it was all over, it was as though she came out again from dusk into hard, glittering sunshine. There was no sorrow possible; it was impossible to wish the end had not come, and yet the hard, glittering, usual sunshine was more than she could bear. She and Martin were again alone. The other two presences—that welded, warm, other life—were gone, quite gone. Her very body had been possessed by Allie as by a spirit, and now the spirit had departed, leaving her empty, leaving her what she had been before.

But in her emptiness she was not the same. She had for a time lived another, a fuller, life. For a time, she had been translated into another atmosphere, an atmosphere where love had been so tender, so powerful, that a quarrel withered before it sprang, and she was still dazed by it. She prodded into her memory, so that she might understand. Going about the emptied house, taking up her small habitual duties, she remembered what in her childhood she had taken for granted, the love her parents bore each other. She had grown up sheltered and wrapped about, not really with their love for her, but with their love for each other. It was their love for each other that shaped her and made that home her home. Under that radiance she had lived with happiness for her daily mood. That was why they had not minded being poor, any of them.

"Yes," she thought, pausing above the flowers she was setting in a vase for the table, "Dad had his little ways, and Mother could never cook. Not so long as she lived would she have been a good cook. But, somehow, it was only funny and we laughed. It didn't seem to matter. It didn't matter that her hair was always slipping a little, either, or that Dad would forget and let the furnace get too low when he was writing his sermons. Why didn't anything matter, these days? Why were we never lonely in that tiny village?"

Yes, she thought, remembering, thrusting the yellow tulips gravely one by one into their dish, they were never lonely together. Even after her mother died, her father had not been lonely. He said serenely that she could not really die. He had her, he would have her forever. Allie was a part of him, though her body was buried. When the restraint of his reason was gone and his spirit came out untrammeled it came all mingled with hers.

She finished the flowers and set them in a bar of sunshine that fell upon the table, and then she went and sat by the window and looked out into her garden, budding with early spring, and she pondered this mingling, this marriage, in which she had taken so strange and borrowed a part for a little while. It was as though for a moment she had been let into heaven by mistake, a guest uninvited, and had taken an actor's place for an instant before, inexorably, she had been shut out. For now those two were together again, in existence or out of existence, or wherever it was. Even nothingness could not separate those two who were so one.

But they were gone together and she was left alone with Martin, and so she put away like a dream the weeks she had been possessed, and consciously she took up the life with Martin, the only life she now had. She went about the house, mending and making neat. The room where the old man died she made over wholly, changing the very color of the curtains and moving the pictures and the furniture into new places. She must be satisfied with what life she had now. The other was not her own, she kept reminding herself. Her mother had given her back the body she had used for a little while to help her lover to come over into death to be with her. She felt not so much bereft as left behind. She moved about her house silently, working at this small thing and that, left behind. She and Martin were left behind.

She was very gentle with Martin, gentle and considerate and painstaking to do what he liked, and he was kind, too. She began to think, "Perhaps we can go on being kind the rest of our lives, now that we have been kind all these days. Perhaps we have broken the old habit of quarreling. Perhaps we see how we ought to be to each other." She asked herself earnestly if she could not be Allie to Martin, having now learned what Allie was to Robert. But if she were to be Allie, she must be better to Martin. She must fight, for instance, this increasing tendency in her to shrink from him, though she was trying to be kind.

For now, to her wonder, she found herself shrinking from him very much, from the touch of his hand, from any hint of ardor in his kiss. Though she could still see his large, even good looks, she shrank from him. This she must not do. She must rather, she planned, troubled, come nearer to him, tell him more, open herself more fully to his knowledge. "Martin," she must say, "Martin, let's give each other everything. Let's hold nothing back."

So she planned to speak, and she would wait for him to answer. Perhaps then, really, they two also could put their hearts into words each for the other to understand. But suppose he said, and she seemed to hear him say, "I don't know what you mean. I'm not hiding anything from you. . . ."

Then she must say, "No, Martin, not hiding, of course. We wouldn't hide from each other. But I mean . . . just open the door and let me in and come inside me, too.

Why am I lonely, though I eat at your table and sleep in your bed?" Over and over, she planned such talk.

But it all came about in its own way, after all. There was no good in her planning, for life went willfully its own way, in spite of her. An hour would come, she knew it must come, she felt it must come, though she postponed it by her determined kindness and by her planning. For day by day, the memory which had possessed the house grew weaker. Day by day, their own actual life grew stronger, more pressing, more actual. She caught his eyes returning to her coffee cup, and there was an instant's struggle in her before she put down the spoon. After all, why should she not stir if she liked? It was a small thing, but if she liked . . . And then she forced herself to put down the spoon. And why should he begin to answer her abruptly again? Why, if he could be kind, should he not continue kind? But he was very busy and absorbed. There was a new experiment in the laboratory. He looked up at her at the breakfast table one morning and did not see her. He said sharply, "I'm in a hell of a hurry with this damned thing at the laboratory. They want me to report on Saturday. Can you come down and help a bit today?"

She hated herself because she wanted to pluck out the bitter phrase he had flung at her that winter's night. "Never come again . . ." he had said.

"Of course I will come," she said gently, for of course he had forgotten.

At the laboratory she worked all afternoon, and answered nothing when he cried at her for clumsiness, though she was angry and the word "Ungrateful!" hung upon her tongue to cry at him. But it was true, she was somehow very clumsy today. There was a sort of tremendous refusal gathering in her, and to deny that refusal in her heart made her breath come hard and her hands tremble. But still she held it back. Robert would have laughed at Allie's clumsiness, teased her a little, sent her home to rest. But then Allie would not have had this inner battle to fight against a great surging, blind refusal.

. . . Yet if it had not been for the wind she might have held the hour off a long time, perhaps forever, since surely day by day she was growing a little stronger, a little more used to holding it off. But the next day there came that rough, tempestuous March wind, the wind that forced the hour upon them. Who could withstand the wind? It swept through the house in great rocking gusts, it tore at the windows and rattled the doors. Peace was wrenched away. All day she sat in the house waiting for the end of the wind, holding herself hard against it, waiting for darkness.

When darkness fell and the wind dropped into the night, she was spent. She must have something to bring her back to peace. So, unthinking, she went to the piano to find a little quiet for herself. But before she could more than touch the keys once or twice, the door was flung open as though by the wind again and there stood Martin.

"What a day!" she called to him, preparing for the steadying, sonorous chords.

Then his furious eyes struck her. "Noise, noise . . . noise . . ." he said, his voice tight, his face drawn. Her hands dropped. What was in his voice?

"You mean . . . ?" she asked blankly.

He answered, "I've got to have quiet."

"Of course," she agreed, and closed the piano softly.

He came in and threw himself down, but she did not rise from the seat. She sat there, her hands folded on the closed piano.

Of course he was very tired, she told herself—very, very

tired. She ought to go to him and do something for his great weariness. But she couldn't. She didn't, she realized, ever want to do anything for him again.

"What is it?" he asked wearily.

"It's the end of the truce, isn't it?" she murmured helplessly.

"What do you mean?" he replied, searching for his matches. "I'm dog-tired. You aren't going to cook up some trouble again, are you?"

She turned to look at him. So here they were again. The hour had caught them, the hour she had been pushing off with her dread. They were suddenly back again to that winter's night, the night when she had run to the door. But she was not the same woman now. She couldn't quarrel like that—not now—not having once known. . . .

"No," she said, "I'll never quarrel with you again."

"Then what's the matter?" he asked irritably.

She repeated his words bewildered, "I don't know—I honestly don't know—what is the matter, Martin? What is the matter with us?"

But before he could speak, Allie came into the room to answer her. There was Allie so clearly that it was like a picture thrown upon the wall opposite her.

She remembered one day when she had been a girl of seventeen and she had gone into her mother's room and found her mother standing in the clothes closet, her face buried in her father's old brown tweed coat.

"Mother," she had cried, startled, "what are you doing?"

For a frightened instant she thought something had happened and that her mother was crying. But her mother turned quickly to show a laughing, rosy face under her gray hair all curly and awry.

"It's nothing at all," she said, laughing again; "I was

just cleaning out the closet and there was Robert's old brown coat, shaped just like him, and I had to kiss it."

She heard Allie's voice, she saw Allie's shining eyes, only for a second, but long enough to understand what Allie meant. . . . There was no truce possible for her and Martin, Allie said, however they might live together, however determined through however many years, for their flesh and their blood were alien to each other. Though sometimes they might love each other at sudden blind moments of necessity, they never would like each other. They were irrevocably enemies in the blind, deep, secret ways of their natures. That night Martin had said, "Everything I do seems to rub you the wrong way." Now Elizabeth, remembering, understanding Allie, answered him, slowly, comprehending at last, "And I never could have kissed your coat. I never wanted to . . . kiss your coat. I shouldn't have married you unless I wanted to . . ."

"For God's sake," he burst out at her, "talk so that I can understand. . . ."

"I can't," she said simply, "I never can. . . ."

And suddenly, with these words, the truth was said, as though someone else had spoken it, as though Allie had spoken. She turned upon the piano stool and stared at Martin. He was sitting deep in the chair beside the hearth, his small habitual frown above his closed eyes. Of course, she could not speak to make him understand, nor could he reach her understanding. They had no means by which to speak together, and love could never be where there was no speech together. There was no love, there never had been love, and that past attraction which they had forced to take the shape of love was never love. They had so innocently deceived themselves; they had so unknowingly hurt each other; they had been so wrong to try to shape each other through marriage to the secret unfulfilled desire. Of course each had quarreled against such shaping—of course each heart had strained against the other.

"Oh, Martin," she cried aloud, "do forgive me. . . . I never knew how wrong it was, how cruel . . ."

He opened his eyes and answered slowly, patiently, without looking at her, "I hate mysteries. You're always making mysteries. It seems a pity a man can't come home and ask for silence."

She smiled, not minding any more what he might say, now that she knew she did not love him, did not need to try to love him or make love from what he gave to her. He could not hurt her, she did not want to hurt him, now that she knew that what had been between them was not love. She felt a new, fleeting, humorous tenderness for him, as a mother might feel a tenderness for a stubborn, sullen, little boy who did not know what was wrong with him. Some day, some woman would adore his very bluntness and his simplicities, and ask no more than suffering at his hands. She felt no jealousy toward her; no, more than that, she must help to find that woman if she could, in gratitude that she herself was free. Her heart leaped suddenly to sing a little song of freedom, now that she knew what had been was not love, was never love, and never need they be compelled again. She turned instinctively to the piano, eagerly, freely, now that she was not tied by love.

And then she paused and glanced at him. He sat there sturdily, his hands in his pockets, his brows drawn down, his lips pursed about his pipe, the smoke cloudy about his square, handsome head. He was shut into his silence. She closed the piano again softly, smiling secretly. Let her song wait. So let him have his silence, poor Martin, dear Martin, whom she ought never to have married. Allie and Robert, coming into her house to teach her, had made her know how wrong she was. But she'd make it up to him one day, kindly, gently, letting him wander into his freedom, and without quarreling any more. And when she saw him happy and relieved, there would be time for making music. She had a lifetime yet for making music, a happy lifetime for making her own music.

The Refugees

❧❦❧

THEY WALKED through the new capital, alien and from a far country, yes, although their own lands were only a few hundred miles perhaps from this very street upon which they now walked. But to them it was very far. Their eyes were the eyes of those who have been taken suddenly and by some unaccountable force from the world they have always known and always thought safe until this time. They who had been accustomed only to country roads and fields, walked now along the proud street of the new capital, their feet treading upon the new concrete sidewalk, and although the street was full of things they had never seen before, so that there were even automobiles and such things of which they had never even heard, still they looked at nothing but passed as in a dream, seeing nothing.

There were several hundred of them passing at this moment. If they did not look at anything nor at anyone, neither did any look at them. The city was full of refugees, many thousands of them, fed after a fashion, clothed somehow, sheltered in mats in great camps outside the city wall. At any hour of the day lines of ragged men and women and a few children could be seen making their way toward the camps and if any city dweller noticed them it was to think with increased bitterness, "More refugees— will there never be an end to them? We will all starve trying to feed them even a little!"

This bitterness, which is the bitterness of fear, made small shopkeepers bawl out rudely to the many beggars who came hourly to beg at the doors, and it made men ruthless in paying small fares to the ricksha pullers, of which there were ten times as many as could be used, because the refugees were trying to earn something thus. Even the usual pullers of rickshas who followed this as their profession cursed the refugees because, being starving, they would pull for anything given them, and so fares were low for all, and all suffered. With the city full of refugees, then, begging at every door, swarming into every unskilled trade and service, lying dead on the streets at every frozen dawn, why should one look at this fresh horde coming in now at twilight of a winter's day?

But these were no common men and women, no riffraff from some community always poor and easily starving in a flood time. No, these were men and women of which any nation might have been proud. It could be seen they were all from one region, for they wore garments woven out of the same dark blue cotton stuff, plain and cut in an old-fashioned way, the sleeves long and the coats long and full. The men wore smocked aprons, the smocking done in curious, intricate, beautiful designs. The women had bands of the same plain blue stuff wrapped like kerchiefs about their heads. Both men and women were tall and strong in frame, although the women's feet were bound. There were a few lads in the throng, a few children sitting in baskets slung upon a pole across the shoulders of their fathers, but there were no young girls, no young infants. Every man and every lad bore a burden on his shoulder. This burden was always bedding, quilts made of the blue cotton stuff and padded. Clothing and bedding were clean and strongly made. On top of every folded quilt with a bit of mat between was an iron caldron. These caldrons had doubtless been taken from the earthen ovens of the village when the people saw the time had come when they must move. But in no basket was there a vestige of food, nor was there a trace of food having been cooked in them recently.

This lack of food was confirmed when one looked closely into the faces of the people. In the first glance in the twilight they seemed well enough, but when one looked more closely one saw they were the faces of people starving and moving now in despair to a last hope. They saw nothing of the strange sights of a new city because they were too near death to see anything. No new sight could move their curiosity. They were men and women who had stayed by their land until starvation drove them forth. Thus they passed unseeing, silent, alien, as those who know themselves dying are alien to the living.

The last one of this long procession of silent men and women was a little weazened old man. Even he carried a load of two baskets, slung on a pole on his shoulder, the same load of a folded quilt, a caldron. But there was only one caldron. In the other basket it seemed there was but a quilt, extremely ragged and patched, but clean still. Although the load was light it was too much for the old man. It was evident that in usual times he would be beyond the age of work, and was perhaps unaccustomed to such labor in recent years. His breath whistled as he staggered along, and he strained his eyes to watch those who were ahead of him lest he be left behind, and his old wrinkled face was set in a sort of gasping agony.

Suddenly he could go no more. He set his burden down with great gentleness and sank upon the ground, his head sunk between his knees, his eyes closed, panting desperately. Starved as he was, a little blood rose in dark patches on his cheeks. A ragged vendor selling hot noodles set his stand near, and shouted his trade cry, and the light from the stand fell on the old man's drooping figure. A man passing stopped and muttered, looking at him, "I swear I can give no more this day if I am to feed my own even nothing but noodles—but here is this old man. Well, I will give him the bit of silver I earned today against tomorrow and trust to tomorrow again. If my own old father had been alive I would have given it to him."

He fumbled in himself and brought out of his ragged girdle a bit of a silver coin, and after a moment's hesitation and muttering, he added to it a copper penny.

"There, old father," he said with a sort of bitter heartiness, "let me see you eat noodles!"

The old man lifted his head slowly. When he saw the silver he would not put out his hand. He said, "Sir, I did not beg of you. Sir, we have good land and we have never been starving like this before, having such good land. But this year the river rose and men starve even on good land at such times. Sir, we have no seed left, even. We have eaten our seed. I told them, we cannot eat the seed. But they were young and hungry and they ate it."

"Take it," said the man, and he dropped the money into the old man's smocked apron and went on his way, sighing.

The vendor prepared his bowl of noodles and called out, "How many will you eat, old man?"

Then was the old man stirred. He felt eagerly in his apron and when he saw the two coins there, the one copper and the other silver, he said, "One small bowl is enough."

"Can you eat only one small bowl, then?" asked the vendor, astonished.

"It is not for me," the old man answered.

The vendor stared astonished but being a simple man he said no more but prepared the bowl and when it was finished he called out, "Here it is!" And he waited to see who would eat it.

Then the old man rose with a great effort and took the bowl between his shaking hands and he went to the other basket. There, while the vendor watched, the old man pulled aside the quilt until one could see the shrunken face of a small boy lying with his eyes fast closed. One would have said the child was dead except that when the old man lifted his head so his mouth could touch the edge of the little bowl he began to swallow feebly until the hot mixture was finished. The old man kept murmuring to him.

"There, my heart—there, my child—"

"Your grandson?" said the vendor.

"Yes," said the old man. "The son of my only son. Both my son and his wife were drowned as they worked on our land when the dykes broke."

He covered the child tenderly and then, squatting on his haunches, he ran his tongue carefully around the little bowl and removed the last trace of food. Then, as though he had been fed, he handed the bowl back to the vendor.

"But you have the silver bit!" cried the ragged vendor, yet more astonished when he saw the old man ordered no more.

The old man shook his head. "That is for seed," he replied. "As soon as I saw it, I knew I would buy seed with it. They ate up all the seed, and with what shall the land be sown again?"

"If I were not so poor myself," said the vendor, "I might even have given you a bowl. But to give something to a man who has a bit of silver—" He shook his head, puzzled.

"I do not ask you, brother," said the old man. "Well I know you cannot understand. But if you had land you would know it must be put to seed again or there will be starvation yet another year. The best I can do for this grandson of mine is to buy a little seed for the land—yes, even though I die, and others must plant it, the land must be put to seed."

He took up his load again, his old legs trembling, and straining his eyes down the long straight street he staggered on.

Mrs. Mercer and Her Self

❧❦❧

"GOOD-BY, dear."

"Good-by, Harold."

Mrs. Mercer offered her cheek and Mr. Mercer kissed it heartily. She looked up at him with affection. "Sure you have enough clean shirts?"

"One for every day, and an extra one for the dinner."

"I put your studs in myself."

"I'm not going to a desert," Mr. Mercer said smiling. "I can pick up a shirt in New York if I have to."

"I hope you can," Mrs. Mercer said.

She stood at the window and waved while he got into the taxicab. When he was out of sight she sat down in the chintz-covered chair by the window. For the first time since they had been married twenty-two years ago, she would be alone in the house. Last year Elizabeth had still been at home. Now she was at college, too, as Hal Junior was. She looked around the room. What would she do with herself? The room looked tired—faithful but tired. That was the way she felt. She could go upstairs this minute and crawl into bed and sleep as long as she liked. Why not?

She got up, sighing, and as she passed the telephone table in the hall she took off the receiver and locked the front door. Let the neighbors think nobody was at home. So far as she was concerned, nobody *was* at home.

141

She climbed the stairs slowly. The banisters were dusty and she ought to polish them. "But I can't—because I'm not at home," she thought. The small fantasy teased her imagination. If she were not at home, where would she be?

She opened the door of her bedroom and was startled by a face, a figure that seemed strange. Silly—it was herself, her reflection in the oval pier glass that hung on the wall opposite the door. But she had never faced herself in it before—that is, she had not seen herself. She had always hurried upstairs on some errand, and for years she had dressed in a hurry. Now she stood still, looking at the woman she was.

How she had changed! She would not have known herself. She closed the door behind her, still staring at her reflection. This was she, then, Elinor Mercer, forty-two years old!

"I'm a sight," she thought contemptuously.

She walked to the mirror, her heart hardening against herself. Why not face the woman in the mirror?

"I look like every other woman on the street," she thought. She had had her hair waved yesterday. For ten years she had gone to the same hairdresser, and the waves were as set as corrugated roofing. Her hair was brown, the eyes were gray-blue, the complexion nondescript. Most of the time at home she did not bother to use lipstick or rouge, and when she put it on to go out it was a careless ritual. She had forgotten the shape of her mouth. She examined it now—tight lips, set with years of hurrying and suppressed irritation.

"Oh, Mrs. Mercer, how do you keep such a lovely, even disposition?" young Mollie Blaine had wailed yesterday. She had come flying in to declare that she could not, could not endure her Tom another day unless he learned not to throw his clothes on the floor every morning.

"I set my teeth to it," she had told Mollie.

She wet her lips and tried to put them together softly. It was no use. The years had shaped them.

"I'm an ugly, nondescript creature," she thought.

But then she had never liked the way she looked. Her regular, somewhat large features, her square frame and capable hands had dismayed her even as a girl. She had accepted the handicap, submissive to her mother's teaching that what she did was more important than how she looked.

"I don't believe that," she said suddenly. Her voice echoed about the room, and she jumped at the sound of it.

Then she peered at herself more closely. "What sort of woman are you inside?" she muttered at the reflection. Gray-blue eyes stared back at her. The mouth pursed. "I haven't the faintest idea," she replied. "I've never taken time to find out."

She turned away from the mirror, and lay down on the chaise longue and drew the quilted cover over her. Harold had decided yesterday to let the furnace go out. Tomorrow was the first of June, but it had been a late spring. She shut her eyes and lay still. The silence of the house rose like a tide and she sank into it and it closed over her.

. . . She was horribly shy. That she had hidden since she was a girl by staying at home, by being too tired when Harold wanted her to go with him to Ladies' Night at his club, by refusing to be chairman of any committee at her own club, by being always one of the workers behind the scenes. She had never acknowledged that she did all this because she was shy.

"Very well, I'm shy," she said aloud.

A shy woman, but why?

Because she did not do anything well enough. She did not even read good books. When she read at all, she read stories—something to take her mind off—nothing at all educational.

"All right, I don't like anything solid," she said aloud.

But this was so out of character with her solid, responsible-looking body! She had grown stout and lost her figure. It was her own fault—there were plenty of people, if one were to believe the advertisements, who were anxious to restore one's figure. But she was too shy to go to such places. Besides, what did it matter? She thought of her reflection with sudden hostility. Her body betrayed her. It had made her look like somebody else. When she had been about fifteen, she had been very gay. Between fifteen and seventeen she had grown inches taller, and her mother had said, "Elinor, don't romp—you're too big." So her body even then had betrayed her.

She loathed her mortal frame. Imprisoned within it she had been shaped to it as in medieval times traveling showmen had put children into jars until they were shaped into monstrosities.

She got up in profound anger and began to pace the floor. Every time she passed the mirror she threw it hostile looks. Her thickness, her clumsiness, her height, her hair and skin and eyes, her hands—she spread her big hands— she had been so foolish as to let the manicure girl redden her nails.

"Why, Mamma," Harold had said in surprise.

Mamma—she hated the name. But that was what he had always called his own mother. "I'll tell him I hate it," she decided now, recklessly. "I don't really enjoy being a mother," she thought. There—it was out. All women ought to want to be mothers. "Well, I don't," she thought. A dam burst in her soul. She cried aloud in the silent house. "I don't like babies! I don't like housekeeping! I don't like houses! I hate small towns! I hate this town! . . ." She paused. Did she hate Harold? Was that what was really wrong? Down at the bottom of everything?

She sat down to consider this, her hands on her knees. She could not decide. "But I don't want to see him for a long, long time," she thought. "And I don't want to see Hal, either—nor Elizabeth—maybe never."

Layer after layer, she lifted from herself what she did not like and what she was not. . . . But everything she found out about herself was negative. And underneath was —what? She would never know so long as she stayed in this house, doing busy work.

Anger cooled in her. She forgot herself. She would like to pack a suitcase and close the door of her house behind her. She'd cash a check at the bank and get on a train. What train? Well, a westward train. She had never been west of Pittsburgh. Lovely names floated through her brain —Colorado, Wyoming, Arizona, Dakota, Alaska—she'd get off anywhere, at some station that had a pretty name.

She got up smiling—pretty names, pretty words, pretty places—she dressed without once seeing herself in the mirror, put on her brown three-piece suit, packed her bag, went out of the door and locked it.

. . . "But this isn't the station your ticket calls for, madam," the conductor said.

"You oughtn't to mind if it isn't as far," she said briskly. She put on her brown hat without looking in the mirror set in the wall between the Pullman seats. She didn't look in mirrors any more. As far as she was concerned she was a slender, gay, light-minded woman, a gypsy, a gadabout, going where she liked and doing what she would.

The conductor looked at her rather solemnly. "Sure you have friends here, lady?" he inquired. There was something in her eyes that he didn't like.

"Lots of them," she said happily.

She swung off the train. Above her head was the name of the town, printed in white on a green board—*Alameda.* She did not even know what state it was in, but it took her fancy—a pretty sound, the vowels running over her tongue.

She walked down the empty platform, her mind as empty. Maybe she would go back, maybe she wouldn't. She could do anything she wanted. She had scrupulously left half the money in the bank for Harold, in case she did not want to go back.

The morning was silver and gold, the sunshine gold, the great white clouds over the blue mountains silver. The earth was sand-colored and green. The railroad station was a low adobe building, the roof red-tiled. There was no sign of a town. She yawned in the warm sunshine and sat down on a bench and pulled her hat over her eyes. She had always wanted to sleep on a bench in the sun with her hat over her eyes, but being a lady—

"I hate being a lady," she said, though drowsily. The glittering parallel of the rails ran toward the horizon to meet in some infinity. There was no one in sight. She leaned back and stretched out her legs, and the sunlight penetrated to the very marrow of her bones. She felt warmed through, her blood heated, her skin flushing, her mind drowsing in the content of her body. She had eaten an enormous breakfast on the train—eggs, wheat cakes, cream in her coffee—all the things she never ate. The sun was warm but the air was cool. She breathed deeply and felt elixir in her lungs. She smiled, closed her eyes, and went to sleep.

. . . Sometime later, hours it must be, for the sun was now directly overhead, she felt her arm gently shaken.

"Ma'am," someone was saying, "wake up, ma'am. I've come."

She pushed back her hat and opened her eyes. A huge grizzled man was shaking her. He was hatless and the sunshine sparkled on the silvery threads in his tangled black beard.

"I'm sorry I am so late," he said. "But my jalopy broke down. I told you it probably would."

She opened her mouth to tell him that he was mistaken about her and closed it again. She could tell him later.

"Had a good sleep?" he asked, smiling down at her.

"Wonderful," she said, smiling back.

He picked up her suitcase. "You don't look what I expected."

"Neither do you," she retorted.

"But you told me you were old. . . ." he protested.

"I'm forty-two," she said. She got up and straightened her hat.

"That's not old," he said. "I'm sixty-one."

"How far are we going?" she asked.

"Thirty-seven miles, but there's no road—I told you that."

She did not answer, and they climbed into a huge, ancient, sand-colored car. "In fact," he went on, "I didn't think you'd take me up. I said to myself I'd come to Alameda on the chance you were there. But if you weren't —well—you weren't."

"It was nip and tuck with me," she replied. "I was about to go right past Alameda—and then I decided to get off."

"Irresponsible, eh?" he asked, grinning.

"Completely so," she replied.

"So am I," he admitted. "That's why I want to get rid of the place. I'm going to sea, like I've always wanted to. . . ."

"At sixty-one!" she cried.

"Before I die," he said.

"When are you going?" she asked.

"As soon as I land you at the gate," he declared.

"I can't pay for a place," she said.

He looked at her in surprise. "I thought we settled all that."

"Did we?"

"I told you I didn't want your money," he reminded her.

"I don't feel I ought to be given a home," she objected.

"I'm not giving it to you," he said. "I'm lending it. . . ."

"But if you don't come back?"

"Then you can have it."

"Your children . . ."

"I haven't any."

"Your wife . . ."

He looked at her oddly. "Don't you remember? I told you she left me years ago. It's all in my will—if I don't come back."

"Isn't anybody there?" she asked.

"Nobody but old Manuela," he replied.

She sat back and went through a profound and secret struggle with herself. Should she tell him who she was? But who was she? She did not know herself. Certainly, she was not the woman she had last seen in the mirror.

He looked down at her. "I'm a little worried about your being so young, though."

"Don't be silly," she said sharply. "I weigh a hundred and eighty pounds."

"You don't look it—you got good proportions. Well, I'll leave a couple of pistols in case some drunk rides by —though it doesn't happen in a hundred years—"

"All right," she said.

They were riding over the desert toward the blue mountains. She felt a small morality tugging at her conscience. "What if I hadn't come?" she asked.

"I'd have let the place go back to the desert," he said. "I'd have gone anyway."

In an hour and a quarter they drove up to a sand-colored wall in which was set a red-painted gate. They got out of the car, and he took her suitcase and pushed through the gate. Inside was a garden, a small pool, and a square of rooms. An old Mexican woman shuffled out.

"Manuela, this is your new mistress," he told her.

"Why don't you tell her my name?" she asked clearly. What was her name?

He grinned and flushed. "Ma'am, I actually forget it— I lost your letter, and your handwriting isn't too good or maybe my reading isn't . . . ."

She smiled, and he did not seem to expect her to speak the name he had forgotten. Or perhaps he did not care— he was now in a great hurry.

"Manuela, you feed this lady good. And don't get lazy, or else she'll push you out of the gate."

Manuela grinned with white teeth and tossed back her two black plaits.

"Well, good-by," he said. "I'm off. . . . I'll catch the

three-five to Frisco and walk straight on to my ship—
The Golden Arrow, by the way."

He gripped her hand. "The will—if you need it, it's
cached in a hole in the wall, behind the Indian blanket."

He nodded, smiled inside his beard, and the next instant
she heard the car roar. Through the open gate she saw a
wide streak of dust across the desert.

"Well," she said.

"Come, please eat," Manuela said calmly, and twisting
her braids about her head she set pottery dishes of food
upon the garden table.

. . . She grew lean and hard in the desert wind. The
mountains shielded on the west, and there were occasional
days of glittering quiet. Less occasionally on one of these
quiet days it rained. But much of the time the wind blew
in tangles of sand. She liked it. There was always a shelter
to be found if she wanted it in the lee of the adobe walls.
But she spent hours walking across the desert in the wind.
She could feel it blowing through her until her very skeleton felt clean and dry. Manuela had warned her about
rattlesnakes and she carried a stick, forked at the end.
Manuela had taught her how to pin a snake's head with
the fork and then squeeze it off into the sand. But most
of the time she simply frightened the snakes away. She
found she was not afraid of them.

She found out much about herself. She liked color, piles
of it, gaudy and clear. Manuela brought back armsful of
cotton from market days at Alameda, red and green and
blue and yellow. She made dresses for herself, short,
straight garments belted about her waist. As the weeks
passed she took satisfaction in her bones, apparent under
her skin at last. There was not a mirror in the house,
and she broke the one in her vanity case deliberately.

Her hair grew straight and long, and she twisted it into a knot at the back of her head. She ate meat, a great deal of meat, and cornmeal bread, and not any fruit or vegetables, which she had never liked. She slept twelve hours at night and at any time in the day. She talked to no one, not even to Manuela very much. But she laughed very often with Manuela about nothing, and she grew light-hearted and careless. She did not think of Harold or Elizabeth or Hal or anyone. Long ago, Harold would have come back to the locked house. She did not know how many days had passed since she left. But many—the summer was nearly over and autumn was in the night air. She had never heard a word from *The Golden Arrow*.

At first she had thought, "This kind of thing can't go on." But it had gone on, and she had begun to ask, "Why not?" and then she had simply taken it for granted. It could go on forever if she wished.

She let it go on. Sometimes, she wondered if the other woman, the old woman who had wanted the house, would ever come. But no one came, no one that stayed. Sometimes a cowboy stopped Manuela to ask the way to Alameda, and sometimes a Mexican passed and Manuela fed him.

"Manuela, do you get lonely?" she asked one day.

"Lonely—how?" Manuela replied astonished.

She explained and Manuela laughed. She tapped her breast. "I have always . . . me . . . myself."

On the morning of the seventh of September a telegram came, delivered by an astonished man in a broken-down car.

"I never had a telegram for this place before!" he exclaimed.

He waited while she tore open the envelope. There were

a few lines on the yellow paper, signed by a shipping company in Honolulu.

"We regret to inform you that *The Golden Arrow* was sunk in a typhoon off the Java coast with all hands on board."

The man looked over her shoulder and read it aloud.

"That's the end of him," he remarked and went away without mentioning a name.

She sat down with the telegram and considered. It would perhaps be necessary to open the little hole in the adobe wall and take out the papers. Then she decided she would not. Let him be nameless. What did it matter? The will was safe enough in the wall, if ever she needed it. And the house was hers—if she wanted it.

What did she want to do about it? "I don't have to do anything," she thought. The knowledge filled her with peace. It was enough simply to be. To be—what? It did not matter . . . what. A vessel containing life—that was enough. The telegram fell from her hands and upon the floor. The wind, entering through the open door, snatched it and whirled it away.

But she was quite happy, not knowing it gone. Here was the amazing thing—the discovery. She did not care who she was or what she was. She was content to be as anonymous as a plant or a sagebrush.

What was it that made her suddenly completely happy? Simply being alive—that was all. There was no guilt in her joy. She had nothing to do with the dead body floating somewhere in the warm Java seas. The chance of death had merely fallen upon him, not her. She was alive. This was the source of her lightheartedness. It did not matter what she was or whether she did anything. Whatever she did was merely the extension of being alive. When she walked on the sands, when she looked at the sky, when she shared a storm, when she ate, when she drank, when she slept, when she merely sat as she did now, breathing, thinking—to be alive was enough. She had never understood this before. She had always tried to be something more, to do beyond being. It had taken her all these months to find it out. No ... more than that ... it had taken the telegram. *The Golden Arrow* had gone down with all on board. The man who had unwillingly given her the opportunity to live alone with herself was dead.

He was dead, as one day she must die. But now she was alive, her body sentient, her eyes still able to see the blue hills, her ears to hear the wind, her mind to think, her heart to laugh. She stood up, and flung out her hands. At that moment, she felt something slip into her body and fit there snugly.

"My self!" she thought.

Her hands dropped. She felt complete and content.

In the kitchen, Manuela was bent over the charcoal earthen stove. She went up to her.

"Manuela, your master is dead," she said gently.

Manuela stared at her.

"Drowned," she went on, to Manuela's unblinking eyes.

"This house is now mine," she went on. "You stay here, Manuela?"

"Sure," Manuela said.

"I go away, but you stay," she said firmly.

"Sure," Manuela said. "You pay me?"

"Yes, every month."

"You come back?"

"Some day."

*　　　*　　　*

She reached the town in the late afternoon. Mrs. Blaine, Mollie's mother-in-law, passed her on the street, stared at her and went on.

"She doesn't know me," Mrs. Mercer thought, and was pleased.

She waited until Mrs. Blaine had turned the corner and then she went up her own steps and opened the door. It was not locked, and she went in. The hall was dark but she heard the piano in the living room, and she went to the door. Elizabeth's drooping slender figure was at the piano. She was touching the keys halfheartedly. The child looked sad and unkempt. The room was unkempt, too. There were no flowers in the bowls on the table. Before she went away, she had grown tired of putting flowers into the bowls and seeing them die and throwing them out. How foolish of her! It was wonderful to be alive to pick flowers, wonderful to set them on a table to enjoy them, and when they die, as all must die, how wonderful the richness of nature that provides more, always, to come into bud and bloom!

"Elizabeth," she said gently.

The girl leaped to her feet and stared at her.

"Don't you know me, child?" she asked.

Elizabeth turned pale, and her blue eyes stared. She wet her lips and put out her hands.

"We thought you were . . ."

"No, I'm not dead," Mrs. Mercer said cheerfully.

She smiled at her daughter, but Elizabeth's face was working with sobs. "Mother . . . how *could* you?"

"Now, now," Mrs. Mercer said. She put her arms around the girl.

"But you're so thin," Elizabeth sobbed.

"I'm as pleased as punch about that," Mrs. Mercer said briskly.

"You don't look like yourself."

"Yes, I do—at last," Mrs. Mercer said. "What's that, burning?"

"Oh," gasped Elizabeth, "I'm trying to make a pie. . . ."

They ran to the kitchen together and Mrs. Mercer pulled an apple pie out of the oven. It was smoking at the edges. "No harm done," she said. "But why aren't you at college?"

"Somebody had to look after Dad," Elizabeth protested. "He's simply been crushed. Hal's here, too. . . . He comes home Fridays to be with Dad in the office."

"I didn't think he'd take you out of college," Mrs. Mercer remonstrated.

"He didn't," Elizabeth said. "I came home because Mrs. Blaine wrote me he looked sick."

"That was sweet of you," Mrs. Mercer replied. "Now you can just go right back again . . . if you want to. . . ."

She met her daughter's doubtful eyes. "But, Mother, where have you been?"

"Oh, 'most everywhere," Mrs. Mercer said.

"But you didn't write. . . ."

"It was terrible of me," Mrs. Mercer agreed.

"Are you sure you're all right?"

"I'm wonderful," Mrs. Mercer declared.

The hall door opened. There was a subdued murmur of men's voices.

"It's Dad and Hal," Elizabeth whispered. "Shall I tell?"

Mrs. Mercer smiled. "I can't hide myself. . . ."

Elizabeth ran into the hall, and Mrs. Mercer heard Hal's voice. "I'm going upstairs. . . ."

Then Elizabeth's. "But Hal, you've got to . . ."

Hal again. "I say it was mean—"

Then silence fell. Footsteps went upstairs, Hal's heavy, Elizabeth's light.

In the kitchen, Mrs. Mercer opened a drawer and took out a clean white apron and tied it on. She opened the refrigerator and found a raw steak on a plate. Then she heard Harold's voice.

"Elinor . . ."

"Yes, Harold . . ."

She turned and saw him standing there. He had aged. . . . He was thinner, too. Tears rushed into his eyes but he did not come near her.

"Elinor, where have you been?"

She put down the steak. "Living . . . in a house out on the desert."

"Alone?"

"Yes . . . well, there was an old woman servant."

"What were you doing?"

"Nothing."

"Nothing?"

Suspicion dried his eyes. "There must have been . . . someone."

"You mean—a man?"

"Someone . . ." he repeated.

She looked out of the window, considering. Mrs. Blaine was coming home again, her head bent against the wind. What was the use of telling Harold about the man with the grizzled beard? A dead man—it could never be explained or believed that he was nothing—and yet everything to her, an accident, incredible as life.

"Nobody . . . except myself," she repeated.

"But whose house was it?" he asked. His eyes were dazed.

"Mine. . . . It's just an adobe house. . . ."

"You bought it?"

"Yes . . . that is . . . yes, in the end I bought it. In case I ever want to go back . . ."

She heard footsteps, Hal's unwilling ones, Elizabeth's light ones. Elizabeth was propelling Hal in front of her.

"Look at Mother," she said dramatically. Mrs. Mercer smiled.

"Hello, Hal," she said to her sullen son.

"Hello," he said. Then he stared at her for a long instant. "Gee, you don't look the same. . . ." he said suddenly.

"I'm quite myself," she said.

"But Mom . . ." He stood, his hands in his pockets, his face grave. For the first time she saw that he looked astonishingly like her, now that she was her natural self. He saw it and so did she, and the mutual knowledge pulled them toward each other. But he was young and resisting.

She smiled again. "If you're going to ask for a lot of explanations, you won't get them," she said.

He shook his head and kept on staring at her.

Harold spoke in a sudden harsh voice. "I don't feel I can trust you again."

Elizabeth stepped between them, her young face anxious, her hands twisting. . . .

Mrs. Mercer smiled. She threw back her head. "But here I am, Harold," she said gaily. "This is me—as I am. Trust me or not—it's all there is."

She looked from him to Elizabeth to Hal, challenging them to accept her as she was and would be forever—

"Why, Mother," Elizabeth breathed, "you're beautiful! Dad, look at Mother. . . ."

She looked at him and he looked at her—Harold, her good and faithful husband. He was gazing at her as though he had never seen her before.

"Oh, darling . . ." she murmured, "after all these years —I'm still alive!"

He did not understand what she meant, he scarcely heard her words. But he came toward her as to a light.

"Hal," Elizabeth whispered, "Hal . . . we must leave them alone. . . . It's too wonderful. . . ."

She seized his arm and they tiptoed away, their young faces reverent and their eyes tender.

"Of course they don't understand," Mrs. Mercer thought. She held Harold close, and he held her. "Nobody understands . . . except me. But *I'm* enough . . . for my self!"

The Old Mother

❧❦❧

THE OLD MOTHER sat at the table with her son and his wife and their two children. Their noon meal was being served by the elder housemaid. The old mother sat very quietly with her hands folded in her lap, and she looked with subdued eagerness at one dish after another as these were brought on the table. There was one dish she liked especially, but she said nothing. She knew that it had not been prepared for her, but only by accident, since her son and his wife had often told her they could not eat the dishes she wanted because they were such coarse country fare. Therefore, the pepper and beans were not here today because she liked peppers.

As she gazed at this dish her mouth watered. She was very hungry. She would have liked to take up her chopsticks and plunge them in the peppers and take up all she could and pile them on the bowl of rice the maid had placed before her. But this she had been taught not to do. Yes, in the four years she had been living with her son and his wife she had learned many things. Therefore she waited with such patience as she could until her son's wife said formally, after the food had all been placed on the table, "Mother, will you take what you wish?"

Nevertheless, the son's wife contrived, as she passed the bowls one after the other to the old mother, to emphasize the fact that there were in each bowl extra chopsticks, and she watched sharply lest the old mother forget and dip her own into the common dish. It was true it had taken a long time for the old mother to learn not to do this. All her life long as farmer's daughter and farmer's wife she had not seen it held unmannerly to put one's own chopsticks into the dish. No, her son and his wife were the only ones she knew who thought it so. They had come back together from foreign parts where doubtless the people were savage and filthy, and they had cried out in horror on the very first day when she had carefully and decently licked her chopsticks clean between her lips before she dipped them into the dish.

At first hearing their cry she had stared in astonishment, her chopsticks suspended above the bowl, and she said, "What? What?" There must be, she thought, something untoward in the dish, a shred of hair or cloth or a stick or something that even the best of cooks will drop sometimes, not knowing it, into the food as they cook it. But her son had cried out, "You must use the extra chopsticks—you must not dip in with your own that you have had in your mouth!"

She was greatly outraged then, and she said with indignation, "Do you think I have some vile disease, and are you afraid of me?"

When they had tried to explain about some sort of small things, too small even to be seen, but that pass from one person to another and carry illness, she sat stiff and unbelieving, and she said over and over as they told her, "I do not believe I have these things on me. I have never seen worms on myself."

When they answered, "Ah, but they are too small to be seen!" she had said in triumph, "Then how do you know I have them on me if you can not see them?"

This she had thought victory, but her son had said as firmly as though he were his own father, "There is no use in discussing this matter. I will not have these untidy ways in my house. I will not have it!"

The old mother was very hurt then and she sat in silence and ate nothing at all but her rice, refraining from every bowl of meat and vegetable, although she suffered cruelly in doing this, for all her life she had a good and hearty appetite for her food, and now that she was old her meals were her chiefest pleasure.

Nevertheless, she had had to submit. Once she even saw her son's wife do such a thing as this. The maid had brought into the room one night and placed upon the supper table a bowl of very hot melon soup, a dish the old mother loved, and she was overcome with pleasure at the sight. She forgot all else and she plunged her porcelain spoon into the soup and supped up the delicious brew and dipped her spoon in quickly for more. Instantly the son's wife had risen from her seat, and taking the soup she went to the open window and poured it out into the garden. There was the good soup gone!

When the old mother stammered in her astonishment, "But why—but why—" stammering and wondering, the son's wife pressed her thin lips together and answered very quietly:

"We do not care to drink after you."

Then the old mother grew angry. Yes, she had dared to be angry in those early days. She cried out stoutly, "I shall not poison you, I daresay!"

But the son's wife had answered yet more quietly and very cruelly, "You do not even use a toothbrush."

At this the old mother replied with great dignity.

"I have rinsed my mouth all my life in the way I was

taught, when I rise in the morning and after every meal, and in my day we never considered that this was not enough."

At this her son said contemptuously, "In your day! Do not speak of your day, if you please. It is such a day as yours that we must change altogether if this country is to be considered less than barbarous among other nations."

But the old mother had no idea what her son meant by such talk as this. At first when he made such remarks she had laughed in her big country way, and it seemed to her he was like a little boy talking high words he had heard somewhere and did not understand himself. But when she saw his cold patience with her and his gravity when she laughed at him, and when she saw the respect that visitors to the house paid to him, and how they but tolerated her for his sake, she ceased her laughing without knowing she did, since it is very hard for one person to laugh alone when there are only grave faces everywhere about.

Yes, she had learned to eat in silence and to wait until she was served. She did so now, and when she had eaten a bowl of rice she rose silently and went to her own room across the hall. But there at the door she paused. The truth was that she was still hungry. Her years on the farm had made her used to her three bowls of rice at least, and she felt empty and weak with the one scanty bowl in her. They had used big bowls on the farm, too, big blue and white bowls of pottery, but her son had the little fine bowls city people use. Yes, she was still very hungry. But she did not dare to eat all she wanted lest her son say in his half-sneering way, as he did sometimes, "You eat what laborers do! I never heard of a lady who ate like this. What do you do that you need so much as this?"

Yet he did not begrudge her the food, that she knew. No, how could he, since he earned every month for his teaching more than his father and mother had earned in a whole year on the land? No, it was because he was ashamed of her. She knew he was ashamed of her. When they invited guests to dinners they made excuses to have her eat in her own room. Well, at least she could eat as she liked there.

But now she was still hungry. She turned and crept noiselessly down the hall and out of the back door, across the court, to the kitchen. She went in smiling timidly at the servants, and she took a bowl and dipped some rice out of the half-emptied caldron where it was. Then she went to the table where the left-over foods were for the servants to eat. The dish of peppers was there also, but she did not dare to touch them, for there was but a little left, and the servants would not be pleased if she took it. She helped herself therefore only to some of the cabbage, of which there was plenty left. Then she went back to her room, not daring to glance at any of the maids as she went, and frightened lest she meet her son or his wife. As for the servants, she knew they did not like to share their food with her thus, but still they pitied her somewhat, too, and were tolerant of her, while they scorned her, taking her side against their exacting mistress.

Once in her own room the old mother closed the door softly and slipped the bolt. Then she sat down to enjoy the food. She ate it greedily to the last grain of rice, and rising, she washed the bowl and chopsticks in her wash basin, so that no extra trouble might be given the maids.

When she had eaten she went to a small tin box that stood among several others on her table and opened it and took out of it a little piece of cold rice. This she had saved from yesterday. Now she ate that also, munching it in her jaws. She kept all bits of food she could get in these little boxes lest she be hungry out of meal time. Then she sat down and picked her teeth with an old silver pin she wore in her hair.

After the old mother had sat thus awhile she rose and opened her door and peered out. She did this to see if either of the two children were about. She was afraid to call them to her since her son's wife did not like her children to come into their grandmother's room. She said, when the old mother reproached her for this, "You never open your windows and the air in your room is unhealthy for them. You will keep those old musty clothes, and there are mice everywhere because of those bits of food you hoard."

"Those coats were my own mother's and far too good to be thrown away," answered the old mother. "One can not throw away good things, not clothing and food, surely! If you were as old as I am you would know that poverty comes suddenly, and when one does not expect it."

But to this the son's wife had only smiled her little chill smile. Nevertheless, she called to the children to come with her for some cause or other if she saw them go to the grandmother's room. Therefore it became one of the pastimes of this old woman's life to leave her door open and see if she could entice one of the children to her. Besides, they were such dear little things, so fat and so fragrant. She loved to nuzzle her old nose into their little creased necks and make them laugh helplessly.

When these children were born she was very glad. She had always loved children, and although in her early youth she had married a poor man, a man who must earn their rice by extreme labor on the land, still she welcomed every child that came to her. Yes, even the girls she welcomed and she kept every one except the one her mother-in-law had commanded must not be saved because it was so poor a year and so without harvests that they did not know what death lay ahead for any of them. It was true that many had starved that year, and all had come too near it.

But to this day the old mother remembered with sorrow the little girl she had seen but the moment it was born, and never again, and she counted it as one among the four she had lost altogether. Yes, she counted it as one among the four the gods had taken from her.

Of her three children who had lived to grow up, this son was the only son left, for the eldest had died of a cholera eight years ago in the very midst of his manhood. The third was a daughter whom she never saw now, since the woman lived in another village than her old one, and was married to a poor man, and it is not to be expected that a daughter's husband will welcome his wife's mother when she has a son to care for her.

Therefore she had only one son left, but she and her old husband had always considered him the finest they had. Yes, when this son was a baby he was the cleverest and the most willful child of all. From the first they had said to each other that they must give this child more than the others and make a scholar out of him, and so her husband had taken him to a foreigners' school in the nearest city when the boy was not more than ten years old, and they had left him there for ten years. This was because the learning was good enough there, and they did not mind, as some did, that he had to learn a foreign religion of some sort with his other books, because the tuition was very little, and after a year or so when the boy did very well, nothing at all. Yes, those foreigners gave him everything. At first the boy had come home for New Year holidays and in the summer, but after a few years he did not wish to do this, because he had become so fine a scholar he was not comfortable any more in the earthen country house. Well, those foreigners put it into his head even to go to other countries to study even more, and they gave him some money to help him, but not enough either. She remembered that very day when her son had come in unexpectedly and said to her and to his father while they were planting the rice in the water beds, "Mother, I am going away to foreign parts to study more. The foreigners will give me some money, but not enough, and I want to ask you and my father for all you can give me, and in your old age I will care for you uncomplainingly."

At first it had seemed the wildest thing for him to do, but she and her husband had talked here and there with everyone about it, and there were many who said, "We have heard that if men go to foreign parts they get such learning that when they return they make vast sums of money every month. If you let him go you will not need to work in your old age."

Yes, so they heard, and they let him go then, seeing that at that time they had their good elder son, who was a small shopkeeper in the nearest market town, and he did enough business to care for himself and his wife. They let this boy of theirs go without betrothing him, even, before he went, because he was so lordly and so willful with all his learning, and they so much more ignorant than he that they did not know how to force him nor even answer all his great talk.

Well, he had married himself in the new way that men did nowadays, without asking his parents. He married himself while he was in that foreign country, not to be sure, to a foreigner, but she was the same as a foreigner, this pale, finicky woman who spread woolen cloth on her floors and hung cloth at her windows, and who would wash her children all over every day, as though such dear little things could be so dirty!

Well, when her son's return was yet two years off, her good old man died. A lusty, hearty old fellow he was, and yet he died all of a sudden one cold winter, and he died of a pain in his chest and a fever, and before she could call a doctor, thinking it would right itself and he unwilling to go to the expense. There he was, dead, and she had to pay for his coffin and his funeral, and there was nothing for it but to sell some of the land, because they had kept themselves so pinched to send money to the boy in foreign parts.

But she was a woman alone now, and she could not till all the land, anyway, and so she had sold a good big piece, and the old man had a good coffin. Yes, and she was glad she had bought him a new blue coat to lie dead in, and it was better than any coat he had ever worn in his life.

That very year in the autumn her elder son died, too, and since he had no children, his wife went back to her own people, and the old mother had no one left except that son in foreign parts. No, she had only him left, and so when he wrote for more money and he must have more money, she sold the land to the last foot and gave the silver to the foreigner to send to her son. Once an old neighbor said to her, "It is better not to sell your land, for even sons do not love so well a mother who brings them nothing."

But she was not afraid; she answered, "He is a good son, and it is all his land anyway, now, and if he needs it, let him have it. As for me, I am not afraid. He has said he will care for me without complaining, and I am not afraid he will not have a place for me in his house." She laughed as she said this, for she was sure of her son.

But now she sighed as she thought of this answer. Well, here she was in her son's house. It was a very fine house. Every visitor who came exclaimed how fine a foreign house it was. There was a top floor above this one and a stair going to it, but they let her have this room on the lower floor because she could not climb the stairs, or if she did manage to get up somehow, she must be led down again. But when they wanted to be rid of her they took the children and went upstairs and sat there and left her alone. Oh, she knew them very well! Although they thought her so old that she did not see through them, yet she saw.

Suddenly the two children came, fresh and rosy from their sleep, into the room across the hall from her open door. She saw them sit down to play with a toy. Both of them were little girls. When the younger one was born the old mother had cried out to her son, "This one should have been a male!"

But her son had replied very stiffly, "We do not feel in this way any longer. In these times sons and daughters are equal."

The old mother laughed noiselessly and contemptuously to herself as she thought of what her son had said. Yes, but suppose everyone gave birth to girls; who would father the next generation? There must be both male and female. Fools!

When she turned again, she saw the younger child looking at her, and she smiled at her. It was true that these were the sweetest children, and of the two she loved the baby better. She longed suddenly to hold the little round thing in her arms. Yes, she must have her old face there in that sweet soft spot beneath the baby's chin. She clucked softly and cautiously with her tongue to the child and the child stared back at her uncertainly. Then the old mother thought of something. She rose and went to one of her many little tin boxes and opened it. In it she found a little sweet nut cake that she had put there ten days or so before. It had a film of mold over it, but this she blew off and wiped the cake clean with her hands. Then she held it out silently to the baby.

The child looked at it and, having but newly learned to walk, she rose painstakingly and toddled to the old mother, holding out her hand for the cake. The old mother seized the little thing and gave her the cake and the child ate it gravely. The old mother closed the door, then, and sat down on her bed, the child in her arms, and she buried her wrinkled face in the little warm neck. She hugged the sweet morsel to her. Ah, little children—little children—

But they had already taught the children to hate her. Yes, for the older child, left alone, went and told her mother and suddenly the door opened and the son's wife came in swiftly and she said very gently, but with what cold, compelled gentleness, "Mother, thank you, but it is time now for the child to go out into the garden." Then, seeing crumbs upon the child's red lips, she cried out, forgetting her gentleness, "What have you given her to eat?"

The old mother tried to answer boldly, for after all, how could a little sweet cake hurt anyone?

"It is only a little cake I had."

But the child's mother seized the child and pried her little jaws open.

"Nuts!" she said angrily. Then she pressed her own lips together and said no more, but she took the child in her arms and carried her away, and the child cried with fright.

The old mother sat down again in great indignation. She told herself that she had done nothing wrong—nothing at all wrong. Nevertheless, she had been so subdued by these four years that she felt a vague guiltiness within herself. She sat muttering in her room. Yes, a little small sweet cake such as all children love, and it is called a crime! Poor little things that must be fed on such pap as their mother gave them!

Then as she sat there muttering she heard a noise. At the door stood the elder child. The old mother forgot the cake and the trouble it had brought her, and she smiled and reached out her hand to the child. But the child shook her head and backed away from her and the old mother's hand dropped and she murmured in a whisper, "They have taught you, too, haven't they?" And she smiled painfully.

But the child only stared at her half afraid, and sat down again to play, with her back to the old woman. Every now and again she turned and stole a glance at her grandmother.

Nevertheless, that night the younger child became ill. Whether it could have been the small nut cake or what it was, the child fell ill. The young mother tended the child through the night, and the son was sleepless also, but by the next morning the child was over the worst and could rest. The old mother when she heard this from a passing servant was much relieved, for she had been very much frightened by the bustle in the night. So therefore when she came into the dining room for the morning meal and found only her son there, she said to him as she seated herself at the table, "Ah, it was nothing serious, then!

Children will have these little illnesses. I remember when you were small also—"

But he interrupted her. She saw at once that he had something to say to her, and that he was very pale and angry. Instantly she could not eat any more and she put down her chopsticks. She stared at him. She tried to remember that he was her son, and but a younger son, and she tried to remember him when he was a small, crying child, coming to find her breast. But she could not. It seemed to her he had always been what he was now, a very proud and learned man, dressed in these foreign clothes he wore, his gold spectacles on his nose. He was a merciless and unsmiling man, and she was desperately afraid of him. For a moment she even wished her daughter-in-law were there, for sometimes she stopped her husband when he spoke too harshly to his own mother.

But there were only the two of them, mother and son. He had even sent the maid from the room. . . . Would he kill her then—his old mother? . . . He was saying:

"I do not wish to be unjust, my mother. I know my duty and you have your place in my house. Nevertheless, if you are to be here, you must do as I say. You shall not spoil my children. I am responsible for my children. Yesterday in spite of all we have begged you before, and we have told you that you are not to give the children food, and particularly not any one of those stale bits you keep in your room as though we starved you—" He stopped an instant to control an old irritation. Then he went on very coldly. "In spite of our wishes you gave the younger child a thing she had never eaten in the best of times. Last night she was ill."

"It was a very small, good cake," muttered the old mother, still rebellious.

"But we have asked you to give her nothing," repeated the son firmly.

Suddenly the old mother gave way. She could not bear any more, and she began to weep aloud and to sob out as she wept.

"I shall go away! Oh, let me go away! I have no home here—I must go away!"

The son waited patiently until she grew a little quieter. Then he said, "Mother, be reasonable. How can you go away? Where will you go in the whole world?"

"I can go to my daughter's house!" cried the old mother violently. "Yes, I will go and hire myself out to my daughter's husband. I am strong yet, and I can gather grass on the hills and pick up manure and look after the children and sweep the floor and burn the fuel in the oven. I could earn the little I eat!"

But the son smiled bitterly. "Do you think I have not thought of that?" he said. "Last year I wrote and offered them money, yes, so much a month if they would take you, because my wife felt it was so hard to have you here because you will not learn or adapt yourself to our house. They answered that, even so, it was more than they could do and that their house was full with their own children."

At this the old mother fell suddenly silent. It was true she had not really thought they would ever have her. But all these years it had been something to say. Yes, when she was angry at her son or his wife she would mutter to the servants behind their back, or to anyone who came to the house, or even to a vendor who was selling fish or vegetables at the kitchen door, "I have a daughter who has land and I can go there if I do not like it here with my son and his wife!"

But now she knew she could never say this again. No,

for if she did her son's eyes would fall on her with bitter knowledge. He had offered to pay out money to have his mother out of his house, and they would not have her, no, not though they were paid for it. She dropped her head and listened as her son went on.

"You see, my mother, my wife is an educated woman and you are but an ignorant country woman. I can say this since we are alone. It is right that my children should be reared in modern ways. I desire it so. My house cannot be like the house you lived in. We will not spit on the floors and let the fowls run in and out, and my children cannot eat this and that as your children did."

At this the last spark of rebellion rose in the old mother's heart and she cried out, feebly, "Yet you are one of my children!"

The son said forcibly and plainly then, "I do not care to lose four out of seven of my children as you did."

At this the old mother drew herself up trembling and looked at him once more and cried out, "Do you accuse me of killing my own children, then?"

The son said loudly, as though his patience were ended and he could not keep his voice quiet any more, "I accuse you only of ignorance and of unwillingness to learn better!"

He rose, then. He had no more to say. Yes, he was going out and leaving her there alone with those last bitter words. She must stay him somehow. She shrieked after him in her old quavering voice, "Well, I can die—at any rate, I can die! I can hang myself—"

Her son turned swiftly at that. He looked at her in great anger and he saw some sort of final courage and despair on that old face he knew so well.

"You say that to me!" he shouted in a sudden, towering rage. "You dare say that to me! You would disgrace

me and have it known everywhere that my mother hung
herself in my own house!"

He pressed a bell fixed in the wall and a maidservant
came in. He strove to say in his usual voice, very cold and
firm, "My mother needs a maidservant of her own. There
are signs she is failing in her mind. Hire a maid who shall
not leave her day or night. I put this responsibility on you."

The maid bowed, and went away.

It was not the first time the servants had heard high
voices in this house and they could be heard even without
listening at keyholes. They knew well enough what had
happened today. But the maid was pleased to have it turn
this way. She had often complained to her master and
mistress that their old mother was more trouble than a
child, and that there should be a special servant to care for
her as children have. Therefore she was glad now and she
had in mind a sister of hers who would be willing and
pleased to have the work. But the old mother turned trembling and sobbing to the servant maid.

"He will not even let me die! I can not even die!" she
wailed, and she went stumbling toward the servant as a
child does who must go for comfort to anyone in its desperate need. But the servant led her to a seat and said
briskly and carelessly, in haste to be away:

"There—there, Old Lady! You do not appreciate your
son. He gives you shelter and food and clothes, and you
really ought to try to be a little more—yes, yes, he is a very
good, filial son. Everybody says so!"

Home to Heaven

❦

"MARIAN, I've got the passports!"

Henry Allen burst into the kitchen of their small rented bungalow and whirled his wife's slender figure away from the sink. Her arms were dripping dishwater and she wiped them on her apron.

"Henry!" she breathed.

"Take off that apron, Madame," he ordered. "No more dishpan hands, if you please!"

She held up her narrow reddened hands, bare of everything except her wedding ring. "I can wear my jade again!" she cried.

"All your pretties," he agreed.

They looked at one another and saw their future as bright as heaven before them. It was clear because it was exactly like their past. They knew what it was going to be. She glanced around the kitchen. Oh, if it could only begin now, this instant, without another day of the hateful present!

"When can we get passage?" she asked with passionate concern.

"Two weeks from today," he replied. He sat down on one of the flimsy kitchen chairs. "And if you think it was easy, you're wrong. The big boss didn't wake up until I told him that the Sunflower people already had their man over there in Shanghai."

"I guess that waked him up," she said, laughing.

"You bet it did!" he said, and laughed with her.

Suddenly, now that it was sure that they were going, nothing seemed to matter. She had been about to put on a beef stew and she ought to get it started. But it didn't matter.

"Did you see anybody else in Washington?" she asked.

He was on his feet again, restlessly. "Halliday was there —trying to get passage for his wife, too. But he couldn't."

Halliday was the Bishop of Soochow. They had known them in Shanghai. "I'll bet *she's* sore," Marian said.

"He said she would be," Henry said with satisfaction. They had not liked the Bishop's lady.

"I can just see her stuck in that suburb of Boston," Marian said with pleasure.

"Maybe she's been able to get a maid," Henry said.

"What's a maid?" Marian's voice was pure scorn. "If they're all like the creature we had . . ." Her accents took on new passion. "Why, just our houseboy in Shanghai did more in an hour than she did in a whole day—and no back talk, either. God, it'll be good to have no back talk again!"

"I'll be glad to get out of the office-boy class, myself," he said. He paused by the kitchen table where she sat and looked down at her solemnly. "I haven't wanted to say anything, Marian, while you were having it so hard here in the house. But it's been hell in the office. The things I've had to do—the orders I've had to take—just to hang on to my job . . ."

"Oh, I *know!*" she cried. "Don't I know. But it would have been awful if you'd lost it. Think of having to live here. . . ." She looked around the barren kitchen.

"Well, we aren't going to live here," he said triumphantly. "You know what saved me?"

"What?"

" 'Member that summer I spent studying Chinese, and you asked me what I wanted to learn Chinese for, when every Chinese we needed to know spoke English?"

"They did, didn't they?"

"Sure they did—they still do—but the big boss has an idea, see? A bran' new, swell idea! He wants all the China staff to know the language."

"Can you imagine!" Marian murmured.

They joined in a duet of laughter.

"Yep, it's the new policy," Henry went on. "So the old gang is out. I'm the only senior member going back."

"But what's the *real* idea?" she asked. "He doesn't expect you to talk to the Chinese yourself, does he?"

"He does," Henry said, "but of course, he doesn't know China. He talks about it being a new day—new day, my hat! Still, you have to humor him."

"Sure you do," she breathed. "Anything he says goes —until we get back, Henry—"

"Yep!"

"Does that mean the Kincaids and the Parcells and all the others won't go back?"

"Yep—it's your old man that's going back to the top. Big boss called me himself and told me—in consideration of the zeal I'd shown in mastering the language . . ."

They laughed again. Then he grew grave. "All the same, I'm going to brush up when I get there—just in case."

"In case of what?"

"In case the juniors get ahead of me . . ."

"Get on to you, you mean," she scoffed.

He was hurt. "Now, Marian, I learned more than you think I did."

She blew him a kiss. "Darling, whatever you learned, I'm respectful. It's saved us."

She had not blown him a kiss in months. She used to do it often in Shanghai, especially when they were first married. They had met in Shanghai. She had been traveling around the world, getting jobs on the way to pay her passage, secretarial jobs, mostly, although sometimes she had to take what she could get. She had gone to his office for a job. He had only been number three in the firm then, but he was young and good-looking and she had become his secretary—his first. It hadn't lasted long. They had been married in less than a year, and in less than five years they had the three children. She had been horrified at their swift appearance, and yet amused. It was so easy to have children in China—one simply hired an amah for each. She had been able to go on with her idle, lovely days, and the children were always somewhere in the periphery, happy and prettily dressed. She heard vague rumors of amahs who fed their charges opium to keep them quiet and of houseboys who meddled with little girls. These rumors she had refused to believe. It was impossible to believe them when she looked at her perfect servants, the amahs so fresh and clean and smiling in their blue coats, and the houseboys immaculate and polite, and Cook at the helm. Even the two coolie gardeners were wonderful. The chrysanthemums they grew! It was fun to give parties to show them off. A party was easy in Shanghai. Twenty guests to dinner, sixty guests to tea. There was nothing to do but give the order and then appear as easy as one of her own guests at the appointed time, dressed and beautiful.

"Suppose we'll get the top company house?" she asked.

"Sure we will," Henry said robustly. "It's going to be put into shape for us."

"We'll need a couple of extra servants," she said. "There'll be more entertaining."

"Listen," he said with energy. "You're going to have all the servants you want, see? And if you don't like the ones we get, you can fire 'em and there's plenty more where they came from, see?"

"Oh . . ." she sighed, "oh . . . oh . . . oh!" She locked her hands behind her head, closed her eyes, and smiled for sheer joy.

Henry watched her and smiled in sympathy. She was still pretty, this woman—the horrible housework hadn't lasted quite long enough to ruin her blond beauty. There was nothing a couple of months of Shanghai life would not mend. Get her hands in shape, her skin, get her hair fixed up—anyway, she hadn't taken on weight, thanks to the housework. She was no housekeeper—he'd be glad to get back to decent living again—his socks hadn't been darned in weeks. The sew-amah had always kept his socks in perfect shape—always.

"Of course, Shanghai's filthy after all those Japs," he warned her.

"Oh, I don't care." She opened her eyes and saw the clock. "Goodness, the kids will be home in no time—it's too late for stew."

"Open a can of beans," he ordered. "I'll go and wash up and come back to help."

This was largess on his part. She knew, and he knew she knew, that his continual secret struggle was over this matter of helping her with the housework. It outraged him, after years in the Far East, where he never so much as took a handkerchief out of the drawer for himself. There had been weeks here when they had had even to do their own laundry. He prayed that this news would never get back to China. He was sorry that he had come back to his home town to live. It would have been easier to keep secrets in a strange community. But when they came back as war refugees, his home had seemed the logical place to stop. They had stayed a month with his parents before his father had spoken plainly to him one day.

"Now, Henry, I hate to say this, but for your mother's sake I've got to—I think you and Marian had better find another place to live. There's a house on Sixth Street—a bungalow—and small enough for Marian to manage."

"Why . . .why . . ." he had blustered.

"No hard feelings," his father had said amiably. "But your mother isn't as young as she could be, and Hannah says she can't keep up with the extra work."

Hannah was the maid.

"I could find an extra maid," he suggested, but his father had stopped him.

"One maid wouldn't do it, Henry. You need a whole raft of servants and nowadays you can't hire 'em. Trouble is, Henry, you've all got out of the way of doing anything for yourselves. Marian doesn't remember there's dishes after every meal, and little Mollie leaves her bed just as she got out of it, and the boys don't even pick up their pajamas. It makes a whole lot of work. And even you, Henry, you don't act as helpful as you used to."

They had moved at once, and while relations were cordial they were not warmly so. His mother's house resumed its look of ordered quiet. Hannah was not helpful about getting a maid. Such as they had found, he had bribed at the employment office and bribed in vain, for the moment they came into the house they were ready to leave.

He strolled upstairs and glanced at the beds still unmade and washed his hands in a bathroom not yet cleaned. Well, never mind—two weeks could be endured in any sort of house.

He whistled cheerfully and then stopped. A wail and a roar came up from the kitchen. The children were home, and Marian had told them. He rushed downstairs, wiping his hands as he went, and flung the towel on the hall table.

"What's this? . . . what's this? . . ." he burst into the kitchen.

"Aw . . . we ain't goin' back to Shanghai." Hal's furious blue eyes met his father's. He flung his strapped books across the kitchen.

"Hal, stop that! Pick up your books."

"I'll be glad to get you back to a place where you'll learn decent English. . . ."

His voice and Marian's were in duet again.

Robert, his second son, stood statue still. "Do we have to go?" His voice was small and chill.

"Of course you do," Henry said roughly. "And mighty lucky, too."

"Your father is going to be number one," Marian said. She was dumping the beans into a bowl. "Get washed, now—dinner's ready."

"Oh, heck—beans again," Hal growled.

But Mollie was silent. She had dropped her books and hat and coat on the floor as she always did. Only yesterday Henry had yelled at her, "Hang up your things, darn you—who do you think is going to pick up after you around here?"

Now he saw and said nothing. It was only two more weeks. A strange dreamy look had come over his daughter's pretty face. She was the youngest, ten on her last birthday.

"Are we really going back to China, Daddy?" she asked.

"We really are. Glad?"

The curious look in her dark eyes deepened and her lids flickered. She looked away from him. "Will Ah Fong be our houseboy again?" she asked.

"I'll bet the whole gang will be on the dock to meet us," he said gaily.

"And the house will be clean and dinner ready to serve when we get there," Marian said. She was slicing bread and now she sliced her thumb. "Oh, damn—again . . ." she wailed. She held the dripping thumb over the sink. "Do something, somebody!" she cried. Henry reached for the bandaid in the kitchen drawer.

"Good thing you don't have to cut bread the rest of your life. . . . You wouldn't have ten fingers left," he said with good humor. Yesterday he would have bawled at her, "Can't you keep your fingers out of the way?"

They sat down to the hot beans and a bowl of cold canned tomatoes, bread and jam. Hal was still furious.

"Just when I was goin' to get on the baseball team," he groaned. His eyes were full of tears which he blinked back.

"You'll go to the American School in Shanghai," Marian soothed him. "They'll have a baseball team there."

"Not a real one," he spluttered. "Over there nobody wants to run—I can remember how it was. They weren't regular fellows there like they are here. The team wasn't worth a cent."

He threw down his napkin, burst into tears and rushed from the table. Henry rose, but Marian stopped him.

"Sit down," she said. "He'll get over it."

"He's damn well got to," Henry said and sat down.

They sat in silence, Robert eating a little, Mollie eating a little, neither saying anything.

Outside the house a trolley turned the corner and screeched. The rough lawn was gray with late winter. Small as it was, it was more than they could keep cut. Henry nagged the boys and then usually cut it himself. They never had flowers. He thought of the great compound in Shanghai. Behind the high walls the wide lawns were green and bordered with flowers. He had accepted them as he accepted all the blessings of their life there. Now, only now, after these dreadful years, would he know how wonderful they were. He glanced at the faces of the two silent children.

"You'd like to go back to China, wouldn't you, daughter?" Henry urged.

"No more old housework," Marian said comfortingly.

Mollie did not lift her eyes from her plate. "I guess so," she said dreamily. "I guess I'd like to go back."

Robert spoke up, Robert the Silent, they always called him. "But we're Americans," he said clearly, "and Americans always do their own work . . . don't they?"

Marian and Henry exchanged amused looks over his dark head and laughed again together.

"Not if they can help it, son," Henry said boisterously.

"No, sir!" Marian agreed.

Robert looked uncertainly from one adult face to the other. "I thought they did," he faltered. "It seems to me they do," he said.

"You're wrong, my son," Henry said, "dead wrong."

*   *   *

The raw March winds which had blown them away from the shore of San Francisco were mild with April when they approached the low flat shores of China. The sky line of Shanghai was untouched. They saw it from the ship's deck.

"It looks the same," Marian murmured.

"Exactly the same," Henry said.

Four of them leaned on the ship's rail, watching the nearing docks. At the last minute Henry and Marian had agreed that it was not worth the struggle to force Hal to come. He had been made captain of the baseball team and they had left him with his grandparents. It had been hard, for a minute, to tell him good-by. "When I see him again he'll be a man," Marian had thought. She had seen already the outlines of the man in his crude young face. Would she blame them some day for leaving him? But he wasn't a sacrifice. He simply didn't want to come back with them. "And stay I cannot," she had told herself and had forced her thoughts away from him.

Now, staring at the familiar Bund, she found herself thinking of him again. "I wonder if we ought to have made Hal come with us," she said.

"No," Henry replied, so quickly that she knew he had been thinking of the boy, too. "Don't get to worrying about that," he went on. "We wanted him to come, didn't we?"

"Yes," she said firmly, and made up her mind not to worry.

Robert and Mollie had not spoken. Indeed, it seemed sometimes as if they had not spoken since they started. "Look," Marian said, suddenly, "isn't that the number one amah, there on the dock? It is!"

"There's the cook!" Henry shouted joyously.

"I hope . . . I hope . . . I hope . . . *he* isn't there. . . ." she heard Mollie whisper.

"Who, dear?" she asked abruptly. She did not hear Mollie's answer. "Oh, I see both the coolies!" she screamed.

In no time at all they were back in the compound. Ah Fong, the old houseboy, was not there. He had been shot as a spy, Cook explained. The number two and number three amahs were also dead, number one amah explained. One had been caught in the bombing of Wing On's department store, and the other one—the young and pretty one —well, the Japanese! Number one amah looked fondly at Mollie and explained no further.

"Is Ah Fong really dead?" Mollie asked abruptly.

"Too bad, missy," cook said, smirking.

But Mollie looked back at him. "I'm glad he's dead," she said calmly. "I don't mind coming back so much, now I'm sure he's dead."

The servants, including the new houseboy, laughed loudly at this, and Henry and Marian, in their joy at being home again, laughed, too.

Really, everything was exactly the same. Marian got up in the morning when she liked, and a pretty tray was always brought to her bed. There was a new flower on it every day. Her hands grew soft and white. Her old massage amah came back and her wash-hair amah, too. There were surprisingly few people dead. Getting herself into condition took most of the morning while the children were at school. People were coming back so quickly that almost every day there were guests for tea or dinner, and she and Henry went out several times a week. It was lovely to wear evening gowns once more, and to see Henry in tails. He looked so handsome, and being number one gave him new dignity. She remembered the little bungalow, but she put it away as a bad dream. Once or twice a month Hal wrote them, and she read his letters quickly and stuffed them into the drawer of her teakwood desk. Half the time she forgot to share them with Henry. But the children always wanted to see them. Together, they pored over the news of Hal in high school. Whatever they thought they told only each other.

But then neither Henry nor Marian had much time for the children. There was a great deal of catching up to do, and as the wife of number one, Marian had duties to the wives of the junior members of the firm. Henry was too busy to take up his Chinese again. Besides, it wasn't necessary. The compradores were there, just as they had always been. He made a good many speeches at men's meetings about the far-flung battle lines of new American trade. "America is in world affairs to stay," he said. Everybody looked up to him, Marian saw with pleasure. And everybody told her how young she looked.

Of course, there were rumors now, as there had always been, although not the same rumors. The Chinese weren't quite the same, perhaps. She and Henry didn't like to acknowledge it, but it was true. Mollie slapped the houseboy and he left. In the old days he would have taken it.

"Oh, Mollie," Marian wailed, "he was so good!"

"That's what *you* think," Mollie answered grimly.

But there were still plenty of houseboys and they soon had another.

Henry said that the new Chinese business corporations were difficult, too. The compradores were not so pliable as they had once been. They took the side of their own people doggedly, and there was trouble over investments.

"Looks like every darn Chinese is hipped on the subject

of fifty-one per cent," Henry grumbled. "How're we going to do business that way?"

"Why don't you tell them so?" Marian inquired.

They were going to a dinner at the British Consulate, and she was trying to decide between white and rose for her gown, between jade and Chinese pearls. Downstairs, Robert was practicing his violin. He had taken it up only recently and was doing rather well under a young Jewish refugee teacher, who was being saved thus from starvation.

"I do tell them," Henry snorted above his white tie. "They just say, 'More better no business'—"

"That's queer," Marian murmured and chose the rose taffeta and the pearls.

"Darn queer," Henry agreed.

But they weren't really worried about anything. Outside the walls of the compound the city was still filthy and partly ruined. That didn't worry them, either. In time it would be cleared up. Beggars roamed the streets, but then there had always been beggars, and they had two company cars, both chauffeured. The children were driven back and forth to school. The beggars tapped on the closed glass panes with their dirt-caked claws when the cars were held up by traffic, and pointed down their open mouths. But nobody paid any attention to them.

Inside the big quiet compound everything was just the same. They lived a perfectly happy life, isolated and safe. Of course it *was* safe? Yes, of course it was. Henry was number one. It was wonderful to be back—it was heaven.

Home Girl

❦

"My mother no like so late," Etsu said.

She looked up, very far up, at the tall American with whom she was walking along the street of her home town. She had lived here all her life but it was a new town since the Americans came. Nobody knew what to make of it, but they were all trying hard to please the conquerors. Etsu held her body stiff in the circle of Ted's arm. "Teddu," she called him.

"You give Mother my chocolate, Etty, and she no care," Teddy replied. He squeezed her tighter. The big obi she wore was a nuisance.

"I wish you'd take the sofa cushion off your back," he complained.

She laughed. This, he knew now, meant that she did not understand what he said and he reached in his pocket for his dictionary.

"Siddown," he commanded her. They were in the park, and there was a bench. She obeyed him and he released his arm. He looked up "sofa" and "cushion" and pointed to her satin obi. She nodded.

"Ah-ha, Teddu," she said. Then she looked grave. "No," she said distinctly. She shook her head for emphasis. "No," she repeated.

It was the first English word she had learned and the one she used most frequently with Ted. Her gravity he instantly understood. She thought he had proposed something improper. He looked at her solemnly.

"Listen, kid, I don't mean take off your clothes—just the sofa cushion. Couldn't you use a string or something?"

He fished in his pockets and produced a string. It had been tied around the box of cookies Sue had made and sent him. Sue was his best girl in Plainfield, New Jersey, which was his home town. It was a good string, and he had kept it. Now he reached his arms around Etsu's waist and demonstrated with the string. She was horrified.

"No, no, Teddu," she said with such passion that he gave up, thrust his hands in his pockets, and stared sulkily across the grass. She sat in her graceful, motionless fashion, stealing looks at him from the corners of her long eyes. She was a very pretty girl, small and slight. Her face was oval and her eyes were black and gentle. But her mouth was her prettiest feature. Ted had looked at it often and long, with speculative eyes. She had never let him kiss her. He had made efforts, both with and without the dictionary, but she had only said, "No, no, Teddu."

It was not as if all Japanese girls refused kisses. The fellows said plenty of them were willing enough, once you showed them how. But Etsu would not let him show her anything. More than once he had decided to give her up and get him an easier girl. But none of them were as pretty as Etsu. Besides, there was something homelike about her house and family. He always called there for her, and her parents hovered around, as anxious as if they'd been Americans. She was the oldest of the family, and they thought a lot of her, anybody could see. There were two girls and a boy younger than she was. They all told Etsu good-by as though she were going to be gone a week, instead of only down the street to the park or the movies. It made him feel responsible.

"To hell with it," he now said aloud.

Etsu laughed and waved to a deer, which came up to them hopefully. The park was full of deer. Even during the war they had been cared for and fed. There had been some talk of eating them, but nobody could bring himself to kill the sacred deer.

"Deer, hungry," she remarked. Study of the dictionary had helped her English very much.

Ted grinned. "Now if you'd just say, 'Hungry, dear.'"

"Hungry, dear?" she said obediently.

"Damned hungry," he replied. He took her little hand and put it to his lips. This she allowed. She had discussed it at home, and Father and Mother had listened, bewildered. She discussed everything about the American with them at night after she came home and the children were in bed.

"Does he bite your hand?" Mother had asked in horror.

"No, he never hurts me," Etsu had replied. She felt tenderness at the thought of him. "He never hurts me at all," she said. "He even helps me by the arm when we cross the street."

Father and Mother had looked at one another.

"You are sure he does not have improper ideas?" Mother asked timidly. Etsu had gazed at them limpidly, anxious to tell them everything. After all, she was in a strange situation, with what danger she did not know.

"He wants to put his mouth on mine," she told them.

The two elders looked away in their horror.

"I forbid it," Father said sternly.

"There are germs in the mouth," Mother explained.

"Promise me you will never allow it," Father commanded, and she had promised.

"But my hand?" she had asked.

They had discussed the hand, and after some hours of deliberation Father and Mother had agreed that the hand might occasionally be allowed if it was necessary to avoid the mouth. But it should not be allowed if it led to the mouth. Since Ted was displeased with her about her obi, she now allowed him the hand.

The deer watched them hopefully.

"He think you eat the hand," Etsu said with amusement.

Ted laughed. "I'll be darned," he said. He forgot that it was Etsu's hand he was kissing. It became a game with the deer. He put her hand down. The deer stared and began to walk away. They saw it look back, and Ted snatched her hand again and put it to his lips. The deer galloped toward them. They laughed and both forgot that a moment before he had been angry and she half frightened.

"Smart deer," Ted said. "For that, I'll buy him something to eat."

They rose and the deer followed, trotting like a dog behind them when it saw them turn in the direction of the vendor who sold the little bean cakes for deer. Ted bought a bagful and they sat down on the grass and he fed them to the deer one by one, while Etsu watched them both with affection. But the sight of the feeding increased her own ever present hunger.

"Feed me, please, Teddu, like deer," she coaxed.

He gave her a cake and she ate it in a swallow. He stared at her.

"Is it good?" he asked.

"Some good," she said.

He put down the bag and leaned toward her. "I'll be damned. . . ." he began. "You aren't sure enough hungry are you, Etty?"

"Some hungry," she admitted.

Father and Mother had both told her that she was never to accept food from him—not real food, that is. Tea and sweets she could take, but no more. Once a man began feeding a woman, he would feel she belonged to him, they said.

"You understand that you cannot belong to an American," Father had said sternly. Father was a tall man, for a Japanese. He had a deep sad voice and sad eyes. None of the children thought of disobeying him. He went on and his voice sank a note deeper. "The Americans are our conquerors and we must show them courtesy. But courtesy does not demand that we give them our women."

"I had rather see Etsu dead," Mother had said. She was a tiny creature, thin as a winter wren.

There had been great difficulty in the town over the matter of Americans and women. It had become clear, within twenty-four hours, that the Americans were used to women and expected to be with them. Some expected more. All through the town anxious fathers and mothers discussed this matter. The Americans did not understand the difference, the vast difference, between home girls and other girls. One of the other girls need not mind if an American came up behind her and put his arm about her middle and pulled out his dictionary. She too bought a dictionary as soon as she could. But a home girl cried and ran if an American put his arm about her. He always ran after her and tried to comfort her, which frightened her more than ever. Ted had run after Etsu and only because the house had been in the same block as the market,

where she bought the family food, had she escaped him.
When she came out the next day, he was there again. She
saw him and slammed the gate and ran back to tell Father
and Mother. Together they had come out to meet the
American and explain matters, which was difficult, since
Mother spoke no English and Father had only what he
had been able to learn out of a dictionary since the
Emperor had announced the defeat of the nation. Ted
had thought they were speaking Japanese, and both had
to use dictionaries to arrive at an understanding.

"I get you. . . ." Ted had said at last. "You mean she's
a nice girl."

Father had beamed at him.

"Mind if I walk with her once in a while?" Ted had
asked.

"No—no," Father had said positively, meaning exactly
what he said.

"Okay, thanks," Ted had said.

He had tipped his cap and walked away with Etsu then,
to the consternation of Father and Mother, who had at
once fallen in behind. But there had been only the block
to go, and when they reached the market Ted had laughed,
tipped his cap again, and sauntered away.

Ted had been there the next day, too, but Etsu had
reported no misbehavior when she got home, and he had
not tried to come in. But at the gate, with the dictionary,
he had conveyed to her that while he walked with her no
other American man must be allowed to do so.

The parents had discussed this solemnly after the children went to bed.

"It is better for only one to follow you than an army,"
Father had declared. "With help from Mother and me, we

can perhaps benefit from this one American, and preserve good relations also."

So it had come to pass that Ted walked with her every day, and after a while she began to come out after supper and walk to the park with him, which was what had happened this evening.

He studied her pretty face. Gosh, but she was pretty—almost as pretty as Sue. He would never have thought a Jap girl could be so pretty. Funny how a few months ago he was shooting every Jap creature in sight! He wouldn't have believed that he could want to be with a girl like this. He couldn't explain it to Sue, so he had not told her anything at all about Etsu. It wasn't as if Etsu made any difference to him and Sue. Sue was the girl he was going to marry—a real honey she was, yellow hair and blue eyes and a figure. She was full of spunk, too—a regular spitfire if you rubbed her the wrong way. Etsu was different —mild and gentle, all the time.

Studying Etsu's cream-colored face, he saw what he had never noticed before—that there were hollows at her temples under her soft black hair, that her neck was childishly thin. "Say," he burst out, "do you get enough to eat?"

She laughed merrily and he tried again, "Etty, listen," he put his hand on her two hands folded on her lap. "Eat, see?" He opened his mouth and pointed down his throat.

"No, no, Teddu," she said quickly.

"I thought not," he said. "You come along with me."

He grasped her wrist and dragged her up and along with him. Behind them the bag of soy cakes fell on the ground and half a dozen deer trotted toward it. But a child ran and snatched the bag first and carried it away. Neither Ted nor Etsu saw it. They were absorbed in struggle, he to pull her toward the restaurant down the street and she to resist him.

"You're going to eat," he said firmly.

"No, no, Teddu!" she wailed.

"Yes, yes, Etty," he said.

In the end he prevailed. He always prevailed, being a man and an American, and she found herself seated at a table in the restaurant. A dozen other couples looked at them and grinned.

"Rope her in, fella," a soldier yelled across the room.

"You shut up," Ted yelled back.

Etsu stared at the menu through tears. "I eat home," she wailed.

"You eat now," Ted ordered sternly.

He took the menu from her hands and pointed at items so recklessly that her Japanese thrift quenched her tears and she took the card away from him again.

"No, no, Teddu," she said.

"*I'm* hungry," he declared. "Order something for me, then."

Under this pressure she said a few soft words to the waitress, who stared at her. Etsu did not meet her eyes. The waitress was certainly not a home girl, and she saw that Etsu was, and her stare was cynical. Etsu did not like it and she looked away.

"Get a move on, kid," Ted said to the waitress.

"Yes, please," she said. The order from the manager was "Obey all Americans."

The food came almost at once, and Ted refused to take a mouthful until he saw Etsu pick up her chopsticks. This she resisted, because she knew that once she began to eat, she would not be able to stop. There would be nothing to stop her, no little brothers and sisters watching her hungrily, no Father and Mother pretending that they were not hungry.

But that was exactly what happened. She began to eat and she could not stop. She ate fish soup and fried shrimps and shredded chicken and cabbage and rice. She ate until even Ted was astonished.

"Boy, you must have been empty," he said.

"Boy?" she repeated.

"Forget it," he said, "it don't mean anything. You just keep on eating." So she kept on eating, until at last she could eat no more. She felt wonderfully warm and comfortable and happy in her body. But in her heart she felt full of sin. She had accepted the food, and now she must pay the price. Tears rose to her eyes. But she could not escape. In honor she must pay for what she had accepted. How would she ever tell Father and Mother?

She was too distressed to protest at the size of the tip that Ted left the waitress. Instead, she followed him in meek misery, her head down, her sleeve to her lips, her geta pattering on the cement floor. The men at the other tables shouted words at Ted which she did not know but which she perfectly understood. They were congratulating him. But why did they whistle as well as shout?

Outside, the twilight was gone and the night come. Soft paper lanterns glowed as people walked along. There were no street lights—the electric works had been destroyed by bombing. In the shadows Ted stopped and put his arms around her and she stood in them, shivering.

"Not here . . ." she murmured.

The blood in his veins stopped, then raced.

"Kid . . ." he gasped, "you don't mean—"

"Not here, Teddu," she said, trying not to cry. She was not thinking about him but about Father and Mother. She would tell them the whole shameful story, how hungry she had been, how at the sight of the hot food she had simply yielded—everything.

"Where can we go, kid?" his voice was thick and breathless. He tried not to think of Sue. Plenty of fellows —married fellows, too—and he and Sue were only engaged.

"We go home," Etsu said gravely.

He knew the Japanese were queer, but this was too queer. "Your people, kid, your father and mother . . ."

"Yes, yes, Teddu," she said faintly.

He gave up after that. They walked side by side down the dark street. He took her hand and held it hard. It was a soft hand, much softer than Sue's. It did not clasp his back as Sue's always did. He did not want to think of Sue. He fixed his whole mind on Etsu—that part of his mind, at least, that did not think, that felt.

Only when they reached the gate of her home did Etsu's soft hand come to life. He felt it pull him through the gate, down the narrow garden walk to the house. The paper wall screens were drawn, and the light in one room shone softly veiled. Against them the figures of Father and Mother moved in flat gray outlines. Etsu drew the screen enough to make a doorway and went into the house, pulling Ted after her. The children were already in bed, and Father and Mother looked at her without smiles.

"I am very late," she said and began to cry.

Father invited Ted to sit down with a wave of his hand. They all sat down on the floor mats, while Etsu continued to cry.

"Don't cry, Etty," Ted muttered. "You don't have to do anything you don't want to do."

But he began to be a little angry. What was the game

now? She had got him all excited and then come home. He listened to the soft outpouring of her voice, understanding nothing. When the Japs really talked, dictionaries were no good. You just had to wait.

"Alas, dear ones," Etsu was saying. She wiped her eyes with one sleeve and the other. "I have fallen so low. I do not deserve to be your child. Yet, I had to return to my home. Where else can I go?"

"Tell us exactly what happened," Father said in a practical voice.

So she told them. "My stomach ached. My eyes became blind. My nostrils were filled with the fragrance of the food. I trembled and felt faint. I thought only of putting the food in my mouth. Once I began, I could not stop. I ate until I could eat no more. He paid how many yen I dare not tell you. Afterward, we went outside and at once he asked me where we could go. I said, we would come home. He refused. But I insisted that you would do what was honorable. He is come in that expectation."

They all looked at Ted. He sat bolt upright on his folded legs, acutely uncomfortable. But the handbook on Japan had said that it was considered rude to stretch the legs out straight.

He grinned at her. "I can't keep it up too long," he remarked.

Father and Mother looked at Etsu. "What does he say?" they asked in unison.

"He says he cannot wait too long," she said faintly.

They sighed, and Father coughed. "We must remember that their ways are not our ways," he said.

"But Etsu is our daughter," Mother wailed.

"That is the difficulty," Father agreed.

"Let's get going, kid," Ted said restlessly. "I can't sit

here much longer." The inner muscles of his legs were beginning to cramp.

"What does he say?" Father and Mother asked again.

"He wants to begin," Etsu said still more faintly.

There was nothing for it. "The Emperor himself said we were to yield to the conquerors," Father said sadly. He motioned to Mother and they rose. "We will go in the other room," Father said. "We will wait there." Mother lifted her sleeve to her face and cried behind it softly. Thus they walked out of the room, and Father drew the screen of the partition behind him.

Ted stared after them. "Mighty decent of the old folks," he remarked. His legs suddenly became unbearable. "Mind if I straighten out?" He got up and stamped his feet, one after the other. "My feet've gone to sleep," he said cheerfully. The room was awfully small, he thought. Queer, how the Japs seem to live in closets! Etsu still knelt, looking up at him. He could make nothing of her look. It was fixed and strange. But her great eyes, under their straight, uplifted lashes, were beautiful. He dropped to the mat again beside her.

"Not scared of me, are you, kid?" he asked tenderly.

She did not answer. He took her in his arms and felt her as soft as a doll, unresponsive, passive, completely yielded. He kissed her at last, full on the mouth, and her face lay against his shoulder. "Why, I can . . . can . . ." He did not finish the sentence. He could do anything with this soft female creature.

At this moment Etsu, against his breast, felt something square and hard under her cheek. Now that the moment was come she was desperately frightened, even with Father and Mother just on the other side of the screen. Fear forced her to seize any delay. She reached inside his coat and pulled out the square. It was a folded leather case.

"This," she said, sitting up, "what?"

"Oh, heck, give that to me," Ted said harshly. He snatched at it, but she held it away from him.

"No, no, Teddu," she said. She tried to laugh. Then it occurred to her that it was his money. She was horrified. Suppose he should think she wanted money! She opened the case hastily and saw a face, a girl's face, twice repeated, one grave, one laughing.

"Oh, Teddu!" she breathed. She looked down into the faces. "Pretty giru!" she said.

It had never come into her mind that he had perhaps a home like her own, with father and mother. He existed for her, as all the Americans existed for everybody, merely as soldiers and conquerors.

"Your sister?" she asked.

"No," he said shortly.

"Your wife!" she declared.

"No—well, not exactly," he said.

She gazed down at Sue's face, so enchanted, so admiring, that he was moved to pride. "She's the girl I'm going to marry," he said.

"Oh, Teddu! Nize!" she said in her little musical voice. Everything she said sounded like singing. "Tell something, please?"

She touched Sue's loose curls. "Black, please?"

•"Gold," Ted said.

"And eyes, please?"

"Blue," he said.

Etsu‾ jumped up nimbly. "Tall, like me?" she asked.

"Much taller," Ted said. He stood up and measured to his eyebrow. "Sue's a tall girl—not fat, though."

"Giru's name, please?" Etsu asked softly.

"Sue," Ted said shortly.

"Sue? So pretty," Etsu murmured, "so pretty . . . pretty! I like!" Impulsively, she put Sue's picture to her cheek. "Nize giru," she said. "She come Japon, too?"

"No," Ted said.

"But you marry?" Etsu said anxiously.

"Sure, when I go home," Ted said.

"Oh, you go home?" Etsu repeated.

"Sure, sometime," Ted said.

"What time?" Etsu urged.

"Oh, maybe next summer."

"Then you marry," Etsu murmured. "You have nize . . ."

"Wedding," Ted supplied.

"Wedding," she repeated, "and then small babies, many small babies . . . so *nize!*" she sighed.

"Yeah," Ted said.

Etsu gazed at the picture affectionately.

She pressed it to one cheek and the other. Then she closed the case and put it back into Ted's breast pocket and buttoned the flap. She patted the pocket with her hand. "Nize," she kept saying, "so nize."

Sue was there in the room with them. He could feel her as plain as anything. All the longing and hunger that had been roused in his strong young body rushed to her. He wanted her, his own girl, and nobody else, the girl he was going to marry, who was going to have his children for him. All the homesickness of the two years he had been away swept over him. He saw the white painted houses, the streets, the green lawns of home. That was where he belonged, in Plainfield, New Jersey, where Sue was waiting for him.

He looked at Etsu in her flowered kimono with the big obi. What the hell had made him think . . .

"Say, I got to be going," he muttered. "It's gettin' late."

She found his cap for him, and he put it on. He stared at her an instant. Queer . . . he didn't even want to kiss her.

"G'night," he muttered.

"Good nigh', Teddu," she said sweetly. She opened the screen for him, and let it be open long enough for the light to shine across the path to the gate. When he had gone out she ran and pushed the bar across. A fine rain was beginning to fall, and by the time she was back in the house again her dark hair was full of silver mist.

Father and Mother were waiting for her.

"He didn't . . ." they began.

"No," she said.

"What happened?" Father asked.

"Nothing," she said. "We talked. There is a girl in America with blue eyes and yellow hair. I saw her picture. He is going home to be married to her."

"But he knew that before," Mother said, bewildered.

"I didn't know it," Estu said. "It was when I knew it that he remembered her."

They stood staring at each other.

"Do you understand?" Mother asked Father.

"No," Father said. "Who can understand Americans?"

Etsu did not speak. She was already pulling down the soft, silken quilts from the wall cupboards. At night Father and Mother slept here on the floor. She slept with the children in the next room.

"At any rate we are safe," she said. "And I will eat his food no more, I promise you."

But hours later, lying wedged between her two little

sisters, she kept thinking of the pretty blond face. Two women, across the seas from one another—and was it possible one had come flying to the aid of the other?

"Who knows?" Etsu asked. Her grateful heart reached through the night. "She is my sister," she thought. "My sister, who saved me. Sue!" She spoke the name aloud. It was like a Japanese name—almost, she thought.

Mr. Right

❦

TED LOOKED across the little park. Like everything else in Tokyo which had not been destroyed by bombs, it was neat. The shrubbery was protected from the deer by almost invisible fencing and the grass was being swept by two old men. By his side Etsu sat, waiting for his advice. He looked down at her small flowery figure and felt the protective tenderness which he had come to accept as his habitual feeling for her. It had nothing to do with the sturdy and aggressive love he had for Sue, his own girl at home in New Jersey. Etsu's plump hands were folded in her lap, and her white-stockinged toes peeped out of her geta, under the edge of her kimono.

He cleared his throat. "Kid," he said, "you gotta stand up for yourself."

Etsu looked at him with astonishment in her round black eyes. She hesitated, then stood up. He laughed. He never knew what Etsu was going to do. One reason he liked her so much was that she kept him laughing. She smiled half timidly.

"No, Teddu?" she inquired.

"Listen—I didn't mean to stand up now, on your feet. It's just the way we talk. You gotta learn English, kid."

She sank to the bench again gracefully, and looked at him with a gaze so exactly like that of a deer that had trotted up to them hopefully, that he laughed again. The deer, encouraged, nosed into his side pocket and he pushed it away.

"Get out, you beggar," he said. "Always thinkin' of eatin', ain't they! No, kid, to stand up for yourself means not to let yourself be run over, see?"

"Run over, Teddu?" Etsu repeated with increased bewilderment. "But in park is no car."

Ted set himself to the earnest teaching of English. "Now, Etty," he began. The deer interfered again, nosing his chest. Sometimes people carried food in their breast pockets or in their kimono bosoms. Ted punched its nose gently and the deer stared in surprise but did not move. "Here—I got to get rid of this wild beast," Ted said grimly. Taking the deer gently by the horns, he rose and ran it backward for twenty feet or so. There it stood, shocked. Etsu laughed heartily behind the sleeve of her kimono raised decently to her face.

"American funny," she remarked when Ted returned to the park bench.

"You gotta act rough with these here deer," Ted said. "They get so nosey."

The deer gazed at them wistfully, but came no nearer. Other deer stared at them, surprised at what had taken place. A few Japanese citizens looked pained but quiescent. Whatever Americans did was not to be questioned. But their looks showed plainly that no Japanese would have thought of running a deer in reverse.

Ted went on with his business. "No, when I say, stand up for yourself, Etty, I mean you gotta think what's best for you. You mustn't just lie down. . . . Your folks say you gotta marry that . . ."

"Lie down where, Teddu?" Etsu asked.

He looked into her round black eyes. Clearly, he was only puzzling her more with every word he said. "Heck, I'll begin all over. I don't mean lie down, Etty. I mean—

gosh, let me think what I do mean. I'm all mixed up now, myself."

He took off his cap and held his head in his hands and shut his eyes for a moment. Etsu was always mixing him up. He would start out as clear as sunshine to say something. In the next minute, she had him in knots.

"Listen, Etty," he began. He kept his eyes shut. "Don't you say anything for a minute—that's a good girl. Let me think as I talk. Your folks want you to marry this old widower guy. You don't want to marry him. . . ."

A small noise as of escaping steam made him open his eyes on Etsu. She had her hand over her mouth and she shook her head.

"Hey—you told me you didn't want to marry him!" Ted cried.

The steam would not be held back. "No, no, Teddu," she cried. She laughed. "So funny you talk . . ." she explained.

"Now, kid, cut out the giggles." He asked her sternly, "Do you—or don't you—want to . . ."

"No, no, Teddu," she said happily. Now they understood one another. She clapped her hands softly.

"Then why in heck don't you tell the old man so, and be done with it?"

Etsu's hands dropped. She looked grave. "In Japon . . ." she began, but Ted cut her off.

"Don't you go telling me what they do here in Japan," he said sternly. "That's what we're here for, to see that they don't do thataway any more in Japan."

"Whataway?" Etsu asked. Was it possible that she was wrong about their understanding each other?

Ted looked harassed. "Now, kid, don't begin getting my English mixed up again. You told me you don't wanta get married to this here widower. Okay! That's clear. I said, why don't you tell your old man that?"

Etsu could not imagine what Father would say, were she to accept this outrageous advice. "In Japon . . ." she began again, forgetting herself. She caught sight of Ted's furious blue eyes and clapped her hands over her mouth. "No, no, Teddu," she said, giggling, *"Not* in Japon . . ."

"I should say not," Ted said sternly. "Forget Japan. Go on, kid."

She cast about for something to take the place of her native land. She looked up at the blue sky, at the blossoming cherry trees, at the deer, licking up the drift of petals beneath them. Some pretty kindergarten children stood with their teacher, decorously watching the deer.

"My father," she began—Teddu had taught her how to say "th." She did it now by sticking her red tongue an inch or more beyond her red lips. Ted laughed and touched the tip of it with his forefinger. They both laughed. The school children turned to stare at them instead of the deer, until admonished by their teacher. Then they stared at the deer again.

Etsu put up her sleeve as a guard against Ted. "My father," she began again, "so kind."

"Queer sort of kindness," Ted remarked, "wanting you to marry an old widower with two children . . ."

"Very hard now," Etsu murmured. "So many young mans dead."

Ted did not answer this. He knew a good many young men dead; he'd never forget the good American fellows who had dropped in the jungles. Every time he'd got a Jap it helped the hurt in him. But it was queer—Etsu having to marry an old widower, maybe, because the young Jap she ought to marry was dead, too! Thank God, it wasn't Sue! Thinking of this, he determined to write Sue a letter this very night and tell her to remember he was alive, *and* kicking, as usual. If any damned old widower at home, with or without two kids, was playing around Sue . . .

"I think," Etsu said carefully. "I more better marry him."

Ted turned on her passionately. "Etty, I'm ashamed of you! You're only a kid. Why don't you wait and see if there isn't somebody else . . . somebody near your own age? You don't have to get married if you don't want to, do you?"

"Yes," Etsu said faintly, "more better."

"That's the way with girls," Ted said, "always wantin' to get married . . . to get married . . . to get married! They don't care who the man is. If they can't get the one they want they take the one they can get—a meal ticket—"

He choked. Had Sue been getting his letters regularly or not? Everything was so balled up these days.

"What do, Teddu?" Etsu said in her soft little voice.

"What do?" he bawled at her. "Why, stay at home and wait till Mr. Right comes along!"

" 'Mr. Right'?" she asked.

"Yeah—a nice young Jap, a coupla years older than you, good-lookin', speaks English . . . a good job . . . never been married before, lookin' around for a pretty kid somewhere—like you—"

A lively interest shone in Etsu's black eyes. "Please," she breathed, "tell my father."

Obviously, she thought Mr. Right was a living young man, and a friend of his. Ted groaned. Etsu believed everything he said right away, the way he said it. It was awful. But that was the way with these Japs. The fellows were always telling stories about the way the Japs hopped to do what they thought you had said. Before you knew it, you were all balled up.

"I didn't say I knew any Mr. Right, Etty," he explained with some exasperation. Plenty of times, he wondered why he bothered with Etty at all. It wasn't as if she was dumb —well, he didn't think she was dumb, but he was never sure, at that. All he knew was that she was so damn pretty that a lot of the fellows were always hanging around the edges, waiting for a chance to horn in. And Etty was too nice and sweet for him to hand her over to just anybody. If she wouldn't let him kiss her, he wasn't going to have anybody else kissing her. Not that he was sorry, really, that she wouldn't let him. When the time came for him to tell Sue about her, he could say that he and Etty had just been friends—nothing else. But he felt responsible for her, just the same. It wouldn't be right to hand Etty over to that bunch of wolves who were his best friends.

"You don't know?" Etsu faltered. "But Teddu, you say, 'wait Mr. Right.' Where Mr. Right?"

Ted took off his cap and scratched his head. He felt in the need of refreshment before he undertook to explain to her the hypothetical nature of the young man he had in mind.

"Let's go find something to eat," he said.

Etsu looked prim. She had an invincible determination, which he could not understand, that she would not accept a meal from him.

"Aw, just tea and a couple cakes," he said.

She smiled, rose, folded her hands inside her sleeves, and pattered along beside him. Even on her geta she did not approach his shoulder. Her tiny figure always moved him to a welter of tenderness. What became of little girls like this in Japan? He remembered stories he had heard of geisha. Maybe the widower would be better than that. He strode along frowning, and Etsu panted a little. So absorbed was he that he did not glare at two American fellows who whistled as they passed.

When they were drinking hot tea and consuming small rice cakes he kept looking at her. He couldn't worry about what happened to pretty Japanese girls. There were too many of them, for one thing. Etty would just have to manage. He'd be leaving for home before long—if you could believe what they said. In a couple of months he'd have forgotten all about Etty. After all, supposing he had never been sent to Japan?

She caught his eye and smiled. Her smile was lovely. Her teeth were very white, and her straight black lashes were long. Hell, she was a nice kid and he knew perfectly well he wouldn't forget her in a coupla months. Maybe he'd never forget her. Certainly he wouldn't forget her if she was unhappy and he knew she was pushed into something hard—a widower with two children couldn't be too easy.

He sighed. "I'm softhearted," he thought sadly. Queer, how one could be softhearted after a war! If you're born soft, you stay soft, maybe. Anyway, a little girl like Etty —even if she was Japanese.

He faced himself reluctantly. If he was going to be happy with himself, and he expected to be and wanted to be, he'd be happier if he knew Etty was happy, even if he never saw her again. If he shirked his duty, he'd feel his conscience gnawing the rest of his life. He'd cursed his tender conscience plenty, but he couldn't down it.

"Etty," he said, sighing. "Gimme a coupla days."

"Coupla days?" she repeated, her eyes rounding.

"Two days, Etty," he said hastily. "See?" He held up two

fingers. "Tomorrow, tomorrow—one, two—I'll try and find Mr. Right for you."

It was folly. It was the last thing he ought to do. Where would he find the man Etty ought to marry? He didn't know any young Japanese. Even if he found one, the likelihood was he couldn't speak a word of English. Besides, what would he say to a strange fellow—how could you go up to a strange fellow and ask him if he wanted to marry a girl you knew? All sorts of horrible complications were possible. He sighed again.

"Gee—war's so simple."

"You say something, Teddu?" Etsu inquired sweetly.

"A mouthful," he muttered.

"In your mout', Teddu? Somesing? Hurt?" Etsu was anxious.

"No, kid, please," he begged her. "Don't get mixed up —lemme think."

The result of some minutes of deep thought on his part, while Etsu quietly but heartily consumed cakes, was that he paid the bill abruptly and ordered her to follow him. He took her straight to her father's door, and then left her with a few stern words.

"You stay home, kid, see? I'll be back in two days— with or without Mr. Right. Tell Father—and don't let him go on gettin' you engaged to that damn widower."

Etsu was completely overcome. She bowed again and again, the little bows that made him think of a fainting butterfly.

"Sank you, Teddu," she murmured over and over, "sank you . . . sank you . . ."

He tipped his cap a little farther over one eye. She was so sweet that he hadn't the heart to correct her English.

"Thass okay, kid," he told her and marched away, feeling her life dependent upon him.

*   *   *

. . . Inside the little paper and wood house Etsu tried to explain the whole thing to Father and Mother. The children were sent to play in the pocket handkerchief of a garden. Clearly, this was not for their ears. There had been nothing so difficult to explain since the night Ted had not stayed with Etsu. That remained inexplicable, but this was more so.

Father put aside his pipe. He felt that the matter was so complex that he could not undertake even that extra occupation. Mother sat in the opposite corner of the room, listening. It was her habitual role in life.

"You say," Father said slowly, "the American brings you a husband?"

"Named Mr. Right, Father," Etsu said timidly.

"Mr. Right," Father repeated. "But it is an American name. I have never heard such a name in Japan."

Etsu stared at Father, smitten with horror. Then she smiled. She remembered distinctly what Teddu had said. "Teddu said Mr. Right is Japanese, two years older than I, Father, and he speaks good English and has a good job."

"There is no such young Japanese," Father declared. "I have searched the city for him. There is only Mr. Matsui, the widower."

"Must I marry him, Father?" Etsu pleaded.

Father sighed. He had a kind heart and he loved his daughter. "Alas, child, what else is there for women to do?" he asked. "Your mother and I cannot live forever.

Your brother will marry some day but he must not be
asked to care for you. And your younger sisters must also
marry. We must get you married first."

The children were playing quietly in the tiny artificial
pool that was in the middle of the garden. Etsu looked out
at their small, bent figures.

"Father, I wish we need not grow up," she said wistfully. "Can I ever have so happy a home as this?"

"Alas," Father said again, "everything is inevitable."

Over in her corner Mother wiped her eyes, one after the
other, on her sleeves, and Etsu drooped her head. Down
her cheeks ran two large clear tears. They splashed on her
knees as she sat with her legs under her. Father saw the
tears.

"At least," he said kindly, "we can wait two days."

*   *   *

. . . In the barracks the men were razzing Ted. He had
broken down after supper. There was no other way to explain his loss of appetite and his nervous state of mind.

His girl had turned him down. That was the way it had
begun. Everybody knew the faithful Etsu. He had braved
their laughter before. He had never denied their accusa-
tions. They wouldn't have believed him if he told them his
relations with Etsu were perfectly pure. They would have
howled like wolves. So why tell them? Anyway, he was
half ashamed of such purity, until he remembered how
much easier it was going to make his life with Sue. How
could he explain to anybody the way he felt toward Etty?
He couldn't explain it to himself. If he had had Sue—well,
he *had* Sue. But Etty had her own hold on him—she was
like a cute kitten, like a little girl about three years old,

something you wanted to cuddle . . . only she wouldn't let him, and he was glad she wouldn't. But still she was like that. She pulled at his heart, even if nothing could ever come of it. Besides, she was a darn nice girl, clean all the way through. He thought of this and grew earnest. He'd try to make the fellows see.

It was night, in the brief half-hour before taps, when he tried. They were lounging around on the cots.

"It's like this . . ." he began. If he could get them on their soft side—they had an awful soft side—all of them did. He reached for it deliberately. "She's decent, that kid. I know what you all think, but it ain't so. Besides, I'm an engaged fella. . . . I got a girl waitin' for me at home. . . ."

He waited for laughter and whistling to subside and went doggedly on. "Seems the old folks want Etty to marry an old fella with kids—two of 'em. She don't want to, see? So what? Well, seems she's gotta, unless someone else can be found. That's the way it is with these Japs. And Japs are scarce—we know why—"

He watched merriment fade away. He was getting them, all right. There was something about Etsu's faithfulness that had touched them, unknown to themselves. There were a few jeers about having to get her married. He waited for these to pass over him and kept on.

"I don't know a doggone Jap. But I've let myself in for it. What I want to know is—any of you know anybody?"

He waited for a few ribald offers to end, grinning patiently. "Gee, I'm in an awful spot," he said. He wiped his forehead. "I gotta deliver. I sure would appreciate some help."

Taps sounded and the lights went out. Nothing could be done that night. He tossed in strange dreams, seeing against a blackness as soft as jungle night the faces of young

Japanese he had been forced to kill. He woke somewhere before dawn with a conviction as clear as consecration. What if one of them was the man that might have married Etty? It was his duty to make it up to her.

*   *   *

. . . He asked and got forty-eight hours leave. Until now it had not seemed worth while to take more leave than a few hours. He had no desire to sight-see, and a couple of hours was as much as he and Etty ever needed. By that time they had run out of conversation, and he had absorbed enough of her soft charm to last him until next time. He felt restless if he was with her longer than that. It was as much of a nice girl as any fellow could take.

But forty-eight hours was none too long to find that nice girl a husband. He relieved his distress by grumbling and complaining to all the men in the mess about his predicament and their inability to help him.

"There ain't no nice Japs," one declared.

"Gotta be," he retorted. "What'll happen to all these nice girls, if there's no men?"

He ignored the answers they flung across the tables to him and returned to his anxiety. "All the same," he persisted, "you fellows might do a little thinkin'. Look at the fix I'm in!"

The hours passed with horrifying swiftness. They had always dragged on his hands, impeded by menial tasks or tiresome drill and almost equally tiresome leisure, but now with nothing at all happening, the hands of his double-duty, guaranteed watch sped around the luminous dial. Sue had sent him the watch for Christmas, but he had never looked at it so often as now. He thought of advertising in *The Tokyo Times* and went so far as to attempt a description of a suitable husband, "Wanted, a young Japanese, good job, nice disposition," but when it came to saying he was to marry Etsu, it became impossible. "Any fellow reading it would say I'd got her in trouble," he groaned to himself.

The search grew so intensive that he looked at every Japanese he saw with a speculative eye. The age limits went lower and higher. From twenty-four they sank to nineteen, since Etsu was eighteen, and from thirty they rose to forty. The widower was forty-five.

But he who seeks, finds. At ten minutes to five as he passed the hotel, he heard a loud voice, swearing admirably with an American accent. A twinge of homesickness seized him and he paused to listen. The voice came from the lobby of the hotel and through the open door.

"I want a seat on that plane—I want to get home. I'll pay any son-of-a-gun what he asks—just so I can get out of this damned country!"

"Lucky guy to be able to go where he wants," Ted thought wistfully. Think of being able to go to a hotel clerk and yell about a seat on a plane for home! He entered the lobby, sank into a comfortable chair, closed his eyes, and listened to the voice.

"It can't be possible that every damned passenger wants to get back as much as I do. . . . There must be some who would take cash. . . ."

"I am sorry, Mr. Fukuda," the clerk said.

Ted's eyes opened. "Mr. Fukuda?" He got up and approached the desk impetuously. A strongly built figure stood belligerently in front of it. The hair was unmistakable, so were the clenched fists, so, as he came cautiously from the side, was the belligerent profile. The fellow was Japanese—with that accent!

He saluted diplomatically. "Excuse me," he said, "but your talk makes me think of home. You ever been in New Jersey?"

"That's where I come from," Mr. Fukuda said.

"Not, by any chance, from Plainfield?" Ted asked anxiously.

"No—Somerville," Mr. Fukuda said.

"God," Teddy cried, "that's where Sue's grandmother lives!"

"What's her name?" Mr. Fukuda asked crisply.

"Mrs. Riley, and her grandfather is Mr. Riley—runs a men's store. . . ."

"Where I bought this suit," Mr. Fukuda said, and his face crinkled in smiles.

Ted put out his hand. "It's the same small little old world," he said feelingly.

They clasped hands and sat down simultaneously on a long couch. Mr. Fukuda had forgotten the plane and Ted forgot Etsu.

"How come?" Ted asked.

"I was born there," Mr. Fukuda said.

"Then you're American!" Ted exclaimed.

"Sure," Mr. Fukuda beamed. He lifted his thick black eyebrows. "Your name, Mr. . . . ah . . ."

"Ted—just Ted—family name's Miller," Ted said promptly.

"My name is Kino," Mr. Fukuda said. "Family name's Fukuda."

Ted took a deep breath. Then he remembered. A gleam stole into his eye. "Kino, do you have to go home right away?" he asked purposefully.

Kino considered. "I want to go home because I don't like this country," he said frankly.

"What did you come here for, anyway?" Ted inquired.

"My father asked me to come here and inquire into his factory," Kino said. "But the factory is blown up—the whole district was bombed. There is nothing left—why should I stay?"

"What kind of a factory was it?" Ted inquired.

"Silk," Kino said. "My father is an importer—was, I had better say."

"What'll he do now?"

"He wants me to stay here to build a new factory," Kino said sadly. "But I cannot stay. I hate the damned country."

"It's yours," Ted said coaxingly.

"No, America is my country," Kino said firmly.

"Why don't you like it here?" Ted inquired. How did one approach a man with matrimony when he wanted to leave the girl's country?

"I . . . just don't like it," Kino said. "It's too slow."

"You know anybody?" Ted inquired.

Kino shook his head. "I have cousins and one uncle, and I never want to see them again."

Ted edged nearer. "Say, I know some swell people." He was so anxious that his voice was tense.

"Yeah?" Kino's voice was full of sound American skepticism.

"There's a pretty girl—nice, too."

"Japanese girls are dumb," Kino remarked.

"Etty isn't," Ted retorted.

"Etty?" Kino repeated.

"Etsu," Ted said. "I call her Etty for American."

Kino looked stern and Ted caught the look from the corner of his eye. "Nothing romantic, you understand, Kino—but, well, I'm nuts on the whole family. They're just like my own, somehow. I mean, her mother's like Mom, and the father's like my old man, and there's a lot of kids younger—like my kid brothers and sisters. Well, now her dad says she's got to marry an old widower with a lot of kids of his own and she don't want to . . . see?"

Kino did not look interested. Ted drew a fresh breath. "So . . . I thought to myself, if I could find some swell fellow, who'd talk the family out of it—a Japanese, that is . . ."

"I am American," Kino said firmly again.

"Sure," Ted agreed, "but your dad is Japanese . . . and you look Japanese. . . . Well, you know what I mean."

Kino sat silent for a moment. "Why do you care?" he asked abruptly.

"Gee, I don't know," Ted said. His blue eyes were honest. "I'm kinda surprised at myself. I guess it's because Etty is one of those girls—you see 'em at home, too—that every fellow kinda feels he has to look after . . . a sweet kid, you know. Not fresh, or anything . . . kind of little and cute . . . and helpless. . . ."

"You don't . . . ah . . ." Kino suggested.

"Certainly not," Ted said hastily. "I gotta girl waiting at home. I only want to see Etty happy with some fella, and I know the widower isn't the one. She cries every time she mentions him, but I guess the home pressure is getting hard. They'll listen to you better'n me."

"I have no interest in people I don't know," Kino said thoughtfully, "but if I could break down some of these damned old hardshell Japs, and make them see the light, I would take pleasure in it. Where does the family live?"

"Come with me," Ted said joyfully.

He walked Kino in such haste to the little house on one of the modest streets of Tokyo that he was afraid Kino might suspect him of something. He did not talk. Ted could not talk and think at the same time, and what he was thinking about was how to get hold of Etty while Kino was talking to Father and Mother, and how to tell her that she must turn on all the works. He sighed. She wouldn't understand "turn on all the works," and he would get all involved trying to explain to her what it was. He wished she understood plain English!

"Etty understands English real good," he told Kino.

"You teach her?" Kino inquired with a grin.

"Well, of course she ain't perfect," Ted replied hastily.

They reached the door of the house, and Mother opened it. Housebroken for Japan, Ted took off his shoes, and Kino slipped his off as a matter of course. Mother spoke no English whatever, but at the sight of Kino she was suddenly overcome with modesty and politeness. She bowed again and again, and she lavished grateful looks upon Ted which he did not comprehend. In her soft voice she called, and Father came hastily out of the inner room, his brown-rimmed horn spectacles on his nose. He had been copying the scrolls which he sold for a meager living.

"Hah-sodeska," he said when he had listened to Mother's whisperings in his ears. Then he beamed, took off his spectacles, and bowed again and again to Kino and only less often to Ted.

Father did not speak English, either. But there was no mistaking his warmth of welcome. He ushered the two young men into the tiny sitting room.

Mother had hurried in before him and had whisked Etsu out. She had been arranging flowers in the alcove, and Mother finished them quickly, bowing many times to Kino in apology while she did so.

Father began to ask Kino a few experimental questions.

Kino shook his head and turned to Ted. "I don't understand what he's trying to ask me," he said frankly. "I'm the youngest of our family, and I just never learned much of the stuff. This is an educated old guy and he uses long words."

Here was a predicament. Kino didn't speak enough Japanese! Then where was Etty? Ted leaned forward on his folded legs. They were sitting on the floor as they always did in this little house. He could only sit so long before he had to stretch his legs.

"Etty," he said distinctly to Father, "where is she?" He made motions.

Father looked distressed. "Hah . . ." he said. He looked at Mother, and Mother bowed her head. A few words passed between them.

"They don't want the girl to come in," Kino said. "They're old-fashioned, like my old folks."

"Then we'll get nowhere," Ted said. "She's got to come in." He lifted his voice and shouted, "Etty—come here!"

There was a rustling outside a panel, and the shadow of a slender, kimonoed figure appeared against the rice paper, but the panel did not slide back. Etsu's pretty voice called her parents. Father wagged his head and issued a sudden order. The panel slid back, and there, against the background of the tiny garden, stood Etsu. She held her fan across the lower part of her face, and her long straight eyelashes lay against her flushed cheeks.

"Come in here, Etty," Ted ordered her. "This is a friend of mine. He don't speak much Japanese, see? He's American. . . ."

He was amazed to see Etty patter into the room and abase herself before Kino. She sank to her knees, her kimono falling in perfect folds about her, and she bowed to the floor until the creamy nape of her neck, under the soft black hair, lay exposed to the view of the young men. Ted looked at Kino, and Kino, feeling that intent look, returned it.

"Cute, ain't she?" Ted said, out of the corner of his mouth.

"H-m-m," Kino replied, without committing himself to a nod.

"That's why I feel kinda sorry for the kid," Ted said in a low voice. He didn't want to rush Kino. But certainly he couldn't take the next plane now.

Etsu had risen gracefully and was preparing tea. She placed a bowl before Kino with both hands, and bowed again.

"Thanks," Kino said abruptly. Etsu flashed him a smile as soft and bright as a baby's.

Father said something.

"What's he say, Etty?" Ted inquired.

Etsu shook her head. "No . . . no . . . no . . ." she said. Her eyelashes swept downward, and she was covered with new shyness.

"Now, Etty," Ted said severely, "don't begin that." He turned to Kino. "She's always saying no . . . no . . . no."

Kino burst into laughter. "Why?" he asked with twinkling eyes.

"No, no," Ted said hastily, "it hasn't anything to do with me."

Etsu was suddenly grave. "No . . . no?" she inquired. She clasped her chubby hands together and looked at Kino with pleading in her face. "No . . . no . . . Mr. Right?" she asked.

Ted turned to Kino. "She's got something mixed up

again," he said in a low voice. "She's always gettin' mixed up. I'll just find out how things are."

He hooked a finger at Etsu and she followed him obediently. Outside, in the small garden, he looked at her. "What's the idea?" he asked severely. "Acting like you was already engaged! Don't you know you have to lead a man on easylike? You can't just take it for granted that the minute he lays eyes on you he's going to ask you to be his little ball and chain. You gotta manoover!"

"Many?" Etsu said. A light came into her round black eyes.

"No . . . no . . ." Ted said. "It ain't whatever it is you think. *Manoover!*"

She looked at him helplessly. "Not Mr. Right?" she asked.

"Yes, Mr. Right—I think so, that is, but he don't know it."

"No?" she asked.

"Yes . . . not no, Etty . . . he no savvy, see? You got to let him know gradual—oh, heck!—she can't understand! Etty look . . ."

"Where look?" Etsu inquired gazing around the garden helpfully.

"Here, Etty . . . right here . . ." Ted pointed to himself fiercely. "Now, listen! Concentrate, Etty, I'll go slow. You tell Father . . ."

"I tell Father," she repeated adorably.

"Ask Mr. Right . . ."

"Ask Mr. Right . . ."

"Stay to supper . . ."

"Supper?"

"Yeah . . ." he made signs of shoveling food into his mouth.

"Ah . . . ha . . ." Etsu understood and was overcome with amusement. She turned at once and trotted back into the house, Ted following her in triumph. In the room again, where Kino sat in silence waiting, she poured out a stream of soft, eager talk to Father and Mother.

"*Hah-sodeska!*" Father said co-operatively.

He turned to Mother and the three of them argued something politely. Then Etsu turned to Ted.

"Fishu?" she asked prettily, pointing her forefinger at Kino. "Shikinu? Isucreemu?"

"Swell," Ted said heartily. He explained to Kino with condescension. "The folks want to ask you to stay to eat. Fish, chicken, ice cream. 'Course they'll buy the ice cream. They got a fish pond, and they raise chickens."

Kino consulted his watch. His face had changed its expression. He looked benign or, perhaps, ready to laugh. "I've missed any chance for the plane," he said meditatively.

"Sure have," Ted said. "You'll have a swell time now you know these folks. They'll be hurt if you leave. Whyn't you stay a while?"

Kino hesitated. Then he caught sight of Etsu. She had quite forgotten to conceal her eagerness, and she stood posed unconsciously like a little girl, gazing at her hero.

"I don't care if I do," Kino said in a lordly American fashion.

"I've landed the big fish," Ted thought with secret joy. But aloud he was very cautious. "I gotta stretch my legs," he said indifferently. "Stretch your legs, Kino, old fella— Etty and the folks won't mind—they're used to Americans."

Mother and Sons

❦

"HERE THEY ARE, Freda!" Mrs. Barclay called to her maid. She rose from her chair by the window as a roadster swept around the curve of the drive, and stood while her sons, Lane and Harry, leaped out.

Freda came running into the room and now she peered from behind Mrs. Barclay. "Harry's most as tall as Lane," she breathed. "But don't Lane look wonderful in his uniform!"

Mrs. Barclay repressed her irritation. She had never been able to make Freda say "Master Lane." She did not believe that Freda would ever leave her, but in these days one never knew, and so now she said nothing. Instead, she hurried to the door, opened it, and threw her arms about Lane. She was tall but he was taller, and she trembled with adoration while she held him. His shaved cheek brushed her temple, and he kissed her quickly. She smelled soap and leather but beneath that the precious clean odor of his flesh, which she recognized for her own.

"Oh, darling!" she whispered. Then she let him go instantly, aware of his muscles repelling her while they held her. "Well, Lane," she cried, holding him at arm's length.

He was in his second lieutenant's uniform and he was so handsome that she could have wept for joy. Again and again in his lifetime she had been blinded by his beauty, but never so much as now. She would like to have fallen at his feet and worshiped him; literally, she could have done this, but she knew better.

"Aren't you ashamed to be so handsome?" she said, her

225

mouth twisting and teasing. "You look like an advertisement for Brooks Brothers."

"As a matter of fact, I am," he said. "That's where my stuff came from." He put down his cap and gloves and overcoat on the hall settee, rubbed his hands and blew on them. "It's getting cold—there'll be frost tonight, Mother."

"It's the end of your roses, I'm afraid," Harry added.

"I picked them all today, to the last buds, because you were coming, Lane," she said, and waved her hand at the bowl on the table. His hands and hers were extraordinarily alike, long and slender, but his were a man's hands. She seized his right one and pretended to examine it. "How clean!" she cried, laughing. "When I think how I used to scold you about your hands—the way I still do Harry!"

Harry had followed them into the living room and now he was sprawled in a big chair watching them, his pale blue eyes blinking. He was biting his fingernail when she caught sight of it and said gently:

"Harry, do stop biting your nails."

"Have to have 'em short for my violin," he muttered.

"Then cut them, for heaven's sake," she said.

"Still fiddling, Harry?" Lane asked.

Harry put his hands in his pockets and nodded.

"Harry really plays very well," Mrs. Barclay said. "He is working now on a Beethoven symphony with the school orchestra."

She knew of course that Lane did not care for music, but still she could never quite give up hope that he really was what she wanted him to be. "Harry, you must get your violin after dinner," she went on, when Lane did not answer.

Harry sat up impatiently. "Oh, heck, Mother, Lane doesn't want to hear me fiddle."

Lane grinned. He was walking around the room restlessly, looking at everything. He stopped and squared his elbows in mock fury at his brother. "Want to get me in wrong?" he demanded. "Sure I'll listen to you, kid."

"It's not very nice of you to say such things, Harry," Mrs. Barclay said. She had a pretty voice and nothing she said could sound severe, and yet both of her sons looked at her with apprehension. Lane went over to her quickly and patted her cheek. "Now, Mother," he said coaxingly. "Harry didn't mean anything."

She caught his hand and held it. "Look at Lane's nails, Harry, they're beautiful—the way yours ought to look."

"His hands are like yours, mine are like Dad's," Harry said shortly.

She dropped Lane's hand and stared at Harry. How did he know that was what she was thinking? Tom's thick pale hands, their stubby fingertips, the scoop-shaped nails —could she ever forget them? He had been dead for five years, but sometimes the sight of Harry's hands brought him back into the room alive again, the huge, sandy-haired, pale-skinned man whom she had married and loathed. How silly it had been for her to marry him to spite Arnold Foster, who did not love her! She had only broken her own heart.

"That has nothing to do with biting your nails," she said.

Lane was prowling around the room again. "Where's the dog?" he now asked.

"Oh, Lane." Mrs. Barclay's voice was tender. "I didn't want to write you—he got run over last month. I don't know how it happened except that he would keep running in front of the cars on the drive. It was the laundry truck that did it. We found him in the bushes, poor old fellow, quite stiff. He'd crawled in there to die all by himself. Harry gave him a beautiful funeral."

"Stupid dog," Lane said.

Harry's pale eyelashes lifted and his small blue eyes were furious. "He wasn't stupid—you never trained him properly. You can't expect a dog to know how to behave if you don't take the trouble to teach him."

"Getting another dog?" Lane asked calmly. He was lighting a cigarette.

"I don't want another dog," Harry muttered.

No one spoke for a moment. "I'm going to call Elise," Lane said suddenly.

"Now, Lane, you must be here for dinner tonight," Mrs. Barclay said. "Freda would be hurt."

"Of course," Lane agreed easily. "But I promised Elise that afterward we might go somewhere—dance or something."

He went out of the room and Mrs. Barclay gazed at his graceful back. "Lane looks wonderful in a uniform, doesn't he?" she said brightly. Harry was cross, she thought, when he did not answer, and when he was cross he was more like Tom than ever. His brown tweed suit was rumpled and his thick hair too long. It would do him good to get into a uniform, but he was only seventeen and she did not know exactly what to do with the year between. She had a strange illusion, as she looked at him, that it was not Harry sitting there, but Tom himself. Tom was so young, even when he died at forty-six. He was what other women called "just a big boy." But she had never been attracted by such big boys, men whose bodies aged while their minds remained juvenile, men who took refuge in remaining children in the eyes of women.

But she had married Tom, knowing what he was, and

knowing that she did not love him. When she accepted him she had, to do her own self justice, no idea of how wicked it was to marry a man she did not love. Her own suffering she had endured with a guilty sense of the injustice she had done him. She remembered this as she looked at Harry, and the old guilt made her say gently, "What's the matter with you today, Harry? Aren't you glad to have Lane come home?"

Lane's gay voice came rolling into the room on laughter. "Quit kidding, Elise—oh, yeah? What do you think I am?"

"Of course I'm glad to have Lane come home," Harry said. He sat up, but he kept the objectionable hands in his pockets. He squared his shoulders and looked at her directly. "Nothing's the matter with me, Mother. Lane and I were having a swell time together. I was awfully glad to see him at the station and we talked all the way home —more than we ever have. But you make everything wrong between us."

Never before had he spoken so bluntly. She felt it a blow and she moved to retaliate blindly. "You're jealous of Lane—that's all it is, Harry. He's handsomer than you are . . . older. . . . It's just the usual younger-brother jealousy."

She perceived at once that the blow in return fell upon his heart, too. The quick red streamed upward into his face and he was scarlet in an instant. "I know Lane is handsome and I am not," he said. "You have let me know that ever since I can remember." His quiet voice, the only thing about him that was not like Tom, cried no anger, only intense suffering.

She gasped and flushed in her turn. Had she indeed been so cruel as this? She refused to believe it. "Now, Harry, that is unjust," she said swiftly. "I have never by any word . . ."

He broke in. "I am not stupid, Mother. I don't need words. I see by your looks and your voice, by lots of ways. I've always known what you felt about me."

She trembled and the tears came into her eyes. Tom could never have spoken like this. It was dreadful that out of Tom's son, the flesh of his flesh, should come these words of articulate accusation. It was as though Tom were taking revenge on her, through this boy. "Harry, how can you talk like this now when Lane is only home for these few hours? Tomorrow he'll be going across—perhaps he'll never come back."

"It is despicable of me to say that," she thought. "It is cowardly to use the possibility of Lane's death to hide myself from Harry—from Tom," she almost said.

Harry looked suddenly as old as Tom. He said calmly: "It's nothing new to me, Mother, though perhaps I have never quite wanted to own, even to myself, how much you love Lane. It has only come over me in the last few minutes that I must face it."

"Of course I love Lane," she cried, "and I love you. You are both my sons."

He smiled so sad a smile that if she had loved him it would have broken her heart afresh and she knew it, and all the old guilt she had felt toward Tom came darkly into her again, to poison her joy.

She rose and went over to him quickly and put her hand on his shoulder. "Harry, we simply must not talk about this now. I am terribly hurt . . . I don't know what I've done to make you think . . . I've tried to be a good mother. . . ."

"You've tried awfully hard," he said, looking up at her. Her hand dropped from his shoulder and she stared down at him aghast. He was pale again. "I wish you would stop trying," he said distinctly, and she knew that he knew it had been an effort to put even her hand on his shoulder. The smell of his flesh was the smell of Tom. She noticed it whenever she came near him. A son could inherit even the odor of his father.

"You've shocked me," she said. "I don't know what to say. But I think we owe it to Lane to keep today happy."

"Of course." Harry rose and stood, tall and stoop-shouldered, his hands still in his pockets. The smile twisted his thick, pale lips. "But you know, Mother, Lane really wouldn't notice anything. He's not like you and me."

She opened her mouth to answer and could not. Her dark-lashed lids fluttered and fell.

"You and Lane look alike," Harry said, "but you and I are alike."

She could not answer the outrageous truth. She had denied it so long, she had hidden it so deeply in herself, sure that none knew it, and this pale ugly boy had shared the knowledge! Now he brought it out and put it before her, on this day of all days, when she wanted to be happy. She was suddenly terrified of him, and she wanted to run out of the house away from him, to run away with Lane. Instead she bent her head and covered her face with her hands.

"How can you be so . . . cruel? . . ." she sobbed.

"Poor Mother," he said, and went shambling out of the room.

She heard the door shut, and, grateful to be alone, she sank into her chair and wiped her eyes. She could hear Lane's farewells—

"Yeah . . . well, so long, Elise. I'll come around about half-past nine. Sure . . . we'll do up the town . . . okay!"

She had barely time to right herself outwardly before he came in. Then, so that he might notice nothing, she said something that would take his attention from her: "You aren't in love with Elise, are you, Lane?"

He laughed as he sat down. "Now, Mother, what a question! How do I know? Maybe I'll find out tonight."

"Elise is a lovely girl," she said. She was amazed at herself. She had always repressed her jealousy of the girls who called Lane up and followed him and sighed after him. She had laughed at him and teased him and so had distilled her jealousy. Now she was not jealous. She wanted her love of him vindicated by another woman's love. If Elise could love him, Elise who was clever and brilliant, it would mean that she was right about Lane and Harry was wrong.

"Do you notice any difference in Harry?" she asked suddenly.

Lane looked surprised. "He's grown a lot taller—I hadn't noticed anything else."

"He's behaving so queerly these days," she said unwillingly. "I don't know what to think."

"He's always been a queer sort of fellow," Lane said absently, "always reading books and practicing music—the sort of things most fellows don't care much about. At least, I don't."

She sat drooping in her chair, looking at him, not answering. The way that children break your heart, she thought, the way they can disappoint you and hurt you, without knowing! The moment the nurse had put Lane into her arms she had fallen in love with him. He was her flesh, he had her dark hair and brown eyes, her smooth olive skin, her slender fine body, even her feet. She had held his feet in her hand when he was a baby, she had scrubbed his rough little boy feet, and she knew the look of his feet now in his young manhood. They were like hers but a man's, long, strong, slim.

"I used to read to you," she said. "Stories and poetry by the hour when you were sick. I used to play to you and sing to you. . . ."

He looked at her, half ashamed. "You've been awfully good to me, but I guess I'm like Dad. You know that, Mother."

She turned her head away. "I suppose so," she said.

She could not face it. She jumped up and smoothed back her hair with both hands. "How shall we use this precious day?" she demanded in a hard clear voice. "Today must be the very best day of our lives. What do you want to do more than anything else in the world?"

"Let's take out the horses," he said eagerly. "I'd like that better than anything."

It was the one thing she and Tom used to do together. After the years had finished their separation, after she knew that he would never like any of the things she loved most to do, after she knew that what he enjoyed bored her beyond endurance, life being so brief, still they had been able to go horseback riding. But she had not once ridden since the day they had quarreled and Tom had gone out alone and been killed. She had kept the horses only for the boys.

"All right," she said now, "all right, Lane."

*　　　*　　　*

. . . She gave herself up to her love for him. The trail led through the woods and against the green gold of the trees his erect and handsome figure stirred her to the heart. The sunshine of the glorious autumn day fell on his dark head and crowned him. She had made this glorious creature, her flesh and her blood had created him in beauty. She tried to hide from him her pride, because he was only her son and not her lover.

"I am sure men who look as you do in a uniform invented war and keep it up," she said drily. "It's too wickedly becoming for permanent peace!"

He laughed his easy laughter that made speech unnecessary. But he had a simple vanity which understood what women felt toward him, even what she felt, and vanity added glitter to his beauty. His eyes were bright, his lips were confident, and his hands were supple upon the reins. When suddenly he broke into a gallop and went ahead of her she drew her own horse back that she might watch him.

"I wonder," she thought, "if Elise can be happy with him."

She had never questioned before the possibility of his making any woman happy. But it was because she had never acknowledged before that he had not made her happy. This heavenly son of hers, whose beauty she had taken for her comfort, had often made her unhappy. "Give him time," his teachers had said. "He has such high spirits. He does not apply himself. When he is older . . ."

She had taken their words to cover her chagrin at his failures. Then before the first year of college was over the war had taken him out of school, and now she could not know what time might have done.

He came galloping back to her, his cap in his hand and his dark hair flying, his eyes alight and his body as graceful as a king's in the saddle. A moment later they were cantering side by side.

"Lane," she said soberly in the midst of the sunshine.

"How do you feel about going to war? I've wanted to ask you, but perhaps we cannot be alone again today. And I want to know, darling—it will comfort me when you are gone—if I feel I know what you are thinking behind all the things you have to do—dangerous things, sometimes. And if something should happen to you . . . it would help me if I thought you might feel you had fought for something worth dying for."

It was true that she had thought of this often, and had longed to know that he had in him a faith which would serve him, if he had to die.

He turned bright and uncomprehending eyes on her. "I guess I haven't thought much about it, Mother. But I expect to have some fun out of it."

Dreadful memories came creeping like ghosts out of the woods and laid their cold hands upon her. So Tom might have answered, so Tom had often answered when, in her desperate attempts to mend their difference, she had laid bare her heart to him.

"Is that all?" she asked Lane.

"What else?" he replied. "What would you want me to feel, Mother?"

"Nothing," she said, "nothing at all."

Harry was not in the house when they came home. He had gone to the school to practice, Freda said, and he did not know when he would be back.

"Then Lane and I will have luncheon together," Mrs. Barclay said. Yesterday she had wondered how she could maneuver to have this luncheon with Lane, and could think of no way to achieve it. Now Harry had done it simply by going away.

But she was not alone with Lane, after all. She kept thinking of Harry. How deeply had she hurt the boy?

She found herself thinking of him with a new feeling, even with a sort of curiosity. Was it possible that she had really never understood him? Perhaps, she thought, with the old guilt that was still connected with Tom, she had been so absorbed in Lane that she had never taken time for Harry. But then she had never had to worry about Harry. He had been a quiet boy who had always known what he wanted, and who had always done well in school. There had been none of the crises which had kept her agitated about Lane. It was only recently that Harry had been restless and impatient and, at times, even disobedient. He had taken to staying out late at night, for instance, not telling her where he had been.

"I wish you weren't going away," she said suddenly to Lane over the beefsteak. It was his favorite food, but today she could not bear it. He loved it rare, and he was eating heartily. "I really feel I need help with Harry," she went on. "I don't understand him."

"Leave him alone," Lane advised. "The Army'll take him off your hands next year." He helped himself to steak again. "Swell lunch, Freda," he said.

Freda smiled and her eyes melted. Lane was her favorite, too.

"I don't feel that having the Army take a son off her hands is exactly enough for a mother," Mrs. Barclay said. "Does he talk to you, Lane?"

"He was talking this morning about wanting to go into chemistry," Lane said carelessly. "I didn't pay much attention. He was jabbering away. I never liked chemistry. Mother, do you mind if I go and look up some of the fellows this afternoon?"

"Of course not," she said. "I want you to do just what makes you happiest."

But it was strange, all the same, to be alone in her house that afternoon, the afternoon before Lane might be leaving forever. And Harry did not come home. She telephoned the school at five o'clock, but no one answered. Everyone had gone.

She felt suddenly under such a tension that she did not want to dine alone with her two sons, who had in the course of this day become strange men, and she went to the telephone after a little thought and called up Elise.

"Elise? I wasn't sure you'd be home."

"Oh, it takes me all afternoon to get ready to go out with Lane," Elise cried, laughing. It was the laughter of a woman in love, and Mrs. Barclay recognized it with a pang of something like fear.

"Will you come to dinner, Elise? You'll make four, and I know Lane would like it."

"I was simply praying you'd ask me, Mrs. Barclay," Elise's voice sang over the wires.

"All right then, dear."

She hung up the receiver, told Freda, and went back to her room and lay for an hour on the chaise longue, the house silent around her. At six she rose and bathed and dressed and went downstairs, and at half-past six Lane burst into the house and opened the living-room doors. "Hello, Beautiful!" he cried. "Waiting for me?"

"Of course," she said, turning her cheek for his kiss. "I asked Elise to dinner. She'll be here in a few minutes."

"Swell," he said. "I wanted to ask her but Harry didn't know if you wanted her."

"Have you seen Harry?" she asked.

He was already out of the room and halfway up the stairs. "Nope, nowhere!" he shouted back.

"I simply will not get anxious about Harry," she told

herself. But she was so absurd as to wonder if he had been so foolish as to . . . to do something like running away. She felt after this morning that now she did not know him at all.

But she showed no sign of her anxiety when ten minutes later Elise came in, looking like a golden lily. They kissed gently, and she felt a rush of affection for the tall, beautiful girl whom she had always known. Elise was very young, only eighteen, to Lane's nineteen. But all the children were being forced to grow up quickly these days. The boys had to be men at eighteen and the girls were falling in love, marrying, hurried into womanhood before their time.

"Lane will be down in a few minutes," she said.

"Where's Harry?" Elise asked.

"He went to orchestra practice—and I haven't seen him since," Mrs. Barclay said.

"He's been given the solo," Elise said. "Did you know?"

"No, I didn't," Mrs. Barclay said. "The rascal—not to tell me!"

"It was only yesterday," Elise said. "I met him and he told me. You must be proud of him, Mrs. Barclay—he really plays beautifully."

"Oh, I am," she said quickly.

And then she heard the front door open and, upon an impulse she could not explain, she rose and went into the hall, and there was Harry. He looked tired and his face was smudged. He had his violin case in his hand.

"Harry, where have you been?" she demanded.

"I went home with my music professor," he said. "I wanted to talk some things over with him—get some special help."

"Why didn't you tell me you had the solo?" she asked. "I've only just heard it from Elise."

"I didn't know you'd care," he answered.

She was beaten again by his honesty. "Well, dinner's ready. . . . You had better go and wash your face."

But when he came down fifteen minutes later, just after Lane, he had changed into his dark blue suit and had brushed his hair neatly. His pale face was quiet. He shook hands with Elise without speaking and they went out to the dining room, and he took his place across from Elise. Lane sat at the head of the table, where his father used to sit.

It was a pleasant dinner, and they gave it to Lane. Lane talked and they listened. Harry said almost nothing. Had this been any other day, Mrs. Barclay would not have noticed his silence. But now she found herself forgetting Lane and thinking of Harry. Two or three times their eyes met and parted quickly. He was thinking of her, too. She could feel it. She began to dread Lane's going. Tomorrow at this time she and Harry would be alone in the house. There would be no screen between them. They would be face to face. She found herself thinking more of this than of Lane's going, and she was so astonished that she, too, was unusually silent.

She slept badly that night and woke early. Yes, clearly, she dreaded Lane's going, because of Harry. "This is nonsense," she told herself. "Why, Harry's nothing but a boy—the baby I had, the little boy I've taken care of and taught."

But she really had not needed to teach him much, she thought honestly. Harry learned somehow, without being taught, and Lane had taken so much of her time. She had never really given up on Lane until the Army took him.

"Perhaps it's the very best thing that could have happened," she thought, "for of course he will make a wonderful soldier."

Tom had been a good soldier too. Laid away somewhere today were the medals Tom had been given in France for extraordinary bravery. "Stupid men are always good soldiers," she had thought bitterly long ago. She remembered it now with a new edge to the bitterness. "Oh, Lane's not stupid," she declared to herself, "at least not the way Tom was. Lane is just young. . . ."

The parting which had loomed so dreadful to her for days was inexplicably lightened. The wholehearted sorrow which she had expected was divided, as though it were not quite Lane to whom she was bidding farewell, but someone whom she did not love as entirely as she loved Lane.

"Good-by, Mother," he said in the midst of a great hug.

"Good-by, dear," she replied, and to her own surprise her eyes were dry.

But Elise was crying when the train pulled out. "How brave you are, Mrs. Barclay!"

"He'll be back," she replied. "I have a feeling that he will."

It was quite true that she did feel so. Tom had gone through the last war unscratched, to die from falling off a horse twenty years later.

Harry drove the car home and she and Elise sat in the back seat until they reached the house where Elise lived and she got out. Then Mrs. Barclay moved into the front seat. Whatever there was to be got through about Harry had better be faced, she thought. But Harry seemed quite tranquil this morning. He drove expertly, his thick hands solidly upon the wheel. He did not speak and she glanced at his profile. It showed no distress, though it was grave.

"I sometimes wonder if Elise and Lane will marry," she said after a while.

"I hope not," he said calmly, but with such conviction that she was astonished and even a little amused.

"Why?" she asked, glancing at him.

"I think they'd both be very unhappy, after the first year or so," he said. "I mean—Lane's awfully handsome—it would take a while for Elise to get over that. But she'd get over it. She is—intelligent."

"And Lane is not?"

"I don't say he is not. But she's extraordinary. That would be very hard on him after a while."

"Oh . . . would it?"

"Hard on them both," Harry said.

They did not speak again until they reached the house, and then he only said, "I'm off to practice again, Mother."

"All right, son," she said.

He gave her a quick look, opened his mouth, and closed it again and went away.

Alone all day she pondered that look and late in the afternoon she suddenly understood it. She had called him "son." It was the first time she had ever done so. She put down her needlework and stared across the room. "Why, I have been cruel," she thought. "He's suffered and I haven't even known it."

He came home early that night and went upstairs and washed before he spoke to her. When he saw her he did not touch her and she understood, with the strange new perception she had of him, that he was convinced that she did not want him to touch her. She remembered now that he never came near to touch her, that he had not since he was a little boy, and she had let it be so. It was her impulse to put out her arms to him now, but she knew it would shock him. There must be more between them first, but she did not know how to begin what must be.

They dined together quietly, and quietly he talked about his music and about his difficulties with a certain adagio passage. He asked her about her day.

"I have done nothing," she said, "except sew."

"I hope you haven't been too lonely," he said.

"No," she replied. "I thought I would be when Lane went away, but somehow I am not."

He threw her one of his strange, comprehending looks. "He knows everything," she thought suddenly. "I have seen nothing in him, and all the time he has been growing up in the house, knowing everything about me."

She rose from the table. The tears which had not filled her eyes this morning came welling into them now, and he saw them and hurried to her side, still without touching her.

"Aren't you feeling well?" he asked anxiously.

She put her hand into his arm. "Come into the living room with me," she said; "I want to talk."

*　　　*　　　*

. . . "No, nobody told me," he said quietly. He was sitting with his hands carefully in his pockets, his hands with their bitten nails. "I don't know when I first knew."

They had talked a long time and she felt the strange ease and rest in her being that comes only with all secrets told.

"I knew it, I think, when I was about seven," he went on. "At first, of course, I thought you just didn't like me. Then I began to wonder why . . . and after a while I knew why. It was because I looked like Dad."

She thought speechlessly that for ten years this child, this boy, had suffered what she had suffered, and she had not known!

"But it was only, of course, when I was older," he was saying, "when I was thirteen, I think . . . yes, it was on my birthday. You remember that knife you gave me? I had wanted it a long time and it was exactly what I wanted."

"But you gave it to Lane . . . right away," she interposed. "I thought you didn't care about it."

"He wanted it as soon as he saw it, and I saw that you wished you had given him one, and so I gave it to him. I knew that day you loved him better than you did me, because you let me give him my knife."

She was speechless again and they sat in silence for a long moment.

"When did you know . . . that you were really like me?" she asked at last.

"I think I always knew that," he said. "Because I have always understood you——I've always known what you were thinking . . . and feeling."

"Oh, my God!" she whispered.

She got up out of her chair and went over to him and put her hands on his shoulders, and he looked up at her, smiling his usual smile, and she was horrified at its sadness. "I feel so different today," she said. "I feel as if now I really knew you . . . after all this time. I blame myself so much . . . for what I've missed. Harry, will you forgive me?"

The quick red flooded his face and she saw tears in his eyes. He looked down and his lips trembled. He wet them and drew his breath. Then he could speak.

"Sure," he said. "It's all right, Mother. People can't help the way they feel. I've known that for a long time."

Margaret Mitchell

— ☆ —

GONE WITH
THE WIND

— ☆ —

*Winner of the Pulitzer Prize,
inspiration for the most popular motion picture
ever made, this flaming epic of Civil War
and Reconstruction is the most widely
read American novel ever written.*

78004/$1.25

If your bookseller does not have this title, you may order
it by sending retail price, plus 15¢ for mailing and handling
to: MAIL SERVICE DEPARTMENT, Simon & Schuster
of Canada, Ltd., 225 Yonge Street North, Richmond Hill,
Ont., Canada. Not responsible for orders containing cash.
Please send check or money order.

PUBLISHED BY
POCKET BOOKS